A STORY-TELLER'S HOLIDAY

WORKS BY GEORGE MOORE

LEWIS SEYMOUR AND SOME WOMEN

A MUMMER'S WIFE

MUSLIN

SPRING DAYS

CONFESSIONS OF A YOUNG MAN

ESTHER WATERS

ESTHER WATERS (*Play*)

CELIBATE LIVES

EVELYN INNES

SISTER TERESA

MODERN PAINTING

CONVERSATIONS IN EBURY STREET

THE LAKE

THE STRIKE AT ARLINGFORD

MEMOIRS OF MY DEAD LIFE

HAIL AND FAREWELL:

I AVE — II SALVE — III VALE

THE BROOK KERITH

A STORY-TELLER'S HOLIDAY

AVOWALS

THE COMING OF GABRIELLE (*Play*)

HÉLOÏSE AND ABÉLARD

THE APOSTLE (*Play*)

PURE POETRY (*Anthology*)

DAPHNIS AND CHLOE

ULICK AND SORACHA

THE MAKING OF AN IMMORTAL (*Play*)

A STORY-TELLER'S HOLIDAY

BY

GEORGE MOORE

VOL. II

London
William Heinemann Ltd.
1928

Printed in Great Britain by T. and A. Constable Ltd.
at the University Press, Edinburgh

A STORY-TELLER'S HOLIDAY

CHAP. XLIV.

A FEW days after my telling of the Garden of Eden I caught sight of Alec under the walls of the old mill looking out for a safe place to cross the river, and whilst watching him jump from boulder to boulder I began to wonder if the new story he was coming to tell me would be about a monk or a nun or a hermit. As soon as he was up the high bank I asked if it were a long one and he answered that it was a good-bye he'd come to bid me, having heard in the town that I was leaving Westport at the end of the week. But I won't be delaying the work, your honour, he said, and on my calling to him he came back saying that there was no place for the imagining of stories like a seat by a brook. Like water they do be coming up, foaming and swirling as if they couldn't get on fast enough. The old story-tellers always looked for their stories by running water, I replied, and asked him if he were sure he hadn't one about him. Well, no, your honour, it's the other way round this time; I thought I'd come to you for a story—the like o' them the publishers do be ferreting in their pockets for the notes and the gold to pay you for. I'd like to be hearing one of them just as it comes out of your head for the first time. I think you must take me for a keg, Alec, always on tap as soon as the spigot has been driven in. Isn't every shanachie like that? he answered, and don't the country people be asking me for stories till the last sod of turf is dwindled down into ash? A story, Alec, without Iahveh or fairies, not even a priest in it nor devils, not so much as a serpent—an English or an Irish story, which? I wouldn't stick your honour to one country, Alec answered, but I might get the hang of an Irish story better than an English one. And sure an Irishman the like of yourself wouldn't be hard put to tell an Irish story. If he have one to tell, Alec. Aren't stories always buzzing in a shanachie's head, trying to get out, the way flies do be on a pane? A Connaught story, Alec? And why for not? Aren't you out of Connaught yourself, and out of the heart of it, out of the county of Mayo, like myself? Faith, it 'll be the Ballinrobe cock against the Westport rooster! I don't know that I can think of an Irish story, Alec, unless . . . Unless what, your honour? Unless I start out of an old memory. The best stories are hatched out of old memories, he answered. An old dog for the road, and an old memory for a tale. Perhaps you are right, Alec. I have a story that I heard bits of from an old man of Kiltamagh, whom I used to meet coming up the drive muttering to himself. He had a story that I never heard the end of, for there never was time to tell it all. My governess or my father or mother would always call me away before the end, and so I never heard what became of Tadhg . . . a long story, Alec. No good story is a long story, he answered, and the day is all in front. I 'm afraid the telling will take more than a day. Sure, if it does your honour can be telling it in chapters till the end of time, or a week itself. It is a long story for telling—— A story for reading? he asked, and a little disheartened, for I felt the words: for reading, to be a disparagement, I reminded Alec of his words: Stories ripen in the mouth like apples on a sunny shelf. They do so, he answered; they do indeed. Trust a good tongue to put a good skin on its stuff. In the third or the fourth telling the pink comes out on it, and from that on 'tis as juicy in the mouth as a blackberry in Samhain.

You 've heard of Richard de Burgo, second Earl of Ulster? I have, and troth, as often nearly as I 've heard tell of Oliver Crummel, the curse of himself on him. But I can't say that I know much more about De Burgo than I do about Crummel, for every time the uncle was about to tell me of the great Earl the pipe broke under his teeth or he'd say: It's as dirty as the bottom of a bog! and by the time he'd cleaned the pipe De Burgo and his red head were forgotten. So now on with you! I have no story to tell of the Earl, Alec, but of Ulick, his son by a Frenchwoman who came over to Ireland with a troop of French singers. A bastard! said Alec. And what of that? I asked. No more than that I never heard the uncle tell of a De Burgo bastard. A man may have had a bastard without your uncle hearing of it. Sure he may and welcome, and unbeknownest to the priest himself for that matter, though 'twould be a job as long as Father M'Loughlin is in the county of Mayo. Or it may be, Alec, that my story is a Mayo story and never got across into Galway. All the same, it was from Timothy Moran of Kiltamagh I got it, or the best part of it. A fine old story-teller he was, and I am not going too far if I say there never was a story-teller in Galway that couldn't learn something from Timothy, whether in the telling of stories or the making of them. I can see him still when I look back into the past, a tall, lean man, well known along the road winding through Mayo from beyond Westport to Castlebar and on to Cong—a familiar figure in our walks, who often met us, garrulous and courteous, and followed us a little way, his old caubeen in his hand, his grey hair floating in the wind; or it might be he would pass without seeing us, walking with bent knees, bobbing his head, composing, my governess told me, and forbade me to run after him, saying that my interruption might cost him a fine bit of story. But one day we came upon him as we approached our gates, which he opened for us, asking if he had my leave to take a short cut across the demesne. It will save me a mile of road, he said, for I 'm on my way to Ballyholly. Ballyholly was one of our villages, and he shuffled along with us up the drive and across the park till we came to the bridge that my great-grandfather built when he came back from Spain, a tall, peaked, three-span bridge, out of proportion to the tiny stream that flows beneath. When your grandfather built that bridge, said Alec, there was more water in the lake than there is now. Lough Carra isn't half the size it was since the drainage. It may be so, Alec; but I 'm thinking now more of Timothy Moran than of the water that was taken out of Lough Carra, and he was half-way up the bridge when I called after him, remembering suddenly that a ten-mile walk makes a man hungry; he had come from Castlebar; so I invited him to the kitchen, saying: The cook will give you your dinner, Tim, and I 'll ask a shilling from father, who if he 's out with the race-horses will give it to you next time you come.

A great old story-teller was Timothy, and many legends I heard from him in the stable-yard, whither I was forbidden to go, and in the woods hiding from my governess—legends long passed out of my mind and out of the mind of the world. However closely I search my memory, I come on names only, a phrase, mayhap a broken outline. Of one story I have a beginning, a middle, and an end, a bare, meagre outline, it is true, but an outline, however thin, is enough for a story-teller, and I remember that it commenced well with an account of a ship bringing a troupe of gleemen and gleemaidens from Honfleur to Galway—— May I be interrupting your honour to ask what are gleemen and gleemaidens? The English word, Alec, for mummers. When I was a child the lads in Mayo would be about in the weeks before Christmas gathering up every bit of ribbon; and cross-gartered and with streamers in their hats, they 'd go from big house to big house dancing and singing: The wren, the wren, the king of all birds! No more than that do I know about our Mayo mummers. Enough, your honour, for me to understand that the gleemen and maidens that came over from France were like our own mummers, cross-gartered fellows. Yes and no, Alec; there were lots of queer leggings and some petticoats among them, but they came with lutes, gitterns and rebecks instead of whistles and bagpipes. I beg your honour's pardon for breaking in on you with a question. The fault is not yours, Alec; had I kept to Timothy's own words and spoken of mummers, you would have understood at once—— And would have had no need to interrupt your honour, just as you interrupted Timothy. No doubt I interrupted Timothy often, and to his great discomfort, for Timothy did not like being stopped in a story to answer questions. He liked better to let his tongue run on, his hearers picking up as much as they could without finding fault with what they heard, leastways not till his back was turned and he was beyond the door. I am that way myself very often, said Alec, for there's nothing that spoils a story more than a snorter in the corner, butting in again and again. So be it, Alec; and in my turn I'll get on with the story, saying that when I pressed Timothy to tell which were the better: our mummers or the French, he'd answer that there was nobody alive now with any knowledge of the mummers that came from France in the beautiful ship with the carven prow in the days of the great Red Earl, and if I pressed him still further, he'd say: I'd like to be getting on with my story, young master. Then begin, Timothy, with the carven prow and tell us again how the sea-woman's breasts looked out over the waves, just as you did last time, and then go on to the Norman nobles who welcomed the mummers with the best of everything in their castles. Whereupon Timothy would break in with a bit of history, telling that the Normans did not conquer Ireland as easily as they did England; and being as good a patriot as he was a story-teller, he was apt to become long-winded in his account of William's victory, saying that he would never have got one if the arrow hadn't fallen into Harold's eye. I always wished that Timothy would skip the battle of Hastings, and now I'll skip it myself, telling you no more than that Timothy believed the mummers were brought over from France much more for the fine reports they would spread of the riches of Ireland than for their jiggings and jugglings. And rightly or wrongly, Timothy would have it that it was touch and go with the Normans in Ireland in the beginning of the fourteenth century. They wore us down, he'd say, for whilst we had but one country they had three, getting soldiers and armour from France and Flanders and England; and in our linen tunics we could do nothing against men in armour, for if we did get a battle we couldn't follow them into their castles, so it was all the same whether we lost or won in the field; we were bet in the end. I often wondered how he would get back from castles, shields, breastplates and swords, to the cross-gartered mummers I was waiting to hear about. He was a long time getting back, but he got back at last, and very ingeniously, saying that if it took William five hours of an afternoon to conquer England, it didn't take Louise Chastel, the lutanist, more than the same number of minutes to capture the Earl. Go on telling about Louise, I'd cry; you didn't tell us enough last time. Even in those days I had an exceeding relish for Louise Chastel's victory in the Galway castle, and did not wish Timothy to skip a single word of it.

Now, gentlemen, ladies, and clergy, he'd say, recalling the address of a shanachie of old time, listen if you would hear how a great man can be undone in body and soul by a sinful woman, sent over from France just as Delilah came over from the Philistines for the undoing of Samson. On the night of a gathering in Richard de Burgo's castle to welcome the mummers the wicked work was done; for the Earl had no head for a woman, and in the first half of Louise's song he was like a gossoon after his first noggin of porter, and she wasn't well into the second half when he was pushing his way through his guests, saying that he must ask the gleemaiden to sing a song he had heard his mother sing in his boyhood. If you will be turning your shoulders a little askew . . . he 'd say to the man in front of him, and the man would move as best he could, for the crowd was very thick. And the Earl continued to struggle through it, never stopping, not even when he came to the big pillar against which his wife was leaning with her children about her; he pushed past her—if the devil were after him he couldn't have pushed harder. So hot was he after Louise that she had barely finished her song when he was in front of her looking into her eyes, and everybody in the castle asking: Now, what is he going to do next? Will he take her in his arms and carry her off? But they didn't think he 'd go so far as that, with all his friends and family looking on. Now, gentlemen and ladies and clergy and all who are listening to my story, understand that what these two felt for each other is what you 'll have heard tell of—love at first sight, and a disgraceful sight it was, and shouldn't have happened before the clergy, and might have ended badly if one of the mummers hadn't had the good thought to start singing; another, guessing that something was up, began to dance, and whilst these were dancing and singing a third mummer threw knives into the air and caught them by their handles; and between the three of them the eyes of the company were distracted from the Earl and his lutanist at the end of the hall. And when the singers and dancers and jugglers had finished their feats of skill the Earl and the lutanist were no longer in sight; and the night was far gone before they came from the window-seat where they had hidden themselves for talking, maybe for kissing, the Earl promising all the while to build Louise the beautifullest house in Ballinrobe and fill it with chairs and tables and carpets and pictures of all sorts, and to put gold bracelets on her arms and diamonds on her head and I know not what else—maybe pearls on her ankles, for he was clean out of his senses that evening.

Such is my best memory, Alec, of Timothy's story of the falling in love of Richard de Burgo and Louise Chastel, the lutanist that came over from France in the ship with the carven prow, but a very poor memory indeed it is of Timothy's patter, which came like the brook yonder, shaping itself into pools and running away again into bubbling eddies. A great talker he was surely, the best that was ever heard in Mayo, saving your presence, Alec. And your honour's too, Alec answered. You know Ballinrobe, Alec? I have been through it going to Cong, your honour. And you remember the river Robe at the bottom of the hill, flowing from Lough Carra into Lough Mask under an avenue of limes? Limes are always, and as likely as not there were limes in the days of the great Earl; but there was no bridge, if we are to believe Timothy, who always described the Earl as dashing through the ford as hot as be damned. His own words this time, your honour, I'll go bail for them! Timothy never used the same words twice over, Alec; he kept to the old framework, introducing new inventions, and it was difficult to say which version, the one you heard last or the one you were listening to, was the better. Nobody could choose between the different versions, for nobody remembered what he had heard before, Timothy himself least of all. I don't know if you know the word gusto, Alec? Faith,

I do not. Well, I can't give you as good a definition as I'd like to—blarney is as near to gusto as any word I can think of at the moment, and Timothy's blarney was so soft and winning that his hearers lifted their heads to it, happy as the flowers themselves when the south wind is blowing.

Five words and a smile were enough to capture us, compelling acceptance of the bits we had heard before without question; none but my insistent little self ever thought of interrupting Timothy. He and the times he lived in are coming back to me now. There's magic in the spoken word, Alec; I remembered Timothy when you told me the story of the nuns of Crith Gaille—— And your honour liked the story of the two priests—— Yes, I liked them all; and your telling of them often set me thinking not only of Timothy but that the written word is a poor thing compared with the spoken. But it's a dirty bird, said I to myself, that fouls its own nest, and I fell to thinking that each has its place in art, the spoken word more buoyant and joyful but less precise and complete than the written word—ah, that was the fault with Timothy's stories. He left out the parts of the story that didn't come to him as he walked the roads; there was no word about Ulick's childhood in Ballinrobe. And your honour thinks there should have been? No, Alec, no; Timothy couldn't have been other than he was; and I being what I am, remember that a child goes to his mother for stories. Louise had no stories to tell her son but French ones, and so a love of France was rooted in him at an early age; and a great love of his mother, too, possessed him, for they were always alone together, and I cannot forget that there must have been times when she could bear her loneliness no longer, waiting for the Earl to come clattering up the street on his horse. But Timothy was not interested in Louise's loneliness; I am, and therefore I hear her in my thoughts confiding her loneliness to her son, and he espousing her cause with childish enthusiasm as they sat before the fire in their high-backed chairs till Louise started to her feet: Bed-time, my child, bed-time! No, mother, not yet; go on talking about lonesomeness. Your honour is coming to a pretty bit, said Alec, but I'm asking myself how Timothy could tell all that passed between mother and son and he roaming the roads always. Since we are story-telling together I'd say to you that he had to choose three or four things, just as I have to myself, leaving the words to chance. All the same, Alec, he might have told us how questions began to arise in Ulick's mind, for even in his early teens the child could not have helped asking himself why he lived in a house different from all the other houses in Ballinrobe, alone with his mother, and why his father never remained with them for more than three or four days at a time, saying he had a castle to build at the other end of Mayo. His father and mother would be careful not to say anything before him that would set him thinking, but sooner or later he'd catch a word spoken by the Earl to Louise whilst he waited for his horse to be brought round from the stables, such words as: A castle is needed in the north; I cannot trust—— Ulick, in my imagination, failed to catch the man's name, and sought it till he wearied of seeking it and began to wonder what the man had done to merit a castle being built to lock him up in; I like to think of Ulick asking himself if nobody lived in castles except under lock and key.

In the time I am telling, Alec, a great harp-maker lived in Ballinrobe, one Donogh O'Brien, and his workshop was such an attraction for Ulick when he came into his teens that he was often truant from his lessons, spending long afternoons learning how to use the adze and chisel and saw when his mother would have had him by her side, her lute between them. But Ulick's truancy from his lessons was not the reason why she forbade him Donogh's workshop; she was afraid lest he should hear in the talk always going about the tables at which the apprentices worked that his father was no other than the great Earl. Was there anything in Timothy's story about the workshop? Alec asked me, and I answered that there must have been some mention of it, for Donogh O'Brien was one of the great harp-makers of Ireland; and I continued that the mother could not do else than forbid Ulick to waste his time trying to become a harp-maker, a thing he wished to be. But she could not answer him why he might not become a harp-maker, nor could she keep him from knowing who his father was indefinitely—she knew that; and missing Ulick from the house, she would sit thinking of him in the workshop. Donogh would tell him nothing, but Donogh could not keep the apprentices from speaking, and even if he succeeded in keeping them from speaking of the Earl in Ulick's presence, Ulick would not fail to notice that on his approach the apprentices' talk would change quickly, one asking another if he had taken his chisel; and a hunt for a chisel or an adze or a mislaid harp-string would carry the talk away from the Earl, who would not again be mentioned. This is how the harp-maker's workshop must have appeared to the mother as she sat thinking of her son, and she would send for him or go and fetch him herself.

And the end of all this would be that Ulick would come to his mother, saying: I know my father, but who is my father? His name, mother—tell it to me. Is he the great Earl himself that I hear talked of wherever I go? Thou art keeping a secret from me; why should I not know my father's name? Louise may have often sought for a name that would satisfy her son's curiosity; she may have even asked the Earl to help her, till at last he said: The boy is growing up and must be told. And a great event in the lives of mother and son it was when she told him his father was the great Earl de Burgo. My father the great Earl de Burgo! But mother, why dost thou cry? for it is a great thing surely to be the son of Earl de Burgo? A great thing it would be, Ulick, if thou couldst inherit thy father's title and estates, but these must go to the Earl's son John, and after John to John's son; and though all the Earl's children by his wife Margaret, daughter of Sir John de Burgh of Lanvalay, were to die, thou wouldst still be no more than Ulick de Burgo, or Ulick Chastel if thou shouldst choose my name instead of thy father's. Louise would beg her son not to repeat to his father anything she had told him, but even if we accept Ulick as one who would keep this promise to his mother, the house in Ballinrobe would lose all its innocency and happiness; the son would be constrained in his talk with his father, and when Louise died—— So she died? Yes, of a chill caught after a day's fishing on Lough Corrib, and according to Timothy, was buried in Ballinrobe at the end of May, 1314. Alec, I have always thought of the Earl and Ulick walking together in the orchard on the hill-side above the Robe, Ulick now somewhere between twenty-two and twenty-five, the Earl over fifty. In that walk the Earl must have spoken to his son of his birth, though he had never spoken of it before, and of his future, telling him that when he, the Earl, died, Ulick would find his bitterest enemies among his half-brothers and sisters, and that it would be better for him to seek a career for himself in France, his mother's country. I shall be better able to help thee in France or in England than I can in Ireland—in every way, with money and by my influence. He might have spoken these very words; most likely he did. He spoke them right enough, your honour; you may bet your bottom dollar on that; for it's never been otherwise in Ireland from that day to this, the man in the big house sending his bye-blow to America when the time came for him to marry a fortune that would pay for the cards and the port wine. But, Alec, this time it was the opposite, for whereas the hunting squires sent their bastards to dig the American railways, the Earl allowed his son to seek a career for himself in France, none being open to him in Ireland because of his disgraceful birth. Once gone, gone for ever, he would say in the walk through the orchard over against the river. But I cannot let thee go, Ulick; it cannot be in the nature of things that I should lose thee too. Nor can it be that I should remain in Ireland to meet enemies in thy children, should I survive thee, Ulick would answer his father.

Father and son must have spoken openly to each other after the funeral, but for one reason or another we do not know, and we shall never know, why Timothy passed over this part of the story, telling no more than that Louise died in May, 1314, and that at the end of September in the same year Ulick, wearying suddenly of hunting grouse with falcons over the hills of Lough Mask, stepped on board the Earl's hooker at Cong, his mind made up to leave Ireland for France and seek a career for himself among the trouvères. I shall be the last, he answered his father, and I beg thee not to oppose my wishes, adding thereby to my misfortunes. And the Earl, seeing that there could be no gainsaying Ulick, said: Son, it breaks my heart to lose thee; after thy mother thou art the dearest thing on earth to me; but I will let thee go to France on a condition. And what condition is that? Thou 'lt need a gleeman in France, and what better gleeman could a trouvère have than my harper, Tadhg O'Dorachy, the greatest in Ireland, the favourite pupil of Finn Lorcan? He will be able to help me, Ulick answered; he will follow my voice in the songs that I shall sing under castle windows or in great assemblies. Thou art a great father and a good father and a kind father (now and again, Alec, I come upon Timothy's own words). Every day that I stop in Ireland will be an uneasy day for me, so let me go to-morrow. Art thou in that haste to leave me? Will not the end of the week do as well? At the end of the week, if it be thy will, father, and if thy little tribe of legitimates are not returning from Portumna before then. For the first time the Earl turned a dark face on his son, and in a perilous moment Ulick became aware of his likeness to his father—they were both tall, lean, white men with blond beards. But it was not the likeness to himself in his son that withheld the Earl's fist, but Ulick's dark eyes, which reflected his mother; to strike his son, he felt, would be like striking Louise. And seeing that his father's anger had died out of his face, Ulick kept back the words that came to his lips: Had I been legitimate, father, thou wouldst have struck me! Instead of speaking these words, which might have separated them for ever—for a long time at least—he put forth a curious hand, and lifting the border of his father's cloak he said: Forgive me, father, but a young man cannot see a cloak handsome as the one hanging from thy shoulders without examining it. Wouldst thou have my cloak as a last present? and lifting it from his shoulders the Earl placed it upon his son's, and stood in admiration of the sable collar and cuffs and the green silk lining. What suits me suits thee! And they were as dear to each other as they had ever been in the interval between the Earl's last words and the entrance of a servant with news that Tadhg O'Dorachy was waiting audience. Bring him to me, the Earl answered, and a moment after a small man with a long, grey face came in, to whom the Earl addressed himself quickly, saying: Tadhg, the news I have for thee to-day is a great advancement in thy fortunes. Thou art bidden by me to France to make known the Irish harp, and thou 'lt journey thither with my son.

With your son I shall not be separated from you, great Earl, the builder of my destiny, and I would make the Irish harp known all over the world, could I see how it can be done. With thy genius, Tadhg, which thou canst not leave behind. Faith, if my harp-playing were taken from me little would be left of poor Tadhg, and I'd walk as shamed as Adam after the fall. You will ride together to Dublin, where you will find a ship in the harbour ready to sail for the Thames. But isn't the Thames an English river, my lord? The Thames is an English river and my son goes thither with despatches; and when he has delivered these to Edward of England thou'lt sail with him from Southampton to Honfleur, and on thy arrival in France thou'lt ride with him from castle to castle, following his voice on thy harp when he sings under his lady's window or stands up in a great assembly. I shall do thy will, great Earl, in exile as I have done it at home. I would not have thee whimper before me, Tadhg. My tears are of joy, my lord, at the honour you do to me. Then weep on, Tadhg, but listen whilst weeping. I can trust thee to remind my son in time of need that it is not my will he should fare without an armed escort, and on arriving at an inn I would have thee keep thine eyes open for the thieves that entice young men with small winnings till they have won all their possessions; even with these they find little content, and are not satisfied till their dupes stake their future fortune on the throw. From the next danger, that of women, my son has naught to fear. His grace and bearing will inspire only thoughts of love; and should it come to pass that my money is not at hand to pay for a needed suit of Italian armour, the lady's jewels will be given to the Jews, so ardent will she be to see my son lay a champion low. Father, it seems to me that thou dost ask too much of my gleeman, for in thinking how he can protect me against the dice box and the ladies we shall meet on our journey he will neglect his chief employment: his harp and the writing of my songs for me. I beg thee to keep silence, Ulick, whilst I give my orders to my harper. All the same, there is truth in thy words, and I will take heed of them. The ladies that will dangle themselves about thee may be left to the care of their own tempers and dispositions, and to keep them from harm is no part of Tadhg's business; but should thy thoughts turn to the graver issue of love: marriage, I would be warned by him. So, father, thou wouldst not see me married? Till a man weds he is his father's son, but wedded he is a woman's thrall. I would not lose my son, Tadhg. There is more to tell, but if my say be prolonged thou 'lt forget more than thou mayest retain of my instructions. But should my son fall into sickness I would hear of it without delay. . . . Something has slipped my mind that was in it a few moments ago. Now, what can I have forgotten? That if I miss him, said Tadhg, from his place in church at the celebration of the Mass, and from the Communion table—— I would have thee keep a friendly watch over my son without spying upon him. Now leave us; my son and I have much to consider, and when Tadhg was without, Ulick said: Father, I did not break thy talk with thy harper to ask why I should go to France by way of England. I would send thee to England with despatches so that Edward may confer a knighthood upon thee, which he will do at my request; and here are letters to many in France that will receive thee more favourably as Sir Ulick than they would . . . If thou hadst not given me thy cloak to wear, dear father. At which the Earl laughed, saying with tears in his voice: Thou art my son truly. And having no more words, the Earl and Ulick walked over to the window, to watch a ship coming up the bay, furling her sails as she approached the wharves. A ship from Honfleur, said the Earl, that calls at London, doubtless. I would sail in her, Ulick answered, and escape the weariness of a long ride across Ireland with thy little harper. It is true that with favouring winds thy faring may be shorter by sea than by land, but I would not have thee blown into the ocean.

After speaking these words the Earl seemed to forget his son, though he was standing by him. He is thinking of mother, not of me! Ulick said to himself, and his own thoughts leaping forward carried him in vision to within a few hours' ride of Dublin, where he was in person five days later, turning in his saddle to ask Tadhg how many days' sailing it was from Dublin to the Thames. Tadhg answered him that if the winds were fair they would reach the Thames within a week. But if this calm continues—look round you, master, and see if there be wind enough to fill a sail. Not enough to lift the thistle-down, for that last lot was caught in yon hedge, where it can do no harm; but there goes another lot, drifting up again, to float far away and settle in somebody else's garden. Even the aspen is quiet, said Ulick, and I would sail from Dublin in a ship with two masts and a square sail on each. Make your mind easy, your honour; we have a day's riding ahead of us, and there'll be many a change in the wind between this and then. But there's no height beneath that branch for a horse and man to pass under; come round this way and overtake the young youth herding pigs in the field yonder. Whither lies the sea, my good man? You'll get a sight of it when you have passed the small hills. Sight of a windless sea, no doubt, cried Ulick, one only fit for oars! Outside Howth there'll be wind enough for plenty of pleasant sailing, the pigherd cried back, if you don't run into one of them noisy gales moving about at this time of year somewhere in the north. God save you both! And from pigherd to pigherd they rode, inquiring out the way, till they came within sight of the sea. As I foresaw it, a waveless sea! said Ulick. We'd do well to keep from talking about waves, and we on our way to England. We'd do better, Tadhg continued, to keep our eyes open for the river Liffey, that we are to meet in a great plain not a day's journey from Dublin. And being near our journey's end, with a great plain before us, I'm thinking the Liffey must be wandering about here. Behind those bushes as likely as not, Tadhg; and riding forward they came to the Liffey gurgling over shingle. A safe ford is before your honour, said Tadhg. And riding their horses into the water they continued their journey along the right bank till they came in sight of a great cathedral, which on inquiry from a passer-by they learnt was Christchurch, built by the Danes, and saw the two churches on the left bank over against Ostman's Bridge. And at the bottom of the steep hill in front of you are the city's gates, said the passer-by. After thanking him for his courtesy, they began the descent of the hill. Now, which is to come first, the Mayor or the city? Ulick said, drawing rein. Tadhg's instructions from the Earl were that Ulick should pay his respects to the Mayor on reaching Dublin. It is true, he began, that the city comes before the Mayor—— Thou hast said it, Tadhg, the city comes before the Mayor; I would not waste an hour sitting within doors taking instructions from Nottingham but would see the city under the evening light, wherefore we'll ride through the western and out by the eastern gate. If your honour would go to the Mayor with an easier mind after having seen *The White Cloud*—The way to the ships? Ulick cried to the soldier on guard. The ships, he answered, are moored in the deep channel off Lazar's Hill or in Salmon Pool beyond Irish Town. He continued to direct them, mentioning the many places they would pass by on their way thither—names unknown to Ulick and Tadhg, who whilst trying to keep in mind the various turnings they were to take, reined in from time to time to admire the buildings and to ask their names. The like of which they had never seen before was the City Hall, and they stopped agape at the strength of Bermingham's Tower. On passing through Dames Gate they were at All Hallows Priory. We must keep to the north of the Priory, said Ulick; the soldier spoke of a marsh—— And of a short cut through the marsh, Tadhg interjected, which we should find as dry as a bone at this season of the year. Yes; and of the archery butts in Hoggen Green, saying that we should keep to the left of St. Patrick's Well so as to be out of the line of chance arrows, the archers being but apprentices. Now will your honour look round, for 'tis a grand evening we have brought to Dublin, one that couldn't be bettered for seeing the city; and since it was the Danes that built her, Brian Boru might have stayed his hand, for wouldn't the Danes have been a great help to us in keeping out the English. There was once a great Danish Empire, said Ulick, including England and Scotland as well as Ireland. All past and gone, Tadhg answered, and they turned their horses' heads to the marsh.

After riding for a quarter of a mile through dying reeds, rushes, and tussocked grass, they came to some firm grassy slopes. Lazar's Hill, said Ulick. Now, isn't it wonderful that your honour should know it, never having laid eyes on it before. I have heard my mother speak of Félicien Aubes, a great gittern player who came from France to Galway with gleemen and gleemaidens. He died in that hospital. But open thine eyes, Tadhg, and admire the river, the bay and its shipping, with the very ship that I would like to take me to London yonder riding the tide—that one with the high forecastle and higher poop. Maybe she is *The White Cloud* herself, Tadhg answered, and we might do worse than ask about her from one of the fishers beyond. And Ulick having no fault to find with Tadhg this time for his opinions, rode towards a little group of shielings put together out of the broken timbers of boats and ships. True dwellings of fishers, he said on catching sight of long nets drying in the sun, lobster pots woven out of osiers, seines, fishing rods and lines. Hast heard of a ship known as *The White Cloud*? he cried to a man mending an old cobble drawn up on the beach. Heard of her? said the man. Aren't we both looking at her! And her captain? Ulick inquired. Her captain was about a few minutes ago. Tadhg gave two shouts without getting an answer, but the third shout brought to them a florid-complexioned man, with clear blue eyes (a Norman Ulick recognised him to be even before he spoke). And guessing the two horsemen to be his passengers, the Earl's son and his harper, the captain of *The White Cloud* said: We have been expecting you, sir, for the last few days, and would like to loose, if it be to your convenience, to-morrow at daybreak. We came into Dublin less than an hour ago, Ulick answered, and I have business at the castle with his Worship, the Mayor. Maybe I should have done my business first, but I could not put *The White Cloud* out of my mind. Well, there she is, sir, a fine, taut ship that with a fair wind will take us to the Thames in ten days, if you could come on board to-night. My business will detain me in Dublin some days—— A pity, indeed, for I have in mind the storms that tear up the sea late in September and early in October. What did the pigherd tell us, master? and it's they that know it; for being out with the pigs from daylight to dark, they are quick as the wild geese themselves in scenting out a storm. A storm is making ready in the north or in the north-east for certain, the captain continued, so I would be on the other side before it breaks. We, too, would be on the other side, Ulick answered; but my father's orders to me were not to leave Dublin without paying my respects to the Mayor.

We have been detained already too long, the captain muttered, and Ulick stood watching the coming storm, unable to decide whether to go or to stay. At last, yielding to his inclination, he went on board and turned into his berth, and it seemed to him that he had not been long asleep when he was awakened by the plunging of the ship from billow to billow. He cried aloud, for he was unable to collect his thoughts, and would have rushed headlong through the door of the poop, leaving it open, mayhap, if Tadhg's voice had not stopped him. Where are we? he asked Tadhg. On board *The White Cloud,* your honour, and in the midst of a storm. So we have run into the storm, Ulick replied, and coming out of the poop they caught a rope that was thrown to them, and belayed themselves to the bulwarks. By the light of two horn lanterns hung high on the masts they distinguished the sailors at work on the yards, taking the captain's order roared to them from the dark deck, and judged him to be standing by the steersman. At intervals they heard the words: Starboard! Port! and in a little while they began to understand that his skill was to dodge the waves, never allowing one to catch the ship on the quarter. Why doesn't the steersman look aft? said Tadhg, and Ulick answered: The steersman is a coward and dare not look behind him. A poor thing it is, your honour, to be out on a night like this and in doubt of one's own steersman! and quaking he listened to the wind preparing on the horizon for another onset; like a charge of cavalry, gathering strength as it came, it fell upon the ship, stopping her in her course, stunning her. There is not a dry rag on board, said Tadhg. Look ahead, for God's sake, captain! Another big fellow is coming, he added under his breath. Port! cried the captain, and the wave carried *The White Cloud* over the crest into the hollow, the sail on her foremast helping her to climb out of it. And hour after hour went by, with the same dangers, the same escapes, till the thought came to them that the speed of the wind was increasing and would carry them beyond England into the Atlantic.

For that or some other reason they heard the captain cry: We are running too fast; take in another reef! But his voice not seeming to reach them aloft, he moved a couple of steps nearer to make himself heard, and in that moment the mischief was done; for the steersman let the ship swing a little sideways and over her came a great wash of water, carrying away a great part of the poop, and breaking the mainmast. In the darkness and disorder of the deck it was hard to find the captain. Ulick and Tadhg deemed him dead, killed by the wave that had killed the steersman, but this was not so; he had saved himself somehow; and starting to his feet he rushed back to the helm, crying to the crew to cut away the raffle and free the ship from the dangers of a broken mast, whereupon it seemed to Ulick and Tadhg that they must untie themselves and work with the others. But they were bidden back to their corner by the captain. Get some sail on the foremast, he cried, and the crew falling to his intention to bring the ship up to the wind, worked amain, getting at last a new sail ready to go up to their mates on the yards. But the ship, being down in the trough of the sea, got little help from the sail and it was not till eight oars were thrust through the rowports that *The White Cloud* came round. All night the waves crashed against the bows. A good sign, betokening strength of thews and sinews of the rowers, said the captain. If they can hold out till dawn the sea may not get us. You hope for a lull in the wind at dawn? Ulick asked, and the captain answered: Maybe we shall get one if we are off the coast. The lash of the captain's whip went out, and the rower caught strength from it and rowed through the night without feeling the weight of his oar, like one in a dream, till a bleak morning broke through grey scudding clouds. By noon the wind blew from the south-east. Two men fell over their oar; the lash went out again, but it could not rouse them. The feel of the deck tells me . . . Ulick and Tadhg heard the captain say as he disappeared under the hatchway, and when he reappeared again they heard what might well be the end of their lives: Her foremast is rocking in its socket, straining open the strakes, and the sail must be got down or she 'll split beneath us. But if we get the sail off her she will steer no longer, and she steers hardly at all with the sail set. Art afraid, Tadhg? I quake, master, for the sea is cold and salt is bitter in the mouth—an awful death! A voice cried: Land ho! and the beetling cliff of Dunmore rose out of the mist. The cliffs of Dunmore! said the captain. But she is leaking like a basket. The pumps would keep her afloat for another few miles if my men were not weary. We have done no work, said Ulick; myself and my harper can pump. Then bend to the pumps, Ulick de Burgo, you and your harper.

The White Cloud dragged herself round the hook of land into the great estuary nearly a mile wide, where she would have split under them if boats had not come to her help and towed her to the wharf. The hulk is saved, said the captain. We are here for many a month, he added, addressing the peasants. There are many good adzemen and smiths among you? To which the peasants answered: The best in Ireland; none better, though you walk the world over! We shall be detained three months in this village! Ulick muttered, and in doubt whether to seek in Waterford a messenger to take a letter to his father, or to wait in Dunmore till some other ship was driven by a gale to find shelter in the river Suir—one that had lost no more than a sail or some rigging and would be ready to proceed on her voyage to the Thames in a week or ten days, in less, perhaps, he asked the villagers who accompanied him to the inn if many ships put into Dunmore during the winter, and learnt from them that a big wind seldom failed to bring in a ship or two. The seasons are never alike, they said. In one season there is plenty of wind, in another the wind doesn't signify. And here we are for three months, Ulick said, turning from the villagers to Tadhg, with nothing to do but to visit the workshop every morning to survey and question the progress that is being made in repairing *The White Cloud,* and to climb the peak every afternoon to watch for a sail; and he cursed the captain for failing to foresee that the storm would break on the very night of their departure from Dublin. Three months will not be long passing, your honour. Tadhg's optimism angered Ulick, and he answered: I would as lief be told that we were here for three years, or for thirty! Tadhg did not understand, and Ulick did not tell his servant that even in his happiest moods he never could rid himself of the belief that he would die in poverty and obscurity in some desolate place; and this inveterate belief was closer to his heart than before as he and Tadhg toiled through the wet woods to the cliffs, his despair revealing itself very often in a single sentence, as when he said whilst disentangling himself from a thorn bush: The wettest village in all Ireland! And the thorniest, Tadhg answered, thinking of the rent in the hosen. Sometimes a ray encouraged Ulick to hope for a fine evening, but the sky darkened and a gust carried the rain up the valley, drenching it from end to end. That last downpour should keep him from the hill, Tadhg said to himself, and taking down their harps from the wall he asked Ulick if it would not be better to cheer the workshop with music than to climb the hill again. But Ulick could not be dissuaded from the hill, and once more they climbed, and once more seated in a cleft well sheltered from the wind he waited, certain that a ship would appear, whilst Tadhg crouched under a rock out of the rain like a rabbit.

Whilst watching a flock of golden clouds driven southwards, Ulick said: I know nothing more beautiful than golden clouds sailing over blue, yet a sail would gladden my eyes more than any array of colours. And these words bringing a small hope to Tadhg that his honour was weary of daily journeys to a hill-top where the winds were so high that the gulls perched hungry on the rocks below rather than take the air, he said: The gulls cannot know of any rocks but these, else they would have gone long ago. Ulick asked Tadhg what sign he had had that the gulls were weary of the rocks of Dunmore, and Tadhg answered that the time was not for fishing, nor for sailing either. Which means, Ulick snapped, that in thy mind we are befooled every day, and that it was no accident that drove *The White Cloud* into Dunmore a wreck. The Lord's breath lifts the fluffs of thistledown and tears the sail, Tadhg answered, hoping to propitiate, but his words not seeming to reach Ulick's ears, he began to wonder if his honour was thinking that some devil had raised the wind that had driven them into Dunmore, never to set forth again till the Judgment. A sail! cried Ulick, and starting to his feet he was caught by a sudden gust, and would have been carried over the cliff's edge of a certainty if Tadhg had not been by to clutch his belt. Ulick was saved, but his cap flew away over the rocks, startling the gulls from their roosts. Our best peaked cap gone! said Tadhg. Now what cap will your honour appear in when you are summoned to the Tower for knighthood? We doff our caps before we go into the King's presence, Tadhg. But he who is called upon to doff a cap must have a cap to doff, Tadhg answered, and together they descended the hill-side, Ulick talking all the time of the building of a great beacon on the top of the rocks, or the building of a belfry and the hanging of a loud-tongued bell in it that would warn the sailors from afar. Tadhg listened to Ulick's plans for the saving of lives whilst thinking how he would do his best on arriving in London to persuade his honour to lose no time in possessing himself of a new tunic, for there was no saying when the King would not send for him; most likely he would send a messenger off at once after reading the Earl's letter. But there will be no London, only four boards for him if he continues to go up this hill in search of ships. It was by this very pool that he started sneezing last week, and every day since the rheum has been sinking deeper into him—— Dost hear what I'm saying, Tadhg? Yes, your honour, I hear you—you would speak with the captain about the beacon and the bell. Dost think we shall find him in the workshops on our way to the inn? Of that I know no more than yourself, but to-morrow morning will be time enough to speak to him of the bell and the beacon.

As if he had not heard him Ulick turned in the direction of the workshops, bent on finding the captain that evening, and failing to get any news more precise than that the captain had spoken of going to Waterford, he rambled up and down the village, asking everybody he met if he or she had seen the captain of *The White Cloud*; and meeting with nobody who had seen him since noon, he ceased at last to doubt the say of the passers-by that the captain had gone to Waterford to buy the timber needed for the ship's mast. He spoke to me yesterday about the ship's mast, said Tadhg, and your honour would do well to come into the inn and let me pull the wet hose off your legs. When his hose and his tunic were taken from him he could not resist the warm shift that Tadhg offered, nor Tadhg's persuasion that he should take to his bed, wherein he did not cease to talk of the captain; and to pacify him Tadhg left him in charge of the servants at the inn and went out to meet the captain at the bridge-head on his way back from Waterford. He will not lie down till he has seen you, he said to the captain when he came across the bridge, and whilst walking with him to the inn Tadhg told of the shivering fits. Keep a fire burning all night, and if he is not better in the morning we'll send to Waterford for a doctor, were the captain's last words. A doctor, said Tadhg, coming from the door—— No doctor can help me, Ulick answered. You should be in the warm, in your bed, master, and not in the middle of the floor. The pain in my back and loins is too severe to be borne lying at length; and he remained out of his bed some time longer, straining over a chair back. Are they worse than before? Tadhg asked. Ulick answered that the pains were all he could bear, and Tadhg passed the night praying that he might be saved from appearing before the Earl with the sad tidings of his son's death. In the early morning somebody knocked. It is the captain, said Tadhg, and going to the door he whispered: He will not let me ride to Waterford for a doctor, and once he has said a thing he will not budge from it. I cannot hear the words you are speaking together, Ulick cried from his bed, but I know you to be talking of doctors and wise women. I shall see neither, but will lie up till I recover my health or lose it altogether. I must leave Dunmore if I am to get well. Come in, captain. The open door let a flood of spring sunlight into the room, and with it came the captain in high spirits, joyous as a boy, to tell that the timber for the new mast had turned out better than he expected. So everything has happened for the best, except . . . he paused a moment . . . except your honour's illness. Yes, except for my illness all would have gone well, Ulick answered; but I am better to-day than yesterday, and if I could leave Dunmore I would soon be myself again, of that I am certain. Whereupon the captain spoke of a house in Waterford standing in the midst of a garden, with wooden staircases in it and glazed windows—the very house he would like to see his honour lodged in, till Ulick bounced to his feet and called to Tadhg to order a pair of saddle-horses to be brought round.

Now, what sort of horses are being saddled? he asked when Tadhg returned, and Tadhg answered that there were but two in the stables, a restive mare and a quiet cob. The cob will carry you quietly and safely—— I will ride the restive mare! said Ulick, and he sprang into the saddle, to bestride a lengthy, ragged animal that tossed her head, pulling hard, flouncing from a fast trot into a boisterous canter whenever she got the chance. But Ulick held her so well together that Tadhg began to wonder if his honour was the sick man he had complained himself to be overnight. All the same, I will choose the grass to ride over, for the cob's hooves set the mare dancing, and she'll tire the master in the end; and no more than half the journey was over when Ulick drew rein, and turning in the saddle begged Tadhg to believe that he had suffered no pain at all since he had put his foot in the stirrup. Tadhg agreed that his honour's sudden recovery was not less than a miracle; and he was not dismayed next morning by the news that his honour had suffered a good deal of pain during the night, but had kept to his bed through it all. I knew that I would begin to get better when I left Dunmore, and I prophesy that I shall be ready to step on board at the end of the month. But we cannot go on board *The White Cloud,* Tadhg answered, till your honour has written to the Earl to tell him how we escaped drowning off Dunmore. True for thee, Tadhg; let me have writing materials. But when they were brought to him the pen dropped from his hand, and he wandered to the window saying he could not collect his thoughts and that his sickness was upon him again.

At the window there was the sky to be seen, with white clouds moving over, and comely poplars, too, at the end of the garden; and behind the poplars there was an orchard descending, so Tadhg told him, to the river bank. Just as the orchard does in Ballinrobe, he answered. Tadhg would have had him tell of Ballinrobe and his mother, whom he knew his honour loved with a sort of idolatry, and of his father, whom he worshipped, but Ulick was too languid for speech, and even for thinking; he could only enjoy the sunlight in the garden and the south wind bringing to him the fragrance of the earth, now tremulous in the agitations of a new birth. He sought for the scent of flowers in the wind, but there was none; he dreamed as he dozed of snowdrop and crocus; and the day passed, and every day he strove to write his letter; but he could only dream; it vanished on his way to the table, and he asked Tadhg if he would ever be able to command his thoughts again. I am not myself; I am like an animal, only able to receive sensations of earth and sky. Tadhg did not answer; he retired to shed a few tears; and when all signs of these were gone he returned with a brave face and cheering words, and when his honour's face was turned away his eyes searched the writing table for the beginning of a letter. But several days had to pass before the letter began to be written. Why, master, you have written half a page! Yes, Tadhg; my head is all right now. Get thee away into the town and seek a messenger. The letter will be finished ere thou hast found one. Remember, Tadhg, we have been five months here. More than that, said Tadhg, a little more; and we shall need money in London; nearly all we took with us is spent. We shall find money waiting for us in London, Ulick answered, and he took down his harp, which he had not touched since his sickness.

CHAP. XLV.

THE WHITE CLOUD lay along the wharf spruce and taut in her new apparel of sails and rigging, and on stepping on board Ulick de Burgo said to the captain and

Tadhg together: In the high wood up yonder the rooks are hatching, and if there be a rookery along the banks of the Thames—— There is a rookery, the captain replied, at Greenwich. But we shall not land at Greenwich; we shall sail some few miles up the Thames to the Tower; and leaving his passengers he gave orders for *The White Cloud* to be rowed into the sea, for the wind was faint under the hill. There'll be wind enough outside, the captain cried back, and Ulick's eyes followed the sunlight wandering in and out of the woods, lighting up the banks, bringing the rushes into flower and colour to the country and the sea. A month, he said, often spoken of as boisterous and burly, but this year gentle as a child; and spying some daffodils along the bank, he added: I was born in March, and when the news of my coming reached my father's castle he left Galway in his barge, thinking of my mother and of me; but when he reached the house he did not rush in to see us, and never was able to explain how he had been led first into the garden and through the garden into the orchard, out of the orchard into the shaw over against the little river Robe, where he gathered some early daffodils, brought them into the house and laid them in my cradle. . . . Now, Tadhg, in a few minutes more we shall be in the sea, with the big hill and cliffs fading out of our sight; so look whilst there's time, and beg thine eyes to remember things thou'lt never see again. I have no wish to see the hill of Dunmore or those cliffs again, nor to remember them. That hill heartened us whilst at the pumps, Tadhg.

Dunmore had succoured them in their need and indifference to their deliverer was not to his liking. He even regretted leaving the village, though he hoped never to return to it, and to escape from Tadhg's comments he allowed his thoughts to rove among the billows, crashing as they tumbled upwards amid the rocks. And then his eyes delighted in the divers colours of the sea, heaving with feline voluptuousness under a sky densely clouded, with only here and there a hint of the blue beyond the clouds. About the ship gulls snatched their prey from the surface and cormorants pursued theirs into the depths of the sea, and through the gulls and the cormorants *The White Cloud*, herself like a great bird, went tilting over the happy waves. And the wind blowing steadily from the north-west carried them towards the English coast, all of them remembering that it was a north-east wind that had nearly brought them to their doom some five months before, and all of them glad when midnight was past and the sun rose again, for it was at midnight that the wind had raised great waves against *The White Cloud*. A tigress, hungry for their lives, the sea was that night, but now she was pretty as a kitten at play in the sun; and all the crew wondered how such a beautiful weather should continue so long and serve them so well, for a fair wind blew day after day, bringing *The White Cloud* into the Thames estuary on the tenth day. When the Greenwich rookery came into sight Ulick remembered the one above Dunmore, and he asked Tadhg if he had forgotten the words he had spoken to him as they sailed out of the harbour. Did I not say that the young birds would be out of their shells when we arrived in London? You did, faith, and if we were under yon trees we should hear the broods squeaking for the food the parent birds cannot gather quickly enough. And that if we were not delayed more than a month in London, Tadhg, we should see the young birds out on the branches as we rode to Southampton—a prediction that came true, for they were not many miles from Southampton when Ulick turned in his saddle, saying: Tadhg, dost remember what I said to thee as we sailed up the Thames? About the rooks that would be out on the branches in a few weeks, Sir Ulick? And it being the first time that

Tadhg had addressed his honour by his new title, Ulick was swept back into the moment when the King, after reading the Earl's letter, drew his sword, saying: Kneel, sir, and then slapping him on the shoulder, added: Rise, Sir Ulick! and so deep was he in his recollections of the royal gest that Tadhg drew bridle and dropped some paces to the rear. But Ulick needed a confidant; Tadhg was called to the saddle-bow again, and for several miles they talked of Edward II., who would have detained Ulick in London if he had not pleaded that he was on his way to France and would like to be in Normandy in the month of May, when the trouvères rode out of their castles accompanied by their gleemen. So the son of my friend and vassal, Earl de Burgo, would win for himself a fame equal to Adam de la Halle and Jean Bretel. There have been no troubadours for the last thirty years; you were born too late. To soothe the lad, whose face told his disappointment, the King added: But the love of song has not gone with the trouvères; and when Ulick had sung in French and in Irish, Edward asked him to tell the progress the Normans were making in the subjugation of the country. The east has been settled, sir, to the banks of the Shannon, but there are turbulent chiefs—— Of the Irish chieftains I have no fear, much more of the Scots, for my news is that the Bruces would leave their barren lands and seize the fertile soil of Ireland. Let your Majesty put such evil thoughts behind you, Ulick answered, and a cloud came into the King's face, for it was not yet a year since a great English army was defeated at Bannockburn. . . .

But the King could not speak of Bannockburn, Ulick said to himself, and his thoughts passing on to other things, he remembered what Edward had said about the preparation of an army in the north for the invasion of Ireland. The fruits of Bannockburn! he said, reining in his horse to inquire from a party of travellers coming from Southampton if the ship that carried them had returned to Honfleur or was still lying in Southampton water. Prick on, said the travellers, for she looses to-morrow morning, and their horses being fresh, the last twenty miles were ridden at speed. In the commotion of getting on board the thought of an army assembling in Scotland for the invasion of Ireland was laid aside; such news cannot be forgotten though it may be laid aside by the young, and nobody was younger than Sir Ulick de Burgo in his twenty-fifth year when he sailed from Southampton with his gleeman, Tadhg O'Dorachy.

A fair wind is blowing; we shall be in France in a few days, and these should be devoted to the composition of songs, for we shall begin singing at once, Tadhg. Now, tell me, what were the Earl's last instructions? We are to ride from Honfleur to Courancy—— My mother's village! Ulick said. And then from this to that castle, presenting to the lords and ladies the letters of introduction he has given into my keeping. Tadhg drew a list from his tunic and tried to engage his master's attention. Courancy, said Ulick, is within view of the Seine, and we shall ride under poplar-trees whose foliage sweeps gay skies of blue and white clouds; and I have a feeling that it will be under one of those poplar avenues that we shall meet a trouvère riding to a castle whose parapets will show out of a beautifully planted hill-side far away. But did not the King tell your honour that the last trouvère was one Adam de la Halle, who died at Arras about thirty years ago? A trouvère that lived and sang no more than thirty years ago must have left a follower; and we shall find him, for hast not heard that there 's always a last rabbit in the burrow? And though the great trouvères of Arras are dead, Tadhg O'Dorachy lives to make the Irish harp known in France. The Irish harp will make friends wherever it goes, your honour; but I 'd like the letters we have brought with us—— We cannot stop at castle gates to read letters, Tadhg. I shall sound my horn, and the gates will be opened to us by joyous valets. And they had not to follow the winding Seine for many miles before this prophecy came true. It was seldom that they were bidden away by a gatekeeper, and directed by peasants, who left their work in the fields and came down to the hedges to tell them of marriages, baptisms and dances, they rode from castle to castle through the months of June, July, August, and September, till one day in a drizzle of October rain they came upon a long cavalcade wending its way to Paris.

In Paris they found a quiet lodging and spent the mornings composing new songs, and in the afternoons Ulick sang to the lute in salons where all the fashion collected; and leaving Paris when the leaves were green again, they visited all their old friends and made many new ones. A child's holiday their French adventure would have been were it not for rumours that the Bruces were winning battles, and though Ulick often asked Tadhg if he believed these rumours, Tadhg could only answer that if the Bruces were getting the upper hand the Earl would have written recalling them to Ireland. We have not been to Courancy for six months, and a letter may be waiting for us now, Ulick said. But no letter was there. It is strange that the Earl does not even send a message, Tadhg; and the twain rode away, Ulick deep in perplexity, certain that every Norman should return to put the Scots out of Ireland, but dissuaded easily from a return thither by the sight of a castle. We have never sung at that castle, Tadhg, and I have a thought that we shall be well received. As well received at the castle beyond as at the next one, no better and no worse, Tadhg answered. A lady may be embroidering in this one and not in the next, Ulick replied. In this hope he blew his horn; the gates were opened and the Bruces forgotten for a month or for three; and in such variety of entertainment the seasons wore away, till one day in the summer of 1318—it must have been in June, for they always remembered it as a day that still retained something of springlike freshness in the skies and in the trees—they turned their horses' heads once more towards Courancy and Ulick broke silence with the words: Of what art thou thinking, Tadhg? And without waiting for Tadhg's answer, he continued: I am asking myself if it is a wholesome destiny for a man to ride always to castles singing songs. We all fall homesick now and again, your honour. Homesick, Tadhg! With thee it may be homesickness. Tadhg waited for him to say more, but Ulick seemed to be away. At last he said: There are in life diversions; and seemingly on second thoughts he added: And there are preparations. But how may we distinguish between diversion and preparation? And how may it be in the fair order of things that a father should let years go by without sending his son a letter? How many times have we left Courancy downhearted, Tadhg? And leaving Tadhg to his thoughts, Ulick continued: The rumours are persistent that the Bruces are getting the upper hand in Ireland—— I wouldn't go so far as that, Tadhg interjected; the last rumour was that the Earl was back again on his throne. Ulick did not answer, and the horses fell from a trot into a walk. Dost remember Roudier, Tadhg? I remember him well, your honour. But as if he had not heard Tadhg's words, Ulick said: We may well meet him to-morrow in Courancy. Tadhg did not dare to put questions, and their ride ended in silence. He is angry with me! Tadhg said to himself; and next day, during the long ride of some thirty miles, Ulick spoke but few words, and Tadhg grieved, till he saw his master swing himself out of the saddle and ask the taverner if anybody had inquired for him yesterday or to-day. Three days ago a man inquired after Sir Ulick de Burgo, the taverner answered. Ulick entered the inn, and Roudier rose to meet him.

So thou hast returned at last from Ireland, Philippe Roudier! having exceeded by many months the time allowed to thee to make my father's portrait. Has the Comtesse complained, sir, that I was about it too long? for if she have, she 'll forget to blame me in her pleasure, finding in my drawing a likeness that all have admired. Look into it, sir. I 'll look into the portrait and praise it when I have heard thy news, Roudier. My father—where is he? In one of his many castles, sir, in which I cannot tell; he has so many; and his wanderings from one to the other have gained for him the nickname of the Wandering Earl. Tidings of his defeat at Connor cannot have failed to reach you, sir? Rumours have reached me of reverses, Roudier, but each rumour is contradicted by the next, and I know not what to think. In his pride your father would not accept help from Sir Edmund Butler. Help, he said, to drive a few Scots into the sea! a thing he would have done if the crafty Bruce had not contrived to alienate his ally, Felim O'Conor. Betrayed by Felim! Ulick cried. Art sure that thy story is a true one, Roudier? And Roudier answered: Bruce's spies came to Felim with tales that all the Irish were flocking to the Scotsmen's standard, and Felim, though brave, being always mistrustful of his own shadow, as the saying is, dreamed that his sovereignty in Sligo was threatened, and took his leave of the Earl. Whereupon Bruce turned, and at Connor a battle was fought in which the Earl's army was put to flight. Thousands died on the field of battle, and thousands more were overtaken in their flight and killed; and among the prisoners was William, cousin to the Red Earl, who was held to ransom—— To a great ransom, no doubt, said Ulick, one that will help to complete the conquest of

Ireland. The conquest of Ireland is not yet, Roudier answered. Edward Bruce was crowned King of Ireland at Carrickfergus—— Yet thou sayest that the conquest of Ireland is not yet complete! Edward Bruce having defeated the Normans everywhere, Roudier continued, Felim O'Conor fell to thinking that he, too, was a great commander, and assembling an army of ten thousand men, marched through Mayo into Galway, where he was met at Athenry by a great army under the command of Richard Bermingham—— And was defeated? Ulick cried. Killed on the battlefield, Roudier answered, the battle of Athenry restoring the authority of your father, sir.

Ulick called for Tadhg, and before Tadhg had passed the threshold he said: We start for Ireland to-morrow; and if no ship sails to-morrow, then on the next day or the next—by the first ship that looses for Southampton or Galway. Ireland, Tadhg, is in the power of the Bruces, who are everywhere, spreading ruin, killing and burning and destroying. But, master—— Ask no questions, Tadhg; come back from Honfleur with news of the ship. We shall have time for talk during the voyage. . . . There is much more to tell, Roudier said, but you can inquire it all out on board the ship you sail in. I can but repeat gossip. I beg you to calm yourself, sir, for I have here your father's portrait—— I have no eyes for portraits, Roudier. Sir, your father's portrait! True: my thoughts are astray; and after taking the portrait and looking at it, Ulick said: With my father's portrait thou hast passed over another. The portrait you are looking at, sir, is of King O'Melaghlin's youngest daughter, a nun. I thought there were no more kings in Ireland, Roudier. Chieftains or kings, whichever it may please you to call them, Roudier answered; and seeing that Sir Ulick's thoughts were distracted from Ireland for the moment, he said:

I drew portraits of Sir John Bermingham, Sir Richard

Bermingham, and Sir Edmund Butler, and was kept busy drawing portraits of the noble and mighty till one day, at the end of a long talk with the Earl about you, sir, he said: The fame of thy portraits has reached far into Ireland, even to Lough Ennel, the partial kingdom of King O'Melaghlin (we allow him the title out of courtesy, for he favours our cause). He writes asking me to send to him the Comtesse d'Artois' craftsman, for he would have portraits of himself and of his daughters, three beautiful girls often spoken of as the Three Celtic Graces. I answered your father, sir, that I had been in Ireland longer than the holiday the Comtesse d'Artois had granted me, and that my thoughts were on the decoration of the horse-litter I had left unfinished, and on the cage I was making for her parrot. The same Comtesse that I knew thirty years ago, said the Earl, intent on acquisitions: tapestries, embroideries, ivories, psalters, reliquaries. Is Hesdin still full of these? Fuller than ever, I replied, adding that you were often at Hesdin, sir, at which he seemed pleased. I would that my boon to King O'Melaghlin should detach him finally from the mere Irish, the Earl continued; and I went to Lough Ennel under escort. At every stage of the journey horses awaited us, a journey of three days; and at the end of the journey I received a welcome greater than I had expected from the King. Almost a familiar welcome it was—the Irish are a courteous nation, from king to shepherd, and O'Melaghlin was flattered that Earl de Burgo had granted his request.

My first portrait was of the King himself, and I had little trouble with it, for he never asked to see my drawing, and on the third day was still sitting like a statue when the Princesses Liadin and Muirgil came in, two beautiful girls who spoke in Irish to their father, translating what they had said into Latin afterwards so that I might understand them, saying that the water in a well could not give back a truer image of their father. Clapping their hands they withdrew, smiling to reward me for my work. I hope my drawing of your daughters will please you, sir, I said, as well as my drawing of you seems to please them. Two beautiful girls will make a more attractive picture than one old man, he answered, and to turn his thoughts from a mournful subject, I continued: Earl de Burgo spoke of a third daughter, and three would make a happier picture than two. A happier picture, the King muttered; but for whom? And afraid that his third daughter might have died lately, I said no more. But the desire of speech was upon the King, and he continued: My youngest daughter has turned from the paths of this world into the path that leads heavenward. A great blow this was to me, Philippe Roudier, for the flesh is weak. I loved my daughter Soracha better, perhaps, than Liadin and Muirgil, and it may be for that weakness God in his wisdom chose to take her from me. But though my daughter is taken from me, my confessor will not deem it a sin if I tell him that I would have a portrait of her. . . .

The convent of Durrow is but seven miles from Lough Ennel, and I went thither bearing a letter from King O'Melaghlin to the Abbess, who entertained me with pleasant talk about your father and Ireland, till our converse grew wearisome. Perhaps you would like to see Sister Soracha? she said. I answered that I would, and she returned bringing with her the Princess. And we sat talking about the King and her sisters, till at last taking courage I began: Princess—— Sister Soracha, please, she interjected. Shall I begin your portrait to-day, I continued, or shall we leave it over until to-morrow? Why not begin at once? the Abbess asked, and I answered: I am ready. But I did not draw Sister Soracha's portrait easily; I tore up two drawings. And one day she said: The French come to Ireland to help the Normans. Who have, I replied, become Irish. They come hither to rob our country, she continued, and to do this they have to oppress, and Ireland will never be at peace again. Tears rose to her eyes which I feigned not to see, and to distract her thoughts, I said: I came from France to draw a portrait of Earl de Burgo for his son, Sir Ulick de Burgo, a trouvère. I thought there were no more trouvères, she replied. So you have heard here in Ireland of our trouvères and troubadours? I asked. Their impieties and wanton lives, she answered, have been reported. Reports, I said, which have no doubt contained some grain of truth, but no more. A grain of wheat in a bushel of chaff, she answered smiling, and seeing that for a nun her mind was freer from conventional beliefs than I had supposed it to be, I continued: Yes, Sir Ulick is a trouvère, the last of them. We spoke of the great trouvères of the twelfth century, and I sang some of their songs to her. Why do you not sing to me some of Sir Ulick de Burgo's songs? she asked. I sang snatches from your songs, sir, all I could remember, and even in my poor singing they seemed admirable, superior in many little ways to the songs of Thibaut de Champagne and Colin Muset, and she asked me if I could make a drawing of you from memory. I said I could put some lines upon paper, and after looking at the drawing I had done of you, she left me to continue my altar-piece (the crowning of the Virgin in heaven by her son, with all the saints about them), the nuns coming and going; and when I had drawn them all, the Princess Soracha returned, and we spent some more time talking of you.

I would have you make a portrait of me to take to Sir Ulick de Burgo, she said. Will you do one for him? And when the sitting was over, and she came round to see what I had done, she asked me if Sir Ulick would see her with my eyes or quite differently. I am a nun, she said, and men do not consider nuns as they do other women—or rarely, she added after a pause. I asked her why she had taken the veil, and she answered that when she was nearly eighteen she could think only of Jesus, but she had resisted the craving for her father's sake till her eighteenth birthday. He is a pious man, she said, and would have God's will on earth as it is in heaven, however great the pain may be. My father loves me dearly, above the love that he gives to my sisters—so I have been led to think. And when I asked her if she were happy in the convent, she answered: Jesus was nearer to me before I came hither, and sometimes it seems to me that I love him no longer. As she spoke these words her face and voice told me that the stories I had related of you, sir, and your picture, were as sparks fallen on tinder, and I watched her, wondering, for she seemed to have been absent from herself for a very long while. The woman is never the same as the girl, she said, breaking into speech suddenly. We make promises that we cannot fulfil, or fulfil indifferently. And until the woman within her dies, every nun dreams of being carried away. She knows that she will be buried in her habit, but she puts a taper in her window and lies down watching it, uncertain whether she would follow the knight if he came, only certain that she is guilty of a sin in putting the light there, though it lure nobody. She falls asleep watching the taper, and finds the charred wick in the morning. So her life goes by. Shall I tell all you have told me, Princess Soracha, to Sir Ulick de Burgo? I asked. Tell him what you please, she answered. Yes, tell him that I burn tapers in my window, knowing well that no knight will climb the pear-tree that grows beneath. . . .

You do not think, sir, that I came here with the fable of a discontented nun to amuse a man distracted by news of his country's disasters? No, Roudier; the story of thy nun is true enough; I doubt it not. And the drawing thou hast made of her is beautiful; I have wits about me to see that, but no more. I return the drawing—— But your father's portrait? Ah, I had forgotten it! And Soracha's portrait—will you not keep it, sir? Yes, in remembrance of thee, Roudier. And now we part. The Comtesse d'Artois was a friend of my father, and thy portrait of the Earl, as thou hast said, will help her to forget the long delay. Tell her that when the wars are over I will return, perhaps bringing my father with me; tell her all that. I cannot speak or listen any more, but must think of our departure. Tadhg is in Honfleur asking if a ship sails. A merchant ship will loose, Roudier cried, turning in his saddle. Ulick waved his hand, and unable to bear the strain of waiting for Tadhg any longer, he set forth to meet him. And meeting him half-way between Honfleur and Courancy, he cried: Jump from thy horse at once, for it is not easy to hear in this wind, and thou hast seemingly a long tale to tell.

The White Cloud, your honour, is in harbour for repairs, and a lot of barnacles will have to come off her bottom before she is again ready for sea. Wait two months in Honfleur whilst the Bruces win battles in Ireland! Many battles may be won in two months. I am thinking, Tadhg, of some merchant ship trading between the two ports. The old *Phoenix*, your honour, will loose at the end of the week for Galway. Then return thou to Courancy, Tadhg, and for thy horse and mine take whatever price may be offered thee (remember that thou proclaim them to be Irish), and to-morrow thou'lt come on board. Remember, too, that after the first day at sea thy business will be to bring back to me all the news of the Bruces thou canst gather from the sailors. But as soon as the news goes round that Sir Ulick de Burgo is on board, your honour, the sailors will be as dumb as the stones! A simpleton indeed I should be, Ulick answered, if I had not thought of the need of a different name.

Jules Chastel will come well to the captain's ears. Now away with thee to Courancy, as fast as thy horse can trot. He helped the little man on to his horse, and continued his journey to Honfleur brooding the excellence of his plan. But a plan that cannot be put into practice is never a good one, and they were not many days at sea when Tadhg, eager to hear whether success was going to the Norman-Irish or to the Scotch invaders, began to put questions to the sailors, distracting their attention from their work. A crack from the captain's whip advised him to desist, but he would not be gainsaid, and one day when he stopped a man who had been ordered aloft by the captain to take in sail, the whip whirled and fell across his shoulders and he was bidden to return to his master with the news that the crew did not come on board to talk about the Bruces—news that Tadhg did not care to pass on to Sir Ulick lest it might raise up a quarrel between him and the captain. One blow more or less in a world where there was little else than blows for the mere Irish mattered little. Moreover, the captain was in his right; he must rule his crew. So did Tadhg consider the blow he had received, and the captain, as he walked up and down the deck, half regretted that he had been so ready with his whip. But after all, a stripe is an Irishman's natural lot. And coming upon Ulick next morning staring across the sea, he was moved to pass the remark that they were journeying on a favourable wind and might be in Galway in three weeks.

Ulick, who had spoken to nobody but Tadhg for some days, answered the captain pleasantly, and henceforth whenever they met in the mornings on deck they dropped into talk; and it was from the captain that Ulick learnt that after the battle of Connor Edward Bruce had won battle after battle, defeating Roger Mortimer at Kells, and the royal forces at Sketherys, near Ardscull. Ulick was eager to learn how these battles had been won, but he kept back the questions that rose to his lips lest he might betray himself, and lay awake all night thinking how in the morning he might coax the captain into telling what had happened to Edward Bruce after the defeat of the royal forces. But next day his curiosity was so great that he dared to penetrate into the captain's private room, and, undeterred by the fact that the captain sat with a chart before him, begged that he might be told if the Scots had taken Dublin or any important town. The captain answered that owing to the bravery of Nottingham the Mayor, in burning the suburbs, the Scots had been compelled to leave Dublin and to march on to Limerick, where the Mayor, taking example from Nottingham, burnt the suburbs of his city, and the Scotsmen were forced to retreat through the provinces they had laid waste, only a remnant reaching Ulster. And so ended the dream of the great Celtic empire, the captain added, hoping thereby to rid himself of his visitor. The great Celtic empire! he exclaimed, and the captain with a look of despair on his face told him that the intention of the Bruces was to unite all the Celtic races against the Saxon and the Norman. Scotland, Ireland, Wales and Cornwall—all would be ranged against Edward of England if the Bruces had brought battering-rams, catapults, and other engines of war to Dublin. And why did they not bring these engines? Ulick asked, and the captain answered that the Bruces counted on Earl de Burgo, who was in Dublin at the time, no doubt for the purpose of persuading the citizens to come to terms with the Scots. Remember, sir, that the Earl had married his daughter, Elizabeth, to Robert Bruce, and that his sister is the wife of James the Steward of Scotland. Incensed though he was by these aspersions on his father's honour, Ulick had command enough over his temper to allow himself to retreat with dignity and to keep his own counsel for the rest of that day, arguing with himself from time to time that the captain had only told him the truth, things that he knew already: that his sister was Queen of Scotland and his aunt the wife of James the Steward of Scotland; and at the end of another day's sailing Ulick was tired of his own company, of Tadhg, and was drawing nigh to the belief that if he were Earl de Burgo instead of Earl de Burgo's bastard, he, too, might have gone to Dublin, if not to persuade the citizens to hand over the keys of the city to the enemy, at least to tell them the danger they were in. The Scots were successful everywhere, and Edward of England could give them no help, his armies being fully engaged in holding his own border. Yes, in the circumstance he might have acted just as his father had acted. A few days afterwards Ulick and the captain were again talking of the Bruces, and another fact transpired: that Edward Bruce had refused to take his brother's advice and return to Scotland with the remnant of his army, and was now in Ulster, preparing to descend in the autumn, when the country was full of food, upon Dublin, with the intention of laying siege to the city. If he took Dublin, or defeated the army that Sir John Bermingham would send out to dispute his passage, all the chieftains would rally to his side, and then indeed the dream of the great Celtic empire might come to pass.

All the captain said seemed to Ulick strangely clear; it was as if a light had been brought into a darkened room in which he had been wandering, seeking something, he knew not what. But now he knew why he was going to ask for an army to oppose Bruce's passage into southern Ireland; and till the end of the voyage he brooded the details of this campaign, suddenly revealed to him. But when he arrived in Galway and rushed to the castle, his father in his long cloak lined with green silk standing by the window put out of his mind the words he had come to speak: Father, I am here to help thee in thy need, and instead he blurted out: Thou art the living image of

Roudier's portrait! So thou didst recognise me in his picture? the Earl asked. I did indeed! And the men stood looking at each other, not daring to speak. Roudier bade thee to Ireland? the Earl said at last, and Ulick answered: No; I heard from him and from the captain of the ship I sailed in something of thy story, and I have come to ask thee for an army. Thou must go to Bermingham for an army, or for command in his army, and I doubt if he'll give thee one. It seemed to Ulick hard that he should be punished for his father's mistakes, but he put no wounding questions to the Earl, and telling him without more that he was going to see what Bermingham could do for him, he rode away, to meet a gentleman who talked French like himself and questioned him closely about the Normans in France, the rivalry between the French and the Normans, and the struggle that would soon begin between them, if it had not already begun. Ulick, who knew France only from the castle and from the roadside, could tell him little about the King of France, and pressed him to consider the Irish difficulty, the defeat of Bruce in the east and his own wish to take part in that battle. At these last words a light came into Bermingham's face, and he said: If you have come to Ireland, as I apprehend, sir, to assist the Normans, being a Norman yourself, you can do so by undertaking to defend Mayo against Sligo; and they spent the afternoon together, engaged in deep converse, Ulick learning that what the raiders needed to cease to be raiders was a town. They had tried to take Dublin and failed, and they had tried to take Limerick, and it might well be that, undeterred by their losses at Athenry, they might send an expedition into Galway to seize the town. That they would not succeed in getting the town is certain, Bermingham said, but they would distract many from my army. I should have to garrison Galway heavily, and I need all my soldiers in the east of Ireland, for

Robert, King of Scotland, will reinforce his brother's army.

Bermingham spoke so clearly and haughtily that Ulick was much impressed, and he went back to his father to tell him all he had heard and to ask him which castle he would give him. If thou hast not an army, father, thou hast a castle. And they spent the evening talking of Castle Carra, the Earl saying no word in disparagement of Bermingham lest he might inadvertently quench his son's ardour for battle, and he dropped into remembrances often of his campaigns in Scotland under the banner of the great king, Edward I. of England.

CHAP. XLVI.

EVERY LAKE is a mystery, except the lakes that are merely expansions, overflowings of a great river, like the Shannon lakes, and whosoever is born in a lake district and has lived on lake shores never loses sight of lakes, however far he may wander from them ; and Ulick had often wondered why it was that Lough Carra should suddenly leave its low wooded shores for Lough Mask, a dark pool overhung with mountain forests. From these mountain forests many rivers must flow into Lough Mask, but he knew none of these, only a river that dipped into a cavern to join Lough Corrib, four miles away. Lough Corrib flowed into a river, one that reached the sea, and on the hot breathless journey from Galway to Cong he asked himself if a certain affinity in waters enabled a river to cross a great lake without losing itself in the lake, to appear again and to go on again ; and he thought of birds that are suddenly summoned to cross unknown seas. Salmon came up into Lough Corrib, and he remembered how one day after many hours of vain fishing a fish had risen in the twilight to the fly. They would have remained out even longer in the hope of another rise, but his mother had asked that they might return to Cong, saying she was cold, and his father had bidden the oarsmen put their backs into the oars—a thing which the present oarsmen could not do, so stifling was the heat. Twenty oars dipped into the languid lake, and every hour the overseer dashed buckets of water over the crew lest he should have sunstroke amongst them. All prayed that the sun might sink behind the western mountains and a breeze come up. At last the breeze came, ruffling the lake, and the sails of the Earl's barge drew. If the breeze continues, said the captain, we shall be in Cong before night and you'll be able to get horses and a guide. All of which came true. Ulick, standing in the bow of the boat, cried: A guide to Castle Carra? and was answered by somebody that their horses had arrived the night before from Galway, and that Michael Quin would take them to Castle Carra without missing his way.

You'll be at the castle before midnight! Mike cried, putting his heels into his chestnut nag, leaving them to follow him, a thing which was not easy to do, for the evening had begun to darken and he rode zig-zagging. Sometimes they were in a bog, sometimes in a forest, and after passing through Ballinrobe they seemed to be always in sight of a lake. Lough Carra, your honour; and the green hill away above it goes by the name of Mucloon because of a herd of pigs that a ghost used to trot out of the forest, a ghost that would strangle any man or woman if they so much as looked back on the road from Carnacun to Ballinrobe, or from Ballinrobe to Carnacun. Soon we'll be taking the ford at the foot of Mucloon and you'll be lifting your legs, for the water will be up to your horses' girths; and keep your eyes all to the right or the ghost will be on you—you won't be quit of him till you come to Carnacun. . . . They rode on for two miles more. You should be hearing a late cock or a too early one crowing as we go through Carnacun, and after that you may look to the right or the left, or wherever you like, for Carnacun is the mearing. Whose mearing? Ulick asked, and Tadhg answered: The ghost's, to be sure! And a little beyond Carnacun the boy said: Now we'll be coming to a bit of tough forest and you would do well to keep close to me, for if you lose the track I shall have a job to find you. We will not leave ten yards between us and thee, said Tadhg; and at the heels of the chestnut nag they rode through the darkness, expecting every moment the trees to divide on a background of grey lake. In answer to their questions Mike cried back: You won't see a sight of the lake again till we come to Castle Carra, so it's no good looking for it; keep your eyes on the tail of my nag.

The trees stopped suddenly and Lough Carra lay in front of them with its castle on their right, atop of a headland, only the keep showing, the parapeted walls and turrets and redoubts lost in mists and shadows. Mike asked whether his honour would be willing that he should run down to the moat with the password. Give thee the password, boy? But it isn't in your honour's mind that I'd be making a bad use of the password if I had it? Ulick did not answer, and whilst waiting for the drawbridge to be lowered he looked into the deep moat and admired the fastness of the twin turrets and their great arch, in which he thought he could espy a portcullis. Gustave Landrey, the captain of the guard, came through it, and after exchanging a few words with Ulick he ordered the drawbridge to be lowered. A dark ride through a wild country, he said; if we had had any warning of your honour's arrival to-night we should have been ready to receive you. Ulick signed to Tadhg to join him. Here is Tadhg O'Dorachy, my harper; I must speak with him. Thou hast paid our guide? Tadhg answered that he had, and whilst the ostlers were leading the horses to their stables Landrey came forward with a lantern picked up in the guard-house and led them up a steep path through the garden that encircled the keep to some steps set sideways along the castle walls, so narrow that the keep could be defended against an enemy. Even with bowmen to pick off the spearmen the keep can be held under cover of shields, Landrey said as he unlocked the great door. But no sooner was he across the threshold than he stumbled over a sleeper, falling on his face, and for a long time they were in darkness amid a hustle of men making off in search of other sleeping-quarters. At last recovering the lost lantern, Landrey said: If the Earl's messenger had warned me of your arrival, sir, these fellows would not be lying about half asleep, half drunk; and in answer to Ulick's questions he told that the roused men were Irish allies, whose fault was that they never knew on which side they had engaged themselves to fight. Do you feed in this hall and sleep in it? Ulick asked. Sometimes we eat and sleep here, but the Earl's message came to me that the hall should be a privy residence for you, sir, whilst staying with us, and in this much I beg that your will shall not conflict with your father's. I have had notice of the coming of carriers from Cong bringing beds and bed-linen, and I shall hope for a louver: one is needed; and he piled logs on the hearth built under a hole in the roof, the smoke passing out, to their admiration—— The wind being favourable, Landrey said; but the words had barely passed his lips when a change in the wind's direction filled the hall with smoke. If the door of the keep be kept shut, Ulick remarked, the smoke will find its way out; but he was told that though the door was closed, winds came down from the loopholes above on the staircases. And raising their eyes Ulick and Tadhg saw that the walls of the castle were solid only to a height of twenty feet; higher up they enclosed stairways, leading to the battlements, and the advantage of these was explained by Landrey. If the spearmen were shot by bowmen, he said, we should draw the ladders up after us and defend the castle from the stairs. But we shall have time to talk of the defence of the castle to-morrow. Here are some rugs. Once more, let me tell you how sorry I am that your first night in Castle Carra will be spent on the cold stones. There is a rug apiece, and here are two more. Now, sleep be with you.

It will be hard to sleep on these stones, Ulick said when Landrey had closed the door behind him. Does your honour remember the round tower at Ardrahan? Thou'rt thinking, said Ulick, of the stairs above us, reached by long ladders; well, think of them and cease thy prate, for I would sleep. Very soon he was calling to Tadhg for another rug, but in spite of it the same chilly discomfort kept him awake, and he despaired. But sleep came at last, and when he opened his eyes his surprise was great. Now, what do I see on the table yonder, Tadhg? Cakes that are still hot, master, and you would do well to eat them whilst they are hot. A good thought, said Ulick; and when he had eaten many hot cakes and drunk a cup of mead, he asked Tadhg if it were true that he liked French wine better than mead. And Tadhg, guessing the aim of the question, answered: I have no quarrel with French wine, your honour; and have good news to tell you about the beds. The steads and sheets and pillows will be here before the week is out. I hear somebody at the door. Captain Gustave Landrey asks if he may accompany your honour round the castle. Why does Captain Landrey remain on the threshold? Tadhg whispered: When I told him that your honour was breaking his fast he said he would wait. Beg him to come in, Ulick said, and Landrey, a full-bellied man with round face and flushed cheeks, came in speaking of the beautiful summertime. I hear that no rain has fallen for seven weeks, Ulick said. Not a drop, answered the captain. A cup of mead for you, Captain Gustave Landrey? A hearty health for you, Sir Ulick de Burgo! and having drunk he laid down the cup and broached his errand. You have lived in Castle Carra longer than I have, Captain Landrey, so I would have you take me round the battlements and tell me how the castle should be defended if the King of Sligo, whoever he may be, should lay siege. I'd like you to see Lough Carra from the battlements, Landrey answered. And I am willing to see it with you; but do not disclose the prospect to me before I see it, Ulick replied. The lake would exceed my telling this fine morning, the sun disclosing—— Hush! Ulick interjected, and they went up the last steps of the stairs laughing, to view a mild and gracious lake amid low shores vanishing into grey distances, the lake curving round island fortresses and forests.

The Welsh were invaders in the twelfth century, Landrey said, and the wandering harpers have long stories to tell. A land that has always inspired invaders, Ulick answered. But I see two lakes, one on my left hand and one on my right. Not two lakes but one lake, for if your honour will follow the line of that long tongue of forest to its very tip, you will see that it does not join the Partry shore. A strait is there, and Lough Carra widens out again. I like the eastern lake better than the western, said Ulick; a lake is always lonely and a lake without islands is desolate. Our lake is not without islands, Landrey answered; and the loveliest island of all lies under our shores, to-day without a hermit; but in the ninth century Marban, a hermit-poet, made his dwelling there. You must see it, sir, and Ballintober Abbey at the end of a long marsh, on a knoll, built by Roderick O'Conor, last King of Ireland. Castle de Burgo stands a little farther down the lake, between Castle Carra and Ballinrobe, and between Ballinrobe and Castlebar there are two castles, and between Ballyglass and Ballinafad there are two more; and all of these castles are garrisoned by Norman soldiers—the smallest garrison is twenty-five men and an officer. There are but three or four miles between the castles, and the lighting of a beacon lantern on any one of them would bring from two hundred and fifty to three hundred men marching to help. Bruce will never wrench Castle Carra from our grip, said Ulick. But I did not come to Castle Carra to defend it, but to lead troops into battle when the Sligo men cross the frontier; for the threat is that they will pour into Mayo as soon as Bruce begins his march southward. Your face bespeaks doubt, Landrey. Mayhap, Sir Ulick, it does. We will talk of invasion from the Sligo border anon; I will now lead you through the gable end to the opposite staircase. Ireland is a rich and beautiful country, so I shall be sorry if we cannot keep her out of the hands of the Bruces. We shall not fail to keep her, Ulick answered. If we keep her we shall have to learn a language rough as the walls about us and live as the Irish live, always at war or quarrel. You speak Irish, Sir Ulick? I was born in Ireland, Landrey, and spoke French with my mother and father, Irish with Tadhg, who came to France with me and learnt to like French wine without giving much thought to the language. Dost hear me, Tadhg? Yes, your honour, I hear; but I'm seeking . . . Seeking what, Tadhg? A chest in which to keep your clothes, master. God grant that the carriers will bring us a couple. God grant they may! Ulick answered.

Landrey asked Ulick if he would care to come round the castle with him to see the eighty men-at-arms, all of whom, he averred, would be pleased to meet their new commander. On our way to the men's quarters we shall pass through the kitchens, sir, and coming from France you will be able to tell that there are other ways of cooking pork than boiling it. We have tried beef and mutton, but so inferior are they that we have returned to boiled pork and beans. Which repeated too often, sets you all grunting, said Ulick. It does indeed, Landrey replied;

our cook, though a Frenchman, is very Irish through no fault of his own, for his father died when he was on the breast. In how many ways, Tadhg, canst thou prepare beans and pork? Ulick asked. In a dozen, Tadhg answered. Then, Tadhg, thou 'lt instruct the cook, for he knows but one. I'd do it gladly, your honour, if I had more French on the tongue. Around the pots and pans you will come to an understanding! And on these words they passed through the great door into the sunny air and waited on top of the steps to admire better the pink bellies of the pigs, whose enjoyment in the sun Landrey explained by the fact that they had just come from the trough and were digesting their meal. I cast no blame upon the pigs, sir (they do all they can to become good pork), but upon the cook and an iron pot. Tadhg, said Ulick, thou 'lt impart thy cooking to the wretched Norman who boils pork in a pot. I would not have believed your story, Captain Landrey, had I not heard it from your own lips! Such stories are sad, but lose some of their sadness when told on a lovely autumn morning on steps above an orchard, when damsons are darkening in the branches and the mint bed loses its scent, and the season of pork in all its multiple varieties is about to begin! Now, what do I hear? said Landrey. The rumbling of cart wheels and the cries of carters that the drawbridge shall be lowered—your beds and bedding arriving from Cong, sir. I must give my orders. Tadhg will give them for you, Captain Landrey, if you will allow him. My father sent me to Castle Carra for I needed a battle; a battle, he said, will be fought at Balla when Bruce leaves the north for Dublin. But you think differently; your face tells me you do. If your father told you—— My father is in Galway out of the way of news from Sligo; but our scouts bring you news from the Sligo border daily or weekly. A scouting party returned yesterday, sir, with the news that 1318 is the richest year within the memory of the oldest man, and that the folk were in the fields shearing sheep, stacking corn and gathering apples—1318 will be such a year for cider as Ireland has never known. But if messengers have brought the Earl your father other news, I would have you ride into Sligo yourself to inquire out the chances of a battle at Balla. It might be well for me to do so, for my hopes are plighted to a battle. Carts and waggons are waiting at the drawbridge, and if you have any orders, Sir Ulick? I will leave the settlement of the beds and benches to you, Captain Landrey, and the business of the castle you will attend to, leaving me to admire the fortifications.

He had not strayed very far when he began to perceive that every yard of the headland had been built over, except a strip of shore that promised no secure foundation for the masses of stone the Irish masons had piled up with a view to building a castle impregnable though battering-rams were used against it. An easy castle to hold, he said, and a hard one to take by assault—or by siege, he added; boats sailing from Ballinrobe could revictual it from time to time; a huddle of men, eighty-three in all, counting Landrey and myself, the keep given over to me and the best house to him, the soldiers lying down in any shelter they can find, a great number lodging in the cellars of the keep. And picking his way over the hot limestone shore and up the withered grass of the hill-side, he passed into the forest, asking himself if he would remain cast away in this outlying fort till the Scots were driven out of Ireland. Bermingham must know that nobody in Sligo is thinking of leaving a rich harvest—Landrey's spies reported it as being the richest for many years; or maybe Bermingham mistrusts the soldiers I would bring with me from Galway, or myself, being a De Burgo. . . . I should have gone to London, to the King; Edward would have received me, mayhap put me at the head of an army on its way to Ireland, and at the head of five hundred English soldiers Bermingham would have accepted me as an ally. But I acted on impulse, without foresight, and here I am in Castle Carra, with nothing in front of me but an unwilling return to a country where I was well received, and might be again. And stooping under boughs he followed the paths of deer, confessing himself all the time, saying: I went to Normandy to find love and met many women anxious to be wheedled, sang, drank wine, and pursued adventures till love, ashamed, called to chastity for protection. A roe deer bounded from the bracken in front of him, scattering his thoughts, and when he recovered them he was not certain that he had not come upon a successor to Jaufre Rudel in himself. Or the germ of one, he said; and he recalled the day he had confided his doubts to the Comtesse d'Artois whilst walking with her through the parakeet room, the room of roses and of lilies, and the room of shields, towards the room in which she transacted the business of her great estates, bedroom and oratory in one. The coverlet, the hangings of the bed—all were distinct, and her voice and his as they sat knee to knee. In youth we are content to let love go, for there is but little pleasure with the beloved. Is pleasure then with the casual rather than with the beloved? In the presence of the beloved we cannot fix our thoughts, and pleasure is overawed, annihilated by the greater emotion. Which do you place the higher, Comtesse, love or passion? I am surprised that a trouvère should be in doubt! And she spoke of Jaufre Rudel, who loved only the Princess of Tripoli and said when he was laid dying at her feet: To see thee is enough! and of Rambaut d'Orange, who loved all his life the Comtesse d'Urgel, whom he never saw and who never saw him. Neither time nor death can rob us of our love, if we love. Men and women have died of love, killed themselves for love, and sought the calm of the cloister so that they might better fix their thoughts on some saint in heaven, and there being only truth yonder, they are the happiest of all lovers, maybe. But it is a mistake to distinguish between lovers, for all who love pass through life hardly aware of life's tribulations and deceptions.

So did she speak, and whilst listening to her it seemed to me that my youth was flitting from me, and that the days in Normandy were taken over by a new spirit of sense. I was not a mile out of Hesdin when the thought came that I should put myself as Sir Galahad into rhyme and music. Fond days of springtide, how quickly over! We outlive you, but we never outgrow you. Even now in this wild forest I feel that a chaste life is the intenser life, and that Soracha, the king's daughter who entered a convent in the belief that a saint in heaven is a more worthy object of love than a knight, will inspire the love that I did not find in Normandy. Thy name, he cried, frightening a bird in the branches, thy name compels me to order that horses be ready at daybreak! But will the recognition on the balcony be a delight to one, or to both? And if neither be what the other imagined, sad indeed will be our plight by the window, Tadhg waiting below with the horses. And if we are overtaken by priests and hirelings and brought back prisoners? Our horses are too swift. Our real danger is that Soracha, overcome by the length of the ride, will be unable to keep the saddle till we reach the bridge-head at Athlone. Once at the bridge-head we shall be safe, and to bring partial forgetfulness of her pains I will sing and teach her to play the lute, and she will tell me how she came to enter a convent when she was seventeen. As I sit watchful at her bed-side I shall hear her say: No blame can be cast upon my good, kind father, who would have had me remain in his court, doing honour to it, but I felt that only the cloister could save me from the storms I could not control. Her story is mine; in it I shall view myself as in a mirror; and receiving her intimate confidences, I shall be able to tell her that I have been through the same transports and ecstasies, saying: A sinner I am, come out of many short-lived loves, desiring one love and only one, a love of many to-morrows. And having fixed her attention with these words, it will be well to pass on to the instruction I received from Mahaut. Didst love her very dearly? she will ask, and I shall answer: Love I can scarcely call it—a grand and beautiful nature, but past her time for love, of which she has had much I shall ask Soracha if it were worth while for the sake of passion to sacrifice love, and she will answer: Ulick, I am thine to love as thou pleasest, with such restraint or ecstasy as may seem to thee good. Or it may be that my avowals will darken her sunny face and that her manner will change towards me, for what more natural than that in her innocence she should think and perhaps say: If I am not to have a real lover I might as well have remained in the convent. I shall answer: I rescued thee from the convent at thy bidding; as a knight I could not do else; but the vows of knighthood do not commit me further than a rescue. If thou shouldst perchance find love to be enough, come with me to Castle Carra, and if thou art not sure thou canst withstand the tests I shall put upon thee, I will send a message to thy father's court to tell him where he will find thee, and with a short good-bye return to defend Castle Carra against imaginary enemies. . . .

To-morrow morning we start for Durrow, he added, as he passed out of the forest into a patch of waste ground where a chill wind shed the gold from some young birch trees. Clouds are gathering; there'll be rain to-night. And Tadhg being still away with the boar hunters, he bethought himself of Soracha's portrait, locked in a box that a soldier would be able to prise open with mallet and chisel. A soldier was sent with these, and when the lid was lifted off and the great door had closed behind the soldier, Ulick was on his feet and then upon his knees in front of the box, marvelling at the beauty of the face. The head drooped a little and the inclination of the body reminded him of a woman in an ivory or a Book of Hours, and he admired the thick hair wound about the head, the long robe open at the neck, the girdle at the waist from which hung a great burden of trinkets; and more than ever certain that the story of the portrait and the message come overseas was a recurrence of an eternal legend, to be lived again, the thought returned to him of a knight riding to receive his reward from Arthur. In my case from the King of Kings, my reward being the liberation of a soul for love's own sake; and in the performance of this knightly errand I shall be the well beloved of the Deity whence all things come and to which all things return. But Tadhg—where is Tadhg? And in search of Tadhg he left the keep to wander again in the forest, his imagination running into a song for her, that he committed to memory as he composed it, changing the rhymes when they did not correspond to his thoughts. Three times he repeated it to himself, and then the melody taking him unawares he walked towards the castle, to hear from the watchman as he passed that Tadhg had returned. A welcome bit of news this was, and taking down his harp from the wall he sought the chords that would enhance the melody, till his gleeman sat up in bed to ask the name of the tune; whereupon followed a little parley, Tadhg declaring that the melody was one that would have stirred the whole of Normandy. Think not of Normandy, Tadhg; we are not riding to Normandy to-morrow but to Ballinrobe. We shall need three horses—— Why three horses, your honour? Tadhg asked. Inquire not at midnight the pleasures of to-morrow, Ulick answered; leave to-morrow to live its own life. Now I bid thee to thy slumbers, with this to dream upon; three horses to be ready at the bridge-head at eight. . . . Three horses! said Tadhg to himself; but who will ride the third? And hearing his master breathing peacefully, he drew the blanket over his chin, muttering: He is back in France in his dreams, his head in a lady's lap. We all have our faults, every one of us! Who will ride the third horse? he repeated on opening his eyes at daybreak, and there being no woman in Ballinrobe he'd as much as look at, one pair of breeches and one hat is as good as another. But it's time the ostlers had their orders; and drawing on his boots he added: There's nothing like a boot to wake up the sluggard! And he remained with them lest they should fall asleep again till the time came for him to return to the keep to help the master in his dressing.

Still asleep! he said as he pushed the great door open warily. I dare not take him by the shoulders, for roused out of his sleep suddenly he is not himself at all. And he busied himself with his master's clothes till Ulick opened his eyes and called for his leather breeches. Here they are, your honour; and timorous he watched the wide shoulders, the ripple of the spine, the lank hips and the small, trim rump, the thin legs and the slender feet. No wonder they're after him, he said to himself. Who wouldn't be, if she were a woman! I had thought to have a dip in the lake, Tadhg, before we started. But an Irish lake is full of cold water in September. My cloak, Tadhg! Which of them? Tadhg asked. The warmest; and my spurs. As he descended the steps of the keep the rowels of his spurs caught in the stonework and Tadhg was bidden to unbuckle them for him. I never spur the mare, but a horseman is hardly a horseman without spurs, said Ulick, and Tadhg muttered to himself: The same on this side as in France! But on whom will the spurs put the comether? In which castle of the many does she live? The portcullis was raised, and as they passed underneath it a tall, restive mare whinnied, laid her ears back, reared, and tried to break away from the ostler, who refused to let her head go till Ulick called: Let her come! Let her come! And being loosed, she quieted at once and walked to him, mayhap with a memory in her handsome brown head of the morsel of honeycomb which she had often licked from his hand. He had brought her carrots that morning, and she followed him about, coaxing him for another and still another whilst he walked to and fro with Landrey, Tadhg viewing the long-plumed hat with suspicion, saying to himself: If Bruce was out in the north the master would wear his helmet. There's a chill wind blowing and your honour would do well to draw your cloak about you. Ulick put his arms through the sleeves and sprang into the saddle. She will outpace the roadsters, he said, turning to an ostler. The grey that Tadhg rides, the ostler answered, is a fast one, and won't be far behind the mare if you match them.

Now, your honour, I'd make bold to ask—— We are going to Donogh O'Brien to buy a harp, Tadhg. Donogh O'Brien? He is at Ballinrobe—don't I know it well—— And I have heard, said Ulick, heedless of his servant's interruption, that by keeping close to the lake we shall shorten our road by three miles at least. Michael Fogarty, the ostler, Tadhg answered, he that comes from Mucloon, the green hill over against the Ballinrobe road (didn't we pass it by on our way from Cong?), told me no later than this morning not to try the short cut if we were riding to Ballinrobe, for it is choked with blackthorn and hazel and we'd be hard set to get the horses through. But we aren't thinking of riding abreast, Tadhg. Even one by one, your honour, we might fail to get through; and coming home in the evening the harp might be scratched off my back, for I'd be loth to trust one of

Donogh's harps to a pack-horse. The harper that can't carry a harp on his own back is—— We shall go round by Carnacun, Ulick answered drily. If I say another word he'll tell me to go home! and they rode without speaking to the muddy pools of Carnacun, out of which snipe rose in hundreds, to go away zig-zagging over the pines. A heron flopping up the sky, his long legs trailing behind him, his spear-like beak in the air, recalled a great falconry on the banks of the Loire, and they rode on again till they came to a piece of green turf that promised so well for a canter that Ulick cried back: Do as well with the grey as thou canst, for the mare won't settle down till she's had a gallop; and pulling hard, she carried Ulick into sight of a green lake curving round low shores, where he reined in to await the arrival of Tadhg and the pack-horse. An ascending road was taken at a fine swinging trot that came to an end on the hill-top, for below them a great marsh seemed to challenge their advance towards Ballinrobe.

We crossed this marsh on the night we rode from Cong; I remember the hill and beyond it the hurdle-bridge over the river Anise. If your honour will take charge of the pack-horse I'll ride on in front, and it won't be long before I find the stepping-stones that we came by. Ulick took the leading-rein, and whilst Tadhg rode among the reeds he watched the wheeling gulls. A cormorant making for a ruined castle that the Welsh had built under the high Brownstown shore helped the time away, and when it lagged unduly he cried to Tadhg: Hast found the causeway? Not yet, your honour, but I'm on the track of it. At last a halloa from Tadhg and the sight of the little man half-way out in the marsh set him thinking of the descent of the hill, not an easy matter because of the pack-horse, a jibber, that for the nonce showed himself tractable enough, venturing out on the causeway, to turn aside, however, at the hurdle-bridge, and it was not till the leading-rein was thrown over to Tadhg that he was persuaded; the mare followed, and the bridge was crossed by all three horses without accident. The red bog ends a mile ahead of us, your honour, and the choice will be to turn to the right and cut off a mile of our journey to Ballinrobe, or—— Why should we not save our horses that mile? Ulick interjected. A mile and a half, Tadhg answered, and they followed the long, straight path, startled by grouse that rose up with a whirr and skimmed away almost out of view. They'll not leave the heather, said Tadhg. You see the village yonder, marked with its poplar-tree? They'll wheel when they get there! A shallow stream at the bog's end was forded with Tadhg trying to tell of the fine castle that had once stood atop of the Brownstown hill, built by a Welshman to defend his lands against all comers: But when your father raided this country thirty years ago he burnt the Welshman's castle. And whilst they rode side by side over the hill Tadhg told a story of burnings and rapine, to which Ulick gave but half an ear, for what his eyes saw interested him more, and what they saw were hazel thickets striving to hold their own against their ancient enemy. It's always hazel against blackthorn, he said, just as it's always Celt against Norman. After a descent through great rocks the country began to improve, so it seemed to him, and he continued: Hazel and blackthorn are rife, but there are many green fields in which cattle graze; elms, too, decorate the roadway and there are walls. And where there are walls and elms there are Normans, he added triumphantly, and looking over one of the walls he beheld deer grazing. Normans and venison imply Ballinrobe; we cannot be more than a mile from the first roofs, Tadhg. The road is becoming strangely familiar. I have seen these fields full of corn; and we shall soon come upon a triangular piece of grass, the village green—where I saw a woman jump through hoops from a bare-backed horse, and a bear dance. Five minutes later he said: We are now in full view of Ballinrobe. In old days there was no bridge; my father rode through the ford up the high street. But look at the limes! Father and mother and I used to walk there in the days when I sailed my boat in the Robe. My father told me I'd barely recognise the high street, rebuilt to the image of Courancy in memory of my mother. Courancy in Ballinrobe! Ulick cried as they rode past peaked gables, impending storeys, and red-tiled roofs with dormer windows. We turn to the right at the top of the hill, and a hundred yards will bring us to Donogh O'Brien's—a stone house with mortared walls and a handsome thatch, standing some dozen or fifteen yards behind the main street. Now, Tadhg, call, and as loudly as you can, for the house is as industrious as a hive, everybody intent on his job. And in answer to Tadhg's repeated calls a lad came. An apprentice, Ulick said, and dressed for the part—a leathern apron from his neck to his knees, and clogs on his feet. Is the master in? he asked, and canst thou manage the three horses? He is in, your honour; but the mare is too game for me. Go to her head, Tadhg; she guesses a stable and the oats are in her mind. On these words Ulick opened a small wooden gate, and he was about half-way down the paved path when the door of the house opened.

God bless the day that gives me sight of you again, Sir Ulick! And an old faded hand grasped Ulick's hand, and he was drawn into a house that he knew full well, for in his boyhood it was his pleasure to come hither to work at the lathe. You see the thrush's cage that you made with your own hands, and the boat with all her sails set that you left behind. But you'll tell me now if this be the first sight you have had of Ballinrobe—what am I saying? When you came up from Cong you must have ridden through Ballinrobe. I did, Ulick answered, but it was dark night; so it was to-day that I saw for the first time Courancy in Ballinrobe. Courancy is the Normandy village in which my mother was born. The old faded hand went to a red beard that curled into grey knots. Well, you'll be telling us all about your travels It would take more than to-day and to-morrow to tell all about our travels, though they were only from castle to castle, spreading the knowledge of Irish music and the instrument for which it was written. I have made better harps since those days, Donogh answered. I have a young man with me, he continued, who can decorate and inlay with any man that ever lived on the top of this earth. And I have a great harper, Donogh; he is in the stables now with the horses, but he'll be here anon. Is your honour talking to me of the great Tadhg O'Dorachy, your father's harper, he who was taught by Finn Lorcan himself? The same, Ulick answered. Here he is. Thou hast heard all the great harpers; to-day thou shalt hear the greatest of all. A bad time it is, said Tadhg, to hear a harper and he after a ten-mile ride, one hand on his own bridle and the other tight on the leading-rein. On the leading-rein? Donogh interjected. We have a third horse, said Ulick, for I would buy a harp from thee, Donogh O'Brien. The harp is safest on the harper's back, Donogh answered. So Tadhg has already told me, Donogh! and he spoke so drily that Tadhg hoped Donogh would find words to carry the talk on. But Donogh waited for Tadhg to release him from his embarrassment.

'Tis the fine drying-room thou hast here, Tadhg said at last. For oak and willow wood, Donogh answered, that will be well seasoned and safe from warp when it comes under the saw and chisel. Yonder are the workers. And when he had thrown open the door of the workroom the apprentices showed in leather aprons and shirt sleeves turned up, some sawing wood laid across trestles, others seated at work-tables set between the windows. Some providence must have chosen your visit to Ballinrobe, Sir Ulick, for to-day I looked over for the last time the harps that I have made for the daughters of King O'Melaghlin, three of the beautifullest women in Ireland and great harp-players all three. Dost know, Donogh, the names of the Princesses who will receive these harps? This one, said Donogh, is for Princess Muirgil and its brother is for Princess Liadin, and this one will be sent by King O'Melaghlin to his youngest daughter, Princess Soracha, who was called by God in all the beauty of her youth away from her father's court to live in a convent, where she is praying night and day that we may all be saved and meet in heaven. The apprentices held down their heads abashed, and Ulick said that the day was not far distant when France would be sending orders to Ballinrobe for more harps than Donogh O'Brien would be able to finish, though he lived till the end of the century; and it seeming to him that the moment had come for a little speech, he enjoined the apprentices to remember always that they were working under the eyes of the greatest harp-maker ever known in Ireland. On coming to the end of his words he took the harp destined for the Princess Soracha from Donogh, and running his fingers over the strings he said: As beautiful to hear as it is to see, but the sight of this harp saddens me. Now why, your honour, is there sadness in the sight of my harp? Donogh asked, and Ulick answered: I came here to-day to buy the loveliest thing in Ireland, and I find the three loveliest things are for the daughters of King O'Melaghlin. Don't you begrudge these harps, said Donogh, for you shall have one equal to them—who knows, superior to them; for though the three harps seem to be my masterpieces to-day, I may not be satisfied with them to-morrow. I did not say I had no oak as good as the oak that went into the making of these harps, and the willow wood I shall put into the harp that I shall make for you, sir, has been seasoning in this warm room since the day you first saw it. I want all thy skill, Donogh, for my harp.

So he is thinking out, Tadhg muttered, a gift of a harp to some great Princess! Shall I send the harp when it is finished to Galway? asked Donogh, or to Castle Carra? Send it to Castle Carra, Ulick answered. So she is coming to Castle Carra! Tadhg said to himself, and he waited trembling, for only a moment seemed to separate him from the name of the Princess—a name that would have been spoken, so he thought, if Donogh had not engaged Sir Ulick's attention on the oak wood which he would use for the upright pillar and the willow wood for the sounding-board, with four sounding-holes, all ornamented with silver bosses and fine carvings. And to show the harp he had in mind, Donogh took a burnt stick and drew, inviting Ulick's admiration (as the harp began to shape itself in his imagination) of the escutcheons charged with bears, carved and gilt, and of the brass tuning-pins which he proposed should be tipped with silver; of these there would be thirty instead of the usual twenty-eight. But I would like to show you, Sir Ulick, some other harps, and my foreman and apprentices will be duly honoured if you will follow me round the workroom and speak some words to them of their skill, should their skill meet with your approval. He led them to the different tables at which the apprentices worked, and Ulick was shown the carved patterns with which the harps were embellished. An ugly harp never comes out of this house, Donogh, but I fear that thou 'lt fail to surpass the harps thou 'rt making for King O'Melaghlin's daughters. The harp I shall make for you, your honour, will equal, as I have said, if it does not beat those I am sending to Lough

Ennel to-morrow or the day after, and by the King's own messenger. And now having seen all that I have to show you, let us get back to the front room, where you will find a table set with bread and meat and beer, poor fare, only fit for a craftsman, his aids and apprentices; but if your honour will partake of it—— Bread and cheese are tasty in the mouth of a man who rose at seven, Donogh, and thy ale will be welcome, and to prove it, pass me that piggin and I'll empty it without drawing breath; which he did. Now tell me, Donogh O'Brien—the house in which my mother lived still stands? Faith, it does, and just as it was the day her ladyship left it for ever, and will stand, with nothing taken from it and nothing put into it, till everything crumbles into the dust out of which all things came and into which all things will go—the Earl's own words to me on the day that he left Ballinrobe, where he spent the happiest years of his life, surely. Every door and shutter is locked and barred—but no doubt these very same words you have heard from himself before you left Galway. Yes, indeed, Ulick answered, and my father will ask me many questions when I return. So we'll walk round the house and garden together, though of little avail it will be to me to see them, for being both in my imagination, reality will merely blot the remembrance. Not blot it, sir. Dim it, alter it, Ulick continued, rob me of something. But since my father wishes it, we will go thither after the meal.

And having eaten they set out together, leaving Tadhg saying to himself: If he does not care to see the old house he was brought up in, why does he go thither with Donogh? And why am I told to wait for him here? Because he would collogue with Donogh about things that he wants me to be in the dark about! And having guessed that this was so, Tadhg pondered as his fingers ran over the strings, pausing from time to time so that he might think better why Sir Ulick had gone to see the house with Donogh O'Brien, leaving him behind—surely because he wished to find out from Donogh any news that might be going round about Bruce? Harpers come hither from the east and the west, from the north and the south; every harper in Ireland has been to Donogh's workshop to buy a harp, or to get new strings, or to have a broken harp mended, so not a thing can fall out in Ireland without Donogh knowing it. The visit to Ballinrobe is but a blind, for he knows well that he couldn't get a harp from Donogh O'Brien under three months; and we are travelling with a third horse to carry harps that are still in the wood! Tadhg recalled Donogh's words: A harp is nowhere as safe as on the harper's back. What I said myself! The mystery is in that third horse. And it's a poor thing that after all these years Donogh O'Brien should be trusted and myself treated like a newcomer. It is, faith! and to stay his tears his hands went again to the strings, this time bringing the apprentices out of the workroom. As if fearing to tread the earth they came, and the spell was not broken till Sir Ulick and Donogh came through the door talking of the shortest way to Dunmore. So we are going to Dunmore! he said to himself, and he watched a chart being made by Donogh; and his faith in being able to reach Dunmore that night by the aid of the chart deserting him suddenly, he said: We shall be lost in brake and forest, your honour, for what is more like one hill than another hill? or one bit of forest than another bit of forest? There's a great sameness even in rivers, all green and slow at the edges, with a stickle in the middle. I'm thinking it would be as well to put a boy from Ballinrobe on the pack-horse. Donogh O'Brien says we cannot miss the road, Ulick answered; and now let us away, for the day will be nigh ended by six.

We are going beyond Dunmore, said Tadhg to himself,

for if we weren't he'd have a boy up on the pack-horse. But ask no questions and you'll be told no lies, as my mother used to say in the Galway kitchen when I asked her what she was putting in the pot. So he climbed into the saddle, and it didn't take them more than five minutes to reach the open country. East by south, said Ulick; isn't that what Donogh said? East by south he said, your honour, Tadhg answered; and the going seeming to them good they cantered and trotted for a few miles, and were able to keep the line, having the sun behind them. We'll be all right whilst the sun is up, said Tadhg, and as Ulick did not answer he began to remember the vow he had made in the presence of the priest that he would have no hand, act, or part again in the deceiving of poor women—not that he pitied them, for they should be able to mind themselves; often enough it was the women started the game, casting their eyes about, looking everywhere except where they were going. But when he is called up before God on the last day it won't help him much to argue that it was the women set him off. Every mother's son of you, God will say, is ready enough for sin, ever since Eve brought the apple to Adam and the two of them ate it in the garden; and it's small sign I see in any one of you, and small wish in any one of you, to keep each other away from the snares the Devil is always laying; rather you are ready to push each other into them. The God of the Day knows that and the rest of it. He will call up the Angel of the Book and it will be all read out, my own share as well as the master's, for if I didn't play the tunes I did the chords, and the bass is as much in the game as the treble is; for I put some fine accompaniments on the tunes the master wrote, and he who works the harmonies is as deep in it as the man that makes the melody. Didn't the priest in Galway say as much when I went to confession? And Tadhg fell to thinking once more of his vow that he would never go out again woman-hunting with the master. Anything else he asks me to do I'll do for him, but the man that makes a vow and breaks a vow is damned and done for. So now Dunmore or beyond Dunmore into Roscommon, it 's all one to me. My conscience is clean, and a man that hasn't a clean conscience might as well be in hell, for then he 'd know all that was coming, and the worst of it.

Of what art thou thinking, Tadhg? Never have I known thy tongue so quiet. Like an eel under a comfortable stone it has been for the last four miles, said Tadhg, and I 'd be hard put to tell your honour what I was thinking. Just riding, taking no note of the country, said Ulick. Hasn't your honour got the chart? and isn't the chart better than my eyes in a country that I 've never seen before? And will you cast your eye over it and tell me if our way is to the right of the hill yonder, or if by going over the hill we might escape that great bit of dark wood stretching up to the horizon. What does the chart say, your honour? Donogh told me that we had better keep a look-out for that dark bit of forest and that we should keep to the right—or was it to the left? Ulick asked. I can't tell, your honour, not being beside yourself at the time. And the talk dropped till Ulick said: I think we did well to keep to the left. Tadhg thought so, too, but he spoke in so aggrieved a tone that Ulick began to wonder what wrong his servant was brooding, and it was to soothe him that he said: Tadhg, when I returned with Donogh from my mother's house I heard thy harp. An angel is playing, I said—— I would not have you say that much, your honour, for no playing in the world could come up to an angel's. How knowest thou? for no more than myself hast thou heard an angel play. I 've heard tell, Tadhg answered, of an angel that came to wrestle with Jacob, but never of a man that heard an angel playing on the harp. And if he did, wouldn't he be caught up on the music and lifted into heaven the way Elijah was?

But if thou camest across such a man? How could that be? for no one that was taken up to heaven on an angel's music could come back again, even if he wanted to, which he wouldn't. Thou speakest well, Tadhg. I try to tell the truth, and no more than the truth. But I would hear from thee why thou wouldst not have me compare thy harp-playing to an angel's. Well, then, the angels play their harps before God, don't they? and it isn't likely that he'd have any but the best. None can outplay thee, Tadhg. Not in the county of Galway, your honour, but heaven's another place. When thou'rt taken out of this life and given a place in heaven, a harp will be put into thy hands and thou'lt play before the Most High. I won't be Tadhg O'Dorachy when I do, and if God should claim my playing to be behind an angel's—— He will not, Tadhg, for didn't I think of an angel when I came up the path? and if thy playing wasn't like an angel's playing why should I have thought of an angel? Never in France did thy fingers draw such music from the strings, and the faces of the apprentices when they left were as if they had been listening to strains from heaven. Well, I won't be saying no to that, your honour, for they are Irish and love their country, and a man's love of his country is close, I'm thinking, to his love of God. More than that, the melodies I played were not of yesterday or the day before that, but those that have come from long ago, shaping the souls of the men without their knowing what was happening any more than the tree knows the wind, or the bee knows the flower, or the fawn knows the dug, and they all taking what the Lord gives without a question or a word. Thou speakest so well, Tadhg, that I'd learn from thee why it is that being Irish as the woods about us and the fields that we walk in and the skies above us are Irish, thou hast ranged thyself with the Normans rather than with thine own chieftains.

Often, whilst watching my mother bending over the

kneading-tray I've thought of Ireland shaping the races that came to conquer her and doing what she liked with them. First were the Firbolgs, and they were but bits of dough under Ireland's knuckles; and the same with the Celts. No sooner were the Firbolgs out of Connaught and the islands beyond Connaught, than Ireland was kneading the Celt, and he taking the fresh shape as easily as the Firbolgs and the Da Danaans did before him. And now the Normans are being kneaded, and many are as kindly Irish as if they were of the seed of Ir and Ever. The Scots left us, there being not room enough for them here, and when our race leaves Ireland for Scotland, they do not become less Irish for the crossing of twenty miles of salt water. The Irish spoken in Scotland is the same as our own, and the songs are our own songs, or so like them that none can tell an Irish from a Scotch song, or the other way about. So it matters not at all to us what race is in Ireland; it's Ireland matters and nothing else, for she is the great plasterer, joiner, carpenter, carver and mason. Now I'll put it to your honour: would I have been a better Irishman if I had followed Richard Bermingham to Athenry, or joined Felim who deserted your father when he went north to chase Bruce out of the country? It was at Connor that William de Burgo was made a prisoner, but he was ransomed by your father in time to take his share of the battle of Athenry—I don't know if your father told you the full story of the battle, for Bruce is always before him, making ready for a pounce on Dublin; or did you talk about the great Celtic kingdom, Scotland, Ireland, Man, Wales and Cornwall? Well, it was a great dream and one that may come true before the story's done, for it's not certain that Sir John Bermingham will prove the better man of the two. My father said the great Celtic kingdom would be no dream at all, Tadhg, if the Irish weren't divided amongst themselves. Maeve all but had it, Brian Kennedy of the Tribute had it, and King Robert said the same before he left Ireland. Now you are talking fair, your honour—if we weren't divided we'd be the top of this earth, and to this no man can say nay; for we have more than any other people the two things that make for greatness. And what are those two things, Tadhg? Love of God and love of country. A man must love himself, Tadhg, if he'd be a man; a race is but a number of men. Now I know what is running in your honour's head; the talk we used to be hearing in France; Nominalism, they called it, and Realism. I'm with the Church always myself, she being a better judge than I am of philosophies and such like. It is enough for me and my likes to have a good religion and a good country, and whoever has them two has enough to be thinking about without thinking of himself into the bargain; without them what better is he than a mouse or a cockroach that lives and dies and has his time behind the wainscot. And which does he get the best worth out of, Tadhg, his religion or his country? His country may be shook to a heap by a quake of the earth or eaten into empty caves by the sea, but his religion cannot be taken from him; like Connla's apple, it never grows less. You know the story, your honour? No, faith, or have forgotten it! None forgets the story of Connla and the girl who came to him from the Shí and threw him an apple which he was to eat; and though he ate of the apple every day it remained the same apple as before; only he was changed; and at last he had to follow the maiden into the sea, for she was a sea-maiden and lived in Tir nan Og; drowned he was in crossing the water.

The story thou tellest, Tadhg, is one of Pagan Ireland. Wasn't Ireland always the same, your honour, not a sword being lifted by a Pagan against a Christian, or by a Christian against a Pagan? and the same is a great honour to us and puts Ireland above the nations for Christianity.

Our soggarts were wiser than the priests of here and there, for without overturning an altar they slipped off their oak leaves and picked up Rome's biretta, and wore it without ever seeking to hush the old stories or to forbid assemblies to do honour to Bel. But, Tadhg, the worship of a false God must have been a great worry to the true God. If it had been indeed, he'd have sent Patrick of the Crozier to us sooner than he did with the news of his son that was born in Galilee. But thou hast said that the Irish do not forget Bel. They'd put it that a false God was better than never a God at all, and now that they have got the true God they think of Bel the way we think of the playthings of our childhood, of the first room we ran about in, of our first walk in the woods, of the lake that we saw for the first time, and the hill, the foxes, the wolves and the stags, and our wonder at a far off mountain, of the music we heard and the prayers that were taught us. Wouldn't it be a sorrowful thing indeed if we had no thought for the past that we come out of? For it would be like having no childhood to look back upon, and Bel was the childhood of religion. A false God your honour says he was, but our fathers would have been badly off without him; and didn't we come upon proof in Castle Carra that the past is never dead in Ireland, no more than our fathers which live again in us? For the men that were called upon ten years ago to dig the moat said that they wouldn't put hand to shovel to disturb the rock that stood in the way of the moat, and it was long enough before the Norman builder could find a why or a wherefore for them not wanting to dig. That rock was Bel's altar once, and every Beltane and Samhain there was a sacrifice on it. By those living now? Ulick asked. By the folk about Castle Carra, your honour. But the rock is no more, and thou hast not told how it was got rid of to make room for the moat. No one would lay finger or hand on the rock, and the work was at a standstill till Father Irnan, who had never approved of dancing or drinking or feasting, came with the bishop and drove the last of Bel out of the rock with holy water and afterwards with fire. They burnt the old God out by the roots. Burnt Bel out by the roots! Ulick repeated, trying once more to disentangle the shrewd harper from the man of prejudices and tradition, persuasions which he had grown up in, hearing with amazement that there being no piping to throw water on the burning rock, water had been brought through the entrails of Brigit Fahy's bull, slain for the purpose and roasted whole afterwards. A strange barbaric people, he said to himself, in whose country I find myself for no very clear reason, and out of whose country it may be I shall never find my way. Tadhg, in our talk we have lost sight of the road we should follow. The last bit of road, your honour, was leading out of Ballinrobe. In the chart that Donogh O'Brien drew for me there are hills and dales and woods and rivers, lakes even; but none of these things can I find in the country before me. He handed the chart to Tadhg, and reining in their horses they tried to recall the country they had passed through, but could remember no more than that they had ridden up some hills and through some valleys, and had seen many woods and fields and some broken steads.

Since we left Ballinrobe we have been through an empty country, wilderness rather than desert, said Ulick. To keep Connaught free from warfare, my father had to collect all the young men in Mayo and Galway, thereby giving so big an army to Bermingham that Bruce will be defeated between Dundalk and Dublin or forced to retreat. Neither ploughing nor digging has been in Ireland, said Tadhg, this many a day, nor hunting of wolves or foxes, so these creatures are commoner now than they were before; and the birds are here in greater numbers than were ever seen or heard of, there being no boys about to climb after their nests or take them in snares. The martens are plentiful in the woods, looking upon them as their own, and as we rode by talking about Bel's altar a badger came out of his hole to walk about in broad daylight. The country is said to be wilder in Roscommon than in Galway, and West Meath is the worst of all, as we shall see if we get so far. Ulick did not answer and they rode on, coming soon after to a field that looked as if wheat had been sown in it, but it was hard to tell whether the stubble was wheat stubble or bean. Above nettles some seven or eight feet high they caught sight of a sagging roof, but the way to it was so overgrown that they deemed it deserted; and when they had left the nettles behind them they came upon thistles spilling their seed all over the land. One year's seeding, seven years' weeding, is a true saying, your honour, and their friend the rain was with them last year month after month; a long guesting it was, I 'm thinking, and Tadhg pointed to mouldering leaves of coltsfoot and charlock. Before the charlock were poppies, groundsel, shepherd's purse and spurry, and every weed of these weeds is as quick a breeder as a rat; a rat whilst you 're looking and another whilst you 're not. Young rats, old rats, thin rats, fat rats, left the field, taking refuge in a barn. A sad country, your honour—— We haven't come here, said Ulick, to watch the rats taking a fall and to count the weeds breeding. Is there any thought in thee for the east or the north or the west? East it is, for the sun is behind us, Tadhg answered. Well, let us fare on; whip up the greys, for it cannot be that we shall not come sooner or later to a grassy hill, a shepherd and his flock. And when they had ridden upwards of two miles in silence, it was Ulick that broke into talk: I 'm thinking, Tadhg, that we are tiring our horses in trying to push through this clough, so hard and strong is the bracken; maybe the wood yonder would be easier. So putting their horses' heads to the sunset they rode out of the clough into the wood. Poor beasts, Ulick continued, they have come thirty miles, and I would tell them if they could understand me of the full manger they 'll eat out of if we reach Dunmore to-night. But what evil wood have we come into? Black earth and blackthorns, trees prone and falling on every side, some quaking, unable to stand, like men coming out of a tavern after midnight; a crapulous wood, full of newt and frog and tadpole pool, stinking rooks and nettles—which is the worser? If we meet nothing worse than a nettle and a rook, Tadhg answered, we 'll do well, for if I didn't see a wolf just now I saw nothing. But how are we to get out of the wood if we don't go back the way we came? We must push on, said Ulick, for to turn back would dishearten our horses. And in pushing on they were very nearly swept from their saddles by boughs, and the paths were so narrow between hazel and blackthorn that they gave themselves up for lost. Cattle have been through these paths, for their tracks are in the mud. Many 's the month since cattle came through this wood, Tadhg answered, a lonesome place, without even a bird in it, and I 'm always afraid of a birdless wood. As he spoke the old path broadened suddenly; fields showed through the trees, and Ulick said: Whatever else may happen to us we have passed out of that evil wood! and the question comes: shall we follow the plain or take to the hills? Tadhg answered: We shall have a better chance of finding our way from the hills, and they rode on for another mile or two in disquiet, feeling their horses tiring under them.

We did well to take to the hills, said Ulick, and he sought for the markings in the landscape that he was told to look out for. My eyes are liars if I do not see a shepherd. Your eyes are no liars, your honour; a shepherd is out before us. But he hears not our horses, nor does his dog smell us though the wind favours him.

Canst tell us the way to Dunmore? Tadhg and Ulick shouted together, and the volume of their voices startled the shepherd out of a great loneliness of mind; but his speech was the harsh, uncouth speech of an almost deaf man. Shout in his ear, Tadhg; keep shouting: Dunmore! till he understands, for maybe by riding on a few paces I may come in sight of a sign. And riding on he came to a few sheep. One of the sheep dead, he said, and forgetting the sign he was seeking on the horizon he returned to the shepherd. The third sheep! The third sheep! The Scots have poisoned the wind! The wind is poisoned! The wind is poisoned! the shepherd muttered again and again. At their approach a raven left off picking at the sheep's eyes. No raven was here a while ago, Ulick said. An evil bird, said the shepherd. An evil bird forsooth! said Tadhg. The raven walked aside, and so grave and melancholy was his gait that the fear he inspired was doubled. An evil bird! cried Tadhg once more, and whoever meets one on his journey would do well to return home, for the journey will not prosper any man who meets a raven on the way. How far are we from Dunmore? he shouted into the shepherd's ear, and this time the shepherd understanding him well, said: A matter of ten miles.

Will your honour believe me that it would be well for us to turn back? A raven is but a crow, Tadhg, and a crow is but a jackdaw, and the flight of one out of a chimney should not turn a brave man from his errand, whatever it may be. Thy cheek blanched when I spilt salt at Donogh's board—— It 's bad luck to spill the salt, your honour. And on passing through Carnacun the cocks did not crow to thy liking, and at Brownstown a lizard on a path frightened thee. I said no word, but I saw the fright in thy face. If you saw my fright why did your honour not call me from my horse to kill the lizard? Is a dead lizard, then, less harmful than a live one,

Tadhg? Most sure and certain it is, your honour. The cocks will crow to-morrow but not with the same crow, and other things mournful and menacing will happen. Wherefore I ask you, master, to turn aside. Our horses are too tired, Ulick answered, to take us back to Ballinrobe even if we wished to return. See, they are beginning to trot of themselves, scenting their stable. Thy mind is like an old loft full of bats. Think of the supper that awaits us, and the oats and the hay that await these poor beasties that have carried us so far; they would reach Dunmore before the rain—they are not afraid of the raven, the rook, the crow, the jackdaw, the lizard or the frog. We are Christians, they are horses! Ulick heard Tadhg mutter, and they rode on through the dusk, Ulick crying back encouragement to his servant. I would not have thee miss Dunmore, for there is an old wife in the town whom thou shalt consult, and she'll read thee thy story out of the stars. So if thy fear troubles thy belly and turns thee from thy food, a bellyful of oracles I promise thee to-night; stars and old wives shall guide thee. To which banter Tadhg listened with a quivering lip and a faint heart, roused a little out of his fears when the lights of Dunmore showed in the distance.

CHAP. XLVII.

REINING IN before a large hovel they asked for shelter and were bidden to come in. But our horses? cried Ulick. The stable is at the far end of the hovel, Tadhg answered, and a woman, lifting down two wooden bars, drove an ass into the backyard, saying: A fine, comfortable stable, and at the service of your honour's horses for to-night and to-morow and the day after, if you'll be here for so long. A great fire was burning in the middle of the floor, the smoke escaping through a hole in the roof, and huddled round it were half-a-dozen men and women, all warming their shins, holding their hands to the blaze. One man, perhaps the man of the house, punched a pig back into his corner out of their way, and the woman who had let them in said: Betsy Egan is with us to-night, the wisest woman in Connaught, and she'll tell you the end of your faring. Give his honour the chance of a warm before he begins to ask a witch to tell him if his journey will end as he wishes it, the man said, and Ulick, who could bear no longer the mingled reek of pig and hen, said he'd rather sleep in the open air. And so that his words should not humble the host, Tadhg added: A wise man he is, too, and great in the reading of the stars. If you'll tell me where the hay is I'll bring him out a couple of trusses to lie himself on. The ass will be munching them, keeping his honour awake, said the woman of the house; and they went out together into the backyard to tie the ass out of reach of the hay. But he brayed so piteously for his fodder later in the night that Ulick untied the halter, yielding some of his bed to the ass for the sake of sleep; and having come some thirty miles sleep fell again so suddenly and heavily upon him that he seemed to have slept but an hour when Tadhg came to him, asking if they should breakfast whilst riding—— Or breakfast in the reek of that fire? Ulick asked, swinging himself into the saddle, and he rode without speaking, breaking silence at last, saying: It wasn't for the warmth of the fire thou wast thinking, Tadhg, to bring me into the hovel, but to hear the end of our faring from the wise woman. I wouldn't be saying it wasn't, Tahdg answered, and he kicked the pack-horse out of his way. Always against my leg! Why can't he leave me my share of leg space? So thou thinkest the wise woman could tell me the end of my faring? She is deep, Tadhg answered. And what dost thou mean by deep? I mean what I say, your honour: deep. She knows things that other people don't know, and she could read your honour in one look. What did she say about me? She said she read a hunger in your eyes which would never be satisfied, though you roamed the country from the Giant's Causeway to the cove of Cork. A hunger in my eyes! What did she mean by that? I can't tell your honour, but there was meaning in it when she said it. Again they rode on, seeking the meaning of the wise woman's words, till Ulick said: And thou, Tadhg, didst sleep as well by the fire as I did under the stars? The jackass was eating the bed from under your honour when I came to you at daybreak. But, Tadhg, I'm asking not how I spent the night, for I know it, but how thou didst spend it by the fire. Seeing sights, Tadhg replied after a pause, that I had hoped never to see again. And what sights may they be? When I was a boy I didn't mind them sights, for I had then no knowledge of the shapes or mis-shapes of womenkind, and wouldn't trouble to look round when they pulled up their smocks so that the warmth of the fire should get at their legs and more than their legs. But now, being a grown man and having come from France and learnt much, I kept on opening an eye to see things that I didn't want to see. But a woman's rump is not an ugly thing, Tadhg. Isn't it, faith? But their rumps wasn't what I feared the most, but when in sleep they turned round the sinful side of them. The sinful side, Tadhg? Well, doesn't your honour know as well as myself that the sin always comes from the bushy side? I can understand thy feelings, Tadhg. No, you can't, your honour, for you're not of my way of thinking and not likely to be, though I shouldn't say it. But as long as there's life there's hope, and I keep on praying that God will bring you back to the Holy Church one day or another when the wickedness has died down in you. But if thou hadst no thought for women's bodies when a boy, how was it the women kept thee awake last night?

Amn't I telling your honour? Lifting their smocks to get the warmth. I am afraid that some wicked thoughts of sins—— No, your honour, I never made a sin with a woman yet, and if God's good I never will. Tadhg, let no lie come from thy lips. I'd bite off the end of my tongue first! But there are things that no man should talk about, unless it be to his own priest. I think a priest would say that a man to whom grace has come should make known his good fortune. I wouldn't keep the secret to myself, your honour, if I could believe that it was the grace of God that helped me, but I'm not so sure of that, and it's a thought that has often troubled me. Well, then, tell thy secret, and in putting it into words perhaps we shall be able to give a fair guess whether it was grace or good luck. I have asked the priest himself, a good priest and a clever priest, but he couldn't tell me. Tell me the story, and thou'lt be able to judge thyself as well as a priest. I wouldn't say that, answered Tadhg. Well, perhaps not altogether, but in some ways, for thou'lt be able to hear how the story sounds in the telling. But your honour is not of the persuasion that in Ireland the weak overcome the strong. Who said that? The wise woman herself, and there's something in it, something I've often felt myself. Tell thy story, Tadhg.

It was long ago, before we went to France, at the time when I was playing the harp behind your father's chair, getting a great renown for myself in Ireland. In the times I'm telling you about there were more harpers than there are now at the Earl's court, and every one of them had a story to tell about women; and listening to their talk I would be ashamed, for I had nothing to tell them, and indeed my understanding was so little that I had to ask what happened between them and the girls. Some of the things I asked set them off in great laughter, but one day I began to think I might go into Galway town and have a talk with one of the girls that

I 'd find sitting about on the benches, and get tales from her which I could tell as if they were my own. She would want a sum of money before she would tell me the kind of stories I was after, but I had saved enough, and I said: She can't well ask more than two pence to tell the stories that will make me seem as well up in the world as the best of them. So away went I to be made a man of for two pence. A big price, but worth it, I said, for no longer shall I be a jeering stock but as bad as the best of them, in appearance at least. Thoughts like that were twisting in my head and keeping me going whilst walking Galway town in search of a punk, and it wasn't long before I came across two sitting on a bench in the sun. After I 'd walked past them two or three times one of them cried: Come and sit by us, bonny boy. For what would I sit beside you? said I. We 'll tell thee that when thou 'rt by us, she answered. So I went to them, and the one nearest to me (for I didn't dare to sit between them) said: Thou 'rt a harper? I said: Yes; wouldst hear me play? And both being of the same mind to hear me, I unslung my harp and began to play. But I hadn't been playing very long before one of the girls rose up and said she must go home to her dinner, and the girl I was left with being more polite, said she would tell me all the stories I needed, but that she, too, would have to be getting her dinner. And, fearing to lose her, I said: I will pay money to hear some stories from thee, and she answered: Come back home with me and I 'll share my dinner with thee and tell thee all the stories I know. When we had had dinner, she said: Now I 'll tell thee a story. I waited for the story, but instead of the story she began to untie her smock, and afraid she might step out of it, I said: Thou canst tell me a story with thy smock on as well as off. Thou 'rt putting a joke upon me, said she, but I 'm not simple as thou thinkest me. It was then I began to understand that the story she had promised to tell me was the sin we were to commit together, so I handed her my two pence and got out of the house, giving thanks to God for his grace which had kept me from sin. But no sooner was I in the street than I began to think it over, asking myself if it was the grace of God or the punk's ugliness that had kept me in the straight path. It may be that your honour can tell me. The wench seemed no wise ugly to thee, Tadhg, whilst sitting with her in the sun? Not till she began to untie her smock, your honour; and I remember to this day saying to myself: What an ugly thing a woman is! But thou hast turned from that belief. France has helped thee to see beauty in women—how much rounder their forms are than a boy's. I should have said that a boy was rounder than a woman, your honour. There is no truth, said Ulick; we know the world through our senses, but as soon as the knowledge that our senses impart enters the mind, it is distorted by what we have seen and heard, and most of all by what we have been taught. Thou hast allowed others to mould thee, Tadhg, but I have turned a deaf ear to all but the inward voice, saying: I am the guardian of God's own work and will bring back to him the self he gave forth, telling him on the Judgment Day that whilst gathering flowers with a woman or talking to her of the stars, I had no thought for stars or flowers but of what her worth might be were we locked in naked battle. Does the sight of men bring lustful thought to women? Tadhg asked. A question thou must put to the priest in thy next confession!

Again they rode on for a mile or more without speaking, and when silence began to weary Ulick he asked Tadhg to tell him of the temptations that had come to him in France. Said Tadhg: Even if the crow isn't hungry he isn't satisfied, and if I wasn't in love I was curious, and the gleemen in whose company I often was whilst waiting for your honour spoke about love as if it were most wonderful. That from which all proceeds, and into which all returns, said Ulick. One day whilst resting at Blois on our way to Franchard, a gleeman in the tavern where we stayed told me that the taverner's wife was in love with me. Faith, it made me laugh! but in the night I said to myself: I'd like well to know what this thing is that all the men and all the women are talking about—this love. So when the taverner's wife raised her eyes to look at me—— To look at thee, Tadhg? Women, your honour, can come to like all kinds of people, tall, handsome folk like yourself, and humble little folk like me. Thou speakest truth; so on with the tale! Well, to give her a chance of liking me better than she did, I asked her to teach me French, and every night I'd sit by her elbow learning the foreign tongue, picking up words here and there and learning to read out of an easy book. Till at last you fell in love with each other? Catherine didn't say much about love, and I had begun to think it all a make-believe when she said: My husband is not sleeping with me to-night; come and seek me in my bed. And curiosity getting the better of my dread of her husband, a tall, sallow, lean, bitter-eyed man, I went shaking into the room; and finding the bed I lay down and waited till a hairy leg put the thought into my mind that maybe I was in the wrong room, for this much I did know: that women are not supposed to be so hairy as men, and the leg that had touched me was more like the shank of a monkey than the proper limb of a man. I am in bed with her husband or with the Devil! said I to myself, and the thought had scarce got into my mind when he turned round; and finding that there was as hairy a leg as his own lying beside him, he leapt out of bed, and with his back against the door he bellowed: Now I'll see who thou art, and it will be bad indeed for thee shouldst thou try to get past me! And knowing him to be a man who spoke the truth, I stayed in the bed till he had struck a light; and seeing me, he cried: Thou shalt have a lesson, thou furry knave, and one that will last thee for this time and the next. He searched about the room, and it wasn't long before he found his belt, and having found it he called upon me to bare my rump. . . . I had to keep to my bed for some days. And thou wouldst not see the doctor lest the truth should be known! I remember the taverner, a tall, gloomy man—— An evil face, your honour, a very evil face. And how was it, Tadhg, that she sent thee into the wrong room? Or maybe, said Tadhg, she sent me to the right one and the mistake was mine; for I like not the thought that Catherine, who taught me French so gently and sweetly in the evening, could play so cruel a trick upon me in the night. Indeed, she wished me to believe that she would recompense me for the beating I had gotten. And what didst thou say to that, Tadhg? I said: Love must be a great thing indeed if it makes good the pain I have suffered; and she answered: Surely it will, and thou shalt not be asked to go into a dark room again; I'll take thee bathing with me. So thy last love adventure, Tadhg, was in a river? Her husband didn't leave Blois, or we left Blois before her husband, and it was on our return that she led me to the river through the garden, not knowing there was a wasp's nest at the end of it; and so many were the stings I got that the doctor said a sting or two more would have had my life.

Worse luck than thine never came to a lover, Tadhg. Worse luck, your honour! I have come to see it all now as the best of luck, for if I had strayed into her bed a big, round, fat, mortal sin, not a doubt of it, would have been committed, and then where should I be, and not an Irish priest within hundreds of miles to hear my confession? But a French priest, Tadhg, can shrive a man as well as an Irish. He can shrive a Frenchman, for they talk the same language, but you couldn't expect him to shrive an Irishman with only a word of the French here and there. So I kept away from the French priests and put my trust in God himself that he 'd keep me going and alive till the ship put in at Galway, and a wonderful peace it was that came over me when I fell on my knees before Father Carabine. One of these days you 'll be finding out for yourself, your honour, that nothing lightens the heart like a good confession. But Tadhg, thy face is overcast. Hast sinned again? Last night—what of it? Faugh! The thought of the unseemly rumps brings the stomach up! No, I haven't sinned, and if my face be glum at times it is for the fear in my heart that our journey may end in a sin. But if I know thee, Tadhg, the wise woman was questioned, and she told thee—— That in Ireland the weak overcome the strong, said Tadhg; 'tis a mysterious saying, surely. And did she tell thee that our quest was a holy hermit, or a lonely lady at her casement window? If I said it was a hermit—— Say it, your honour, say it, and I 'll be the happy man and the contented harper that I was when I returned from the priest in Galway shriven of my sin and as clean and holy as a new-born soul. Of what sin, Tadhg, did he shrive thee? I tried to make it plain to him that I wished to learn from the taverner's wife if the pleasures of love were all that the trouvères and troubadours said and sang. Tadhg, thou 'rt fooling thyself; damn thy conscience! I will beg your honour not to damn my conscience, for without his conscience a man is but a stray. For my conscience sake, say if our quest is hermit or lady. Say, master, and I 'll be gay, and we 'll play our harps together on the banks of the Suck the way the Jews did long ago by the waters of Babylon. Tadhg, thou art a fool and I am weary of thee.

Master, didst thou hear it? I heard the caw of a rook in the air. No rook, your honour, but a raven; watch him, he is going towards the Suck. His caw sounds strange overhead in the still air of the fall, Ulick answered; not another sound. As a dead house the country is. Whip up the greys. And the air being keen and the horses willing, they reached the Suck in half an hour, and failing to find a ford, Ulick rode the mare into the river, Tadhg following with the pack-horse, who chose the deepest place to stop; neither backwards nor forwards could he be persuaded to move. Leave him, Tadhg; as soon as his blood begins to chill he'll follow the other horses; and they had not reached the end of the next field before the brute was after them. Now, Tadhg, tell me the meaning that the wise woman put on an obstinate pack-horse. She put a queer meaning on the raven outside Dunmore, for it's well known that there's no luck for them that meet a raven, 'tis known well since the beginning of the wide world. And ever since meeting the raven, Tadhg, every stick and every stone, every hare and every rabbit, thou takest for an oracle. Thou hearest me? Of neither spells nor omens will I hear another word! But to meet a raven—Tadhg began, and Ulick's anger rising suddenly, he raised his whip to strike Tadhg. Strike me, master, strike me, for a blow will remind me that I am your servant—in this world we are master and servant. And it is well that the servant should be a good servant and the master a good master, Ulick said. And no servant ever found a better master than I have, Tadhg replied.

As they advanced eastward into Ireland they began to read in the fields the story of long wars. For war did not begin with the Scots in Ireland but with the Danes, said Ulick. And before the Danes, your honour. We need not look farther back than the Danes. After the Danes the Normans came, and we were followed by the Scots. And how many burnt steads have we seen, Tadhg, on our way hither, and how many fields over-run by blackthorn and hazel? The field we are in shows but a few patches of grass; only a few more years are needed for it to be forest again. Very little of the great herds of Ireland remain; a few scattered cattle and a few sheep. But herds of deer we have met and herds of wild swine, and wolves and foxes are more numerous than men. As he spoke they came to a low-lying field with drains cut along and across, but reeds and briars had dammed the drains and the field was now nearly marsh despite the long drought. As soon as the rains begin it will be a lake! In the middle of the field was a clump of trees, and guessing it to conceal a spring-head they rode towards it, thinking to water their horses; but at their approach some five or six men and women, with a child or two, ran like wild animals into the woods and could not be brought back by kindly promises of help. Starvelings, living upon cress, said Tadhg. Living upon cress! Ulick repeated. At Dunmore there was talk, your honour, of the food the Scots had taken out of the country, destroying everything that they couldn't carry, leaving only the cress and the berries for people to live on, or—— I could tell stories that would make your honour faint to hear. Well, then, don't tell them! and they rode on in silence till Tadhg said, pointing with his whip: The man that we last asked the way from said we'd find the Abbey of Ballintober in a scoop of the land, with grand trees about it, and cattle feeding. And now, Tadhg, what names shall we give? Your honour's name would have a greater sound than any other in the land. That may be, Tadhg, but I am not willing to give my name. For the night that we are here I am Roger d'Andeli, a trouvère, come to Ireland in search of Irish harps, and thou art my gleeman, Jean Bretel. But if a French monk, your honour, should be here and speak to me in French—— Well, we shall be found out, that's all! Ulick interrupted harshly. And now, Tadhg, listen. Thou hast put thyself between me and my will ever since we set out from Castle Carra, and I'll bear with it no longer but will strike hard across thy shoulders with my whip. Dost hear, Tadhg? Your honour knows that I would do everything and more for your sake. I am Jean Bretel, and will speak the best French I can—— We speak French together, and to the monks I speak in Latin. Thou hast no Latin. A stickle of truth in a flood of falsehood! said Tadhg. Remember, no word of Irish from thee, Tadhg!

The lay brother, who had no Latin, cried to somebody within the porch for a scholar, and when the scholar brother came Ulick gave the name of Roger d'Andeli, a Norman trouvère. Tadhg would have gone to help the lay brother with the horses, but Ulick laid his hand on his arm lest in a moment of forgetfulness he should break into Irish. So he said to him in French: Come thou with me, Jean; the Abbot has sent word that he is willing to receive us. And as trouvère and gleeman journeying together to Athlone to buy harps, they were accepted by the Abbot without suspicion, Rambaud d'Orange's melody serving them for passport excellently well. The Abbot must needs hear it twice over, and after the second hearing he said: When you have gotten your harps it would be well for you to return quickly whence you have come, for a great battle will be fought in Ireland within the next few weeks. Ulick listened with due courtesy to his host, hearing from him the story of Earl de Burgo's imprisonment in Dublin and the Scots' retreat from Limerick with the loss of half their army, and of Bruce, who was still in the north preparing a march southward. But he will be met by Sir John Bermingham with a great army of thirty thousand men, said the Abbot, and it will be well for you to hasten to Athlone, for after the battle there will be parties of soldiers flying from the ranks of the Scotsmen, or perhaps from Bermingham's ranks, and I would not have you fall into their hands. From the Scots you have most to fear, for if the Scottish army be defeated the Scots will scatter north and south and west and wander over Ireland plundering and killing without care or mercy, like men bereft of reason. But when will Bruce begin his march southward? Ulick asked. Our news from the north is that he is waiting for reinforcements from Scotland and mayhap will wait no longer, or he may wait a few weeks more. But the battle will be fought before the middle of October, so hasten to Athlone to buy your harps. Think not that I would bid you away; it is of your safety I am thinking. An early start in the morning I would press upon you. On these words the Abbot rose from his chair, and Tadhg, afraid that he might be dismissed without having obtained the Abbot's blessing, ran forward and threw himself on his knees and began to babble in French. He would have your blessing, my lord Abbot, Ulick said, and he followed Tadhg's example, saying as he rose from his knees: A servant's piety is as welcome in the sight of God as his master's, a remark that found such favour with the Abbot that Tadhg received a pat on the head. You may tell him, said the Abbot, I will remember him in my prayers; a promise that was not transmitted to Tadhg lest in excitement he should break out into Irish. I will tell him, Ulick said to himself, to-morrow, when we are ten miles from Ballintober, but no sooner, lest an evil wind carry my words back to the Abbot.

A lay brother conducted them to their beds, Ulick saying to Tadhg: Rouse thyself betimes, for we should start before the Abbot leaves his bed. The Abbot is an old man and old men lie long abed, Tadhg replied. Sleep was upon them soon after, and next morning whilst waiting at the great door of the Abbey, Ulick said in French to Tadhg: Thy words last night were that old men lie abed—true words, and waiting for him our horses are catching cold. The Abbot is out of his bed, cried a lay brother running towards them, and is dressing quickly so as not to keep you waiting. Whereupon Ulick asked for some horse cloths; but the Abbot arrived before them, and having thanked him and bidden him good-bye they walked their horses through the abbatial domain, it seeming to Ulick that to allow them to trot would show a lack of courtesy. How many miles are there between Ballintober and Roscommon? he asked after passing the gates. About ten, your honour. Well, let the horses trot and get warm, and we shall get warm with them. Tadhg woke up the pack-horse with a cut from his whip, and after a trot of three miles they reined up in front of Lough Ree, a long lake dotted with islands showing dimly through white mist; and riding along the old timbered road under scattered pines Ulick pointed to a shadowy form slinking through the rocks. A dog fox going to earth, said Tadhg, the first living shape we have seen since we started this morning; unless we count the spiders in their glittering snares woven between the door-posts of the barn. Flying from the light into the darkness the insects would go right into them. I 'm thinking there 's not many insects wiser than the spider. How far are we from Athlone? Ulick asked. I 'd say no more than five miles, your honour; but the mare has cast a shoe, the off foreleg, and you 'll have to ride the grey. Tadhg spoke of an old clout or hat to tie round the fetlock, but there being neither clout nor hat to be purchased or picked up on the road, Ulick returned to his thoughts, for in the long walk of an hour and a half he would be able to make up his mind whether he should tell Tadhg the story of the Princess Soracha or keep it from him till they reached Athlone; once across the bridge Tadhg would not be able to return without the password; but to trick his henchman by withholding the password jarred Ulick's sense of knightly honour, and the rather as he was by no means sure that Tadhg's loyalty might not prevail in the end. It certainly would if he could persuade Tadhg that his love for the Princess Soracha was not different from the love with which God is loved in cloisters. But Tadhg could only understand what he had learnt in his youth, and he was afraid that as soon as Tadhg heard that they were on their way to a convent to release a nun from her vows of chastity, he would put his heels into his horse and leave him. Yet it was difficult to think of him deserting a De Burgo in the hour of his need. Moreover, Ulick was not certain that the tale he had been spinning in his head ever since they left the monastery might not prove as fatal to Tadhg as the glittering wheel he admired to the insects. For his tale to have a chance of catching Tadhg it must begin far away, and he could think of nothing more natural than to say: A desolate country thine is, unending wars and forays, murders, burnings, destruction, hard meat everywhere despite the splendid herds that stand knee-deep in succulent herbage, there being no cooking in Ireland. So my mother often said to me, Tadhg answered, and she was the last cook in Ireland, having been learnt by a Frenchman brought over from France. This lake frightens me, Tadhg—the loneliness, I mean. Hast no fear of this desolate country? Why should I fear my own country? said Tadhg. Hast no thought for France? Faith, I have at times; for the eating and the drinking in France, I'll give that in to you, is better than any we get here. Wine is better than mead and it's better than beer, and the first time I lay down between a pair of sheets I thought myself in heaven. And the omelettes, Tadhg! My mother was the last to make an omelette in Ireland, and she died without learning anybody. My father has a cook—— Yes, your honour, a Frenchman, but my mother was the only Irish cook he would ever let nigh the castle. Well now, Tadhg, thinking of the sheets and the wine and the omelettes and the many other good things that are in France, wouldst thou always remain by this desolate lake? I would, faith! and wouldn't it be strange if I didn't like the lakes and hills my forefathers looked upon thousands of years before I was born as well as your honour liked the Seine looping through the green valleys of Normandy, your forefathers being French? The most you can say is that there are three generations of Ireland in you, and these three generations were blotted out by your mother, who was a Frenchwoman. The truth is never far behind thee or in front of thee, Tadhg; it is more often than not up against thy elbow; and never was it nearer to thee than in the words thou hast just spoken. For when I saw Normandy for the first time I seemed to have known always the Seine looping and looping again through the green pasture lands with low hills, and the poplar-trees showing against the sky at evening—yes, and the castles and their gardens, with marble-rimmed fountains. All these were familiar; France to me was like some dim before-time. If it had only been in dim before-times that your honour sang by the marble-rimmed fountains I shouldn't have had a sin at all to confess, said Tadhg. Now again, Tadhg, thou 'rt thinking that it was thine accompaniments on the harp that led the ladies straying from strict paths. And their husbands out and away in Palestine fighting for the Holy Sepulchre, Tadhg answered. But no matter; the time that I've earned in purgatory for the accompaniments has been remitted by Father Carabine, and in Galway town. But thy confession did not save thee from joining friends and returning to the palace next day faint and pale. Well, my sins were forgiven me, and I've done my penance for the drink, saying Paternosters and Hail Marys and telling my beads, and I've given my share of candles to burn in the shrines and got me scapulas to wear and holy medals, and can go to God and the Trinity itself certain I won't be kept in purgatory for long. Nor was that all. Before I left

Father Carabine he made me vow that I'd never play the accompaniment to an ill song again, and it's as well your honour should know this, for it would go to my heart to refuse anything a De Burgo asked for.

But, Tadhg, thine ear is closed when I tell that there must be always a barrier between the lover and the beloved, and that the trouvère does no more than to love the lady in the castle as the monks and nuns in the cloister love the saints in heaven. Jaufre Rudel loved the Princess of Tripoli as a nun loves Christ, as a monk loves Mary, and so great was his love that it consumed him on his voyage to her. No man loves his mistress when he is by her as well as he does when he is away. Rambaud d'Orange never saw the Comtesse d'Urgel nor she him; to sing her praises was enough; hardships, sufferings, afflictions were borne by him cheerfully, for they helped him to appreciate his love. We must suffer if we would enjoy, Tadhg; martyrs and trouvères are alike in this. But in heaven, master, we shall love God better than on earth and he amongst us always. It may be, Tadhg, that the greatest saints will say: We miss the fever and the ecstasies of our convents and monasteries—— And ask God to let them return to earth, master? Among the other questions which thou wilt put to Father Carabine, put this one. No need to put it, for I know well what Father Carabine's answer will be; he will say that no man should sing the praises of any wife but his own. Speak to him, Tadhg, of the need for a barrier, and of Bertran de Born, who was buried in the habit of a Cistercian monk. Folquet de Marseilles, too, repented his sins and was ordained a bishop. I am glad to hear it, and my prayer will be that the grace of God will come to your honour as it came to him. A great day for Ireland and for me, too, it will be when the mitre is put on your head and the crosier in your hand, as they surely will be if you can only keep off the women; and it's for you to think it out, master, if the lady in the portrait is worth all you will have to pay for her in this world and the next. The lady towards whom we are riding is not a wife. How then did it come to pass that Roudier brought her picture over to France? I never liked that man, and if he wasn't a friend of your honour's I 'd say—— Say nothing, Tadhg! After drawing my father's portrait and the portraits of many others, his fame spread over Ireland, and King O'Melaghlin asked my father to send his craftsman to make drawings of himself and his three daughters. The three most beautiful women in Ireland, so I 've always heard it said; and which is the one your honour is after? The two elder sisters are very beautiful, Ulick answered; the youngest is a nun—— And not less beautiful in God's eyes, Tadhg said somewhat sententiously, irritating Ulick thereby. In my eyes, Tadhg, she is more beautiful than her sisters. But we are not chasing a nun, master, are we? She wishes to leave her convent. Faith, if she wishes that, I 'll not waste another good thought about her! But how do you know that she wants to leave her convent if Roudier didn't tell you? I never liked the man, but I didn't think he was one to bring back from Ireland a pocketful of gold and an evil story. I can think of no sadder story, Tadhg, than a woman in a convent wishing to leave it. A story easily put right, Tadhg answered, if she 'll go to her priest; and now that Advent is coming on, with fasting days and extra devotions, all thought of leaving the convent will flow away with her prayers. But we are not all alike, Tadhg. We have all got priests and the blessed sacraments to see us through, your honour. But, Tadhg, nothing is for long the same. A child's thoughts are not a girl's thoughts, and a girl's thoughts are not a woman's. We cannot do else, your honour, than to look upon our fellows as being much the same as ourselves. Ever since your father put a harp into my hand I 've been turning tunes, and before that again I used to be whistling for nobody to hear but the pigs in the sties. One big fellow would stand on his hind legs and grunt till I gave him another tune. Ah, I wept bitter tears when that pig went to the castle to be made into pork. Once more, Tadhg, I'd have thee remember that we are not all alike, and when we aren't alike we don't understand each other.

I would have thee look at her portrait, for it will persuade thee—— I have no need to look at the picture, your honour, for a nun that would leave her convent and break her vows cannot be a holy woman; nor would I put any great faith in Philippe Roudier's stories. Dost think, Tadhg, that he invented the story? Well, he may have heard something like it, but it would have been better for him to have forgotten it—bringing it all this way, and for what, may I ask you honour, unless it be to come between the Mother Abbess and her nun, to bring a great unhappiness on the Princess for certain, for God would not let such a sin go unpunished, be sure of that. Roudier must have been doing scribbles of you and his stories must have turned her head. And how are we going to get her out of the convent—what am I thinking of? I am not thinking at all, and your honour isn't doing much thinking, for a convent isn't easy scaling; walls are high, and dogs and serving-men will come between you and the Princess. The Abbess will put her under lock and key, for no Abbess in the world would make over the King's daughter to you. There are windows, Tadhg, and pear-trees grow by windows. Ah, so you're to climb a pear-tree! O, master darling, let us go home, for this is a game that may cost the pair of us our lives. Tadhg, thou art easily frightened. Not for ourselves, not altogether, but as much for the poor creature herself, who'll have no home to go to when you're tired of her. She can't go back to her father's court and her sisters, for King O'Melaghlin is a pious man of great repute, a founder of monasteries and convents, who is always saying his prayers and going to confession. I ask your honour, where would she go if she left the convent? And what will become of her if she remains in the convent, Tadhg? Bruce is in the north, about to set out to march upon Dublin, and Meath being handy his soldiers will spread over the country after the defeat of Bermingham—— Bermingham won't be defeated, your honour. Bruce has won eighteen battles, and will take risks. Besides, the Scots are like ourselves, the same flesh and blood, and speaking our language, with only trifling differences. A victorious soldier has no God but his appetite, Tadhg. We cannot leave the Princess Soracha—— No great matter, that, for won't she be one of the martyrs, getting a good place in heaven in reward for a bit of an indignity on earth? Leave her to the will of God, your honour, whatever it may be. Let us go back! I am frightened. I have followed thee from castle to castle, falling into great sins for love of thee and for love of thy family. But if I follow thee now—no, I cannot, master, I cannot! And he rode away like one who believes the devil is in pursuit of him.

Ulick sat dumfounded in the saddle. Now, what am I to do? A soldier hired in Athlone could hold the horses under her window, but he, too, might fail me and ride away with my secret. Her portrait was still in his tunic, and having looked on her face again, he said: It cannot be that I shall never see her. Soracha a soldier's booty! A clatter of hooves caused him to turn in his saddle. It is I, master, I've come back to beg you—— To forgive thee? Ulick shouted, his passion leaping into flame. No, to whip me! cried Tadhg, for I shall be easier after I've had a stripe or two. Then take what thou askest! and the lash of Ulick's whip flew out and smote Tadhg across the shoulders, ripping his tunic, again and again and once again, six times in all, and Tadhg would have received a seventh blow if he had not cried out: Master, whip me no more lest I faint and be unable to follow thee to the end. And knee to knee they rode into the town of Athlone, Ulick upholding his servant.

CHAP. XLVIII.

NOW THAT you 've got the heroes safe into Athlone I 'm beginning to feel the want of my tea and shall be glad if your honour will excuse me the rest of the story till to-morrow. And my voice being tired, I was glad of the interruption and spoke to Alec of a cup of tea at the Lodge, it seeming to me that I must offer him some hospitality. I am in the way of taking my tea at Mulligan's, he answered, and you are in the way of taking yours at the Lodge, so we 'll stick to our customs and be friends. But have you no fault to find, Alec, with the story so far as it 's gone? Faith, I have, a fault and a half. We are mostly through the story without coming to a battle; not a word about the battle of Connor, nor of the eighteen battles that the great Bruce won in the south and that made up for the beating of Felim O'Conor at Athenry. My uncle used to talk a lot of that battle; he had it all in his eye; but he hadn't got your honour's words to tell of the poor fellows tumbling over the dead, or limping off with an arrow in the thigh, with a horse shot through the nostrils screaming with pain, trampling on all in his mad way, poor beast. Sure it is as plain to me as if the battle was there in front of me: the cheering at every good shot, and the poor Irish coming on and on in their saffron tunics. The battle was fought in August when the days were long; and I can see the English coming down the hill in the afterglow, sticking and chopping about amid the blind and the lame. I 'd like to have heard your honour tell of all that, but not a word, nor the wind of one! Another thing is that you don't tell of the retreat of the Scots through snowstorms, with troops of starving wolves on their heels eating the dead, aye, and the dying, too. But, Alec, I 'm not writing this history of the Bruces in Ireland. I know that, your honour, but I 've been wondering if the history couldn't be mixed up in some such a way with the story that the reader wouldn't know which he was reading, but would just take it all in, and separate it all out, afterwards, in his mind. I have thought of all that, Alec, I answered with a sigh. Well, if your honour can't do it, no man can. One thing more I 'd say. I 'd have had Edward Bruce the hero of the story, for a finer captain never walked the world. I see, Alec, you 'd have liked history better than a story; I 'm sorry. It 's like bread and butter—they are better together, and so I 'd have liked both the history and the story. But perhaps your honour is right; maybe the two wouldn't mix. Well, to-morrow, by the old mill, you 'll be telling me if he gets the nun or gets fooled. And then there 's the battle of Dundalk and the big fight between Edward Bruce and Sir John Maupas. Once more, your honour: at the same time to-morrow.

And turning from him I watched the rooks coming home through the quiet sky, asking myself if Alec were right and if I should do better to write the story of Edward Bruce, for truly I would not find a doughtier champion in the *Iliad.*

CHAP. XLIX.

THE PASSWORD, Edward of England, opened the gates to them, and the news of Sir Ulick de Burgo's arrival being brought quickly to Sir Roger Mandeville he hurried down the stairs of his house to meet Sir Ulick, who had just dismounted from his horse; and they talked for a while till coming across the courtyard for the second time

Sir Roger caught sight of Tadhg being held on his horse by a soldier. Your servant, said Sir Roger, seems in great pain. For a disobedience I lashed him too severely in a moment of anger, Ulick replied, and Sir Roger answered that in moments of anger we mete out the lash as we would not do if the punishment were postponed till the next day. We have, Sir Roger continued, an old woman here of great repute in the curing of wounds. Have no fear that your servant will not be able to proceed with you within a week. Let a message, he said, turning to the soldiers, be sent to Ann Gregan that she is to come at once to attend on a man who has been flogged. A soldier bent over Tadgh and said: Thy master didn't miss thee when he hit thee; faith, he has laid into thee cruelly. Not harder than I deserved, Tadhg answered. But a faint is coming over thee. Penfold, bring wine from the Governor's house else the man faints again. Courage, Tadhg, for in a little while thou 'lt be easier; a cup of wine is a great help to one in pain. I know it, for I come from thy country, Tadhg answered. Ah! thou hast been in France? Tell us of France. I can think of nothing but my pain, said Tadhg; and after he had drunk some wine he was carried to a comfortable room, where they found the wise woman toasting a piece of linen before the fire. Tell me why the linen is burnt? said a soldier. 'Tis not burnt, she answered, 'tis but scorched. Burnt or scorched, why is it scorched? the soldier persisted. That is the way we have always done it, and our fathers before us, the old woman said. The soldier watched her, and she continued to scorch the linen, and when it was sufficiently burnt Tadhg's torn tunic was lifted from his back, and she said: The skin is only broken in two or three places. Shall I be well to-morrow? asked Tadhg. To-morrow and three weeks from to-morrow thou mayest be well enough to travel, and if thou 'rt well then I shall deserve all the praise I get for curing thee. But the master will be here with the horses to-morrow. The master will have to send the horses back to their stables, she answered.

He'll be sorry for the lashing he gave me, Tadhg said to himself, though I deserved it; and he continued to worry over the delay, confiding from time to time his trouble to Ann, saying that the lashing he had been given had wiped out his fault and would bring him back into his master's favour again if it weren't for the delay. In saying this much he roused Ann's curiosity and was forced to invent a story to satisfy her, and the story he put together in his feebleness was his failure to deliver letters entrusted to his care. Didst lose the letters, honey, or sell them to a spy of the Bruce's? I know naught of Bruce's spies, Tadhg answered; we have come from France. Come from France, my pulse! said the old woman; but thou 'rt not a Norman and speakest good, kindly Irish. Not a Norman, truly, but a man from Galway am I, said Tadhg; and he escaped further questions by feigning a greater feebleness than was upon him. As the pain of his wounds dwindled he thought it well to mutter that they had come from France to buy harps, and would return to France if they could find the harps that suited them. Ann was not interested in harps or the buying of them, but she liked to hear of Ballintober and the Abbot, and was greedy for news of Brother Matthew, Brother Gregory, Brother John, Brother James, saying that they were young when she was a bare-legged girl running about the hen-house bringing in the eggs for them. But I've had my share of trouble, darling, and they have had little. Ah! it's the trouble that ages, and to thine eyes I look ten years older than they. Brother John's thoughts were always in the mead cask and the beer cask, but I wouldn't be repeating idle tales. And Brother Matthew—is he still mad about the east wind? A draught out of the east was an old dread of his. And the same dread lingers on, said Tadhg, who knew not whether the monk was alive or dead, but was concerned to baffle the old woman's curiosity and persuade her that he would be able to travel at the end of the week. To which she answered: Haven't I said three weeks or four weeks, and I should know something about the healing of wounds, having done little else this many a year.

After the skelping your honour gave him he'll be a strong man if he can travel in three weeks from now, she answered Ulick when he came to inquire for his servant. He is in thy hands, Ann Gregan, and it is for thee to say when he will be fit to travel. Have I not said it, your honour—in three weeks? I wouldn't have thee speak to his honour like that, Ann Gregan, said Tadhg from the bed. Have a memory of who he is and what thou art. Well I know the who and the what of it, and I don't need thee to tell me, sonny man! Enough, enough, said Ulick; I would talk to my servant alone about the harps that we are in search of. I'm not standing on your tongue, she answered. He is in thy care, Ann Gregan, said Ulick, his temper rising up against her, and he shall not move from that bed till thou tellest him to rise. All that is thy right, and mine is to talk with my servant alone if it pleases me to do so. So now make thy curtsey and leave us. And when she had closed the door, Ulick took the stool beside the bed. Tadhg, he said, I fear I struck thee too sharply; but no man is always master of his temper. It took me suddenly—— Just as it took me, master, when I rode away; and my temper going out as quickly as it came in, I rode back. Yes, Tadhg; and I lashed thee too harshly. I might have killed thee; another stroke would have done it. But I am alive, your honour; and whilst lying here things have been ripening in my mind and I understanding them better all the while, saying to myself: As likely as not we were brought from France, God not wishing the Princess Soracha to fall into the hands of Bruce's soldiery, a

Princess like her, daughter of a King that has done so much for God's people, for the nuns and the monks of Ireland. I came back to help my father, Tadhg. Would it be wrong for me to be thinking that we were brought back from France to help your father and to get King O'Melaghlin's daughter out of danger? We should get the whole convent out of danger, too, if we could, but we can't carry them all off; there wouldn't be room on the horses, however they clung about us. So thou thinkest, Tadhg, there was something in what I said? Faith, I do, your honour, and lying here I've had time to rue the delay, for the fault was mine. Not all thy fault, Tadhg; we both lost our heads. The news to-day is that Bruce's plan is to come out of the north somewhere about the middle of October, so there's plenty of time for thee to get well. And now tell me if the pain is dying out of thy back. Is it easier to-day than yesterday? It is easier, your honour, and I have often told Ann that a sore back shouldn't prevent a man from riding, but she gives no heed. I'll come to see thee to-morrow, Ulick answered, and every day he came to Tadhg's room to inquire the progress his henchman was making; and it was at the end of three weeks that they cried the pass-word at the bridge-head, Edward of England, and rode into the forest.

Great bronze leaves fell through the branches, and acorns were heard falling on every side. A great year for acorns, said Tadhg to himself, the devil a better; and his thoughts went back to his pigs in Ardrahan and how they would have relished the great feast God had sent them. And now that Ulick was sure of his harper's loyalty, he gave himself wholly over to thoughts of Soracha. In this way each was enough to himself and many miles went by in silence. At last, turning in his saddle Ulick said: Thou'rt the most fortunate of men, Tadhg, knowing nothing of love's torment. An anguish was mine at Athlone that I cannot tell, so great was it; and the sleepless nights! I shall never forget them, the same thoughts going round and round in my head. Had I been with you, master, I'd have played the harp and soothed you. Thou'rt a faithful harper, Tadhg, and to help me to bear uncomplainingly the loneliness of this ride tell me what passed between thee and the old woman. She spoke of the Abbot and his monks—— Whom she said she knew? She knew them by name and by nick-name, and all their little ways were known to her, all their troubles. Then the monks suffer like myself! I wouldn't be saying that, your honour. She is a dirty old woman now, but one day she must have been different. She told me, Tadhg continued, that she had been loved thirty or forty years ago by a Norman, one of the Governors of Athlone, but he left her, for she could never keep away from the casks and the vats. And when he put her out of doors, she asked what his complaint of her was, saying: Has thy dinner ever been kept waiting? and if I drank too much wine it was not for love of wine but for love of thee. All the same, he put me out, and what I get from him now is the rent of one room to live in; that much he'll do for me to the end, he says. And thinking to cheer her, your honour, I answered: All ends are sad, and she said: True for you; all ends are sad till death comes—merciful death, he comes to us all. The old woman of Beare, Tadhg, tells that time was when she wore a new smock every day and that her arms were once wound about kings, arms so lean to-day that carrier boys would scorn them. The old Irish poem awakens sight of Ann Gregan, and I see her in my thoughts watching a herd of swine under these oaks, saying to herself: Every acorn has to drop, and I, that had fine days and nights with kings, drinking mead and wine by the light of shining candles, to-day drink whey water when I can get it, among shrivelled old hags. I see upon my cloak long grey hairs, and the curled patch of my body is grey, too. The flood wave and the second ebb-tide have all come to me. I am the Old Woman of Athlone. The flood wave will not reach the silence of my kitchen; my companions of old time are all laid in darkness. O happy isle of the great sea which the flood reaches after the ebb! But I do not expect flood after ebb to come to me. There is scarce a little place to-day that I can recognise; all is on the ebb.

I think the old woman's story should be put to music, Tadhg. To my thinking, your honour, 'twould be waste of good music, that might better be used on a poem about a woman that led a chaste and holy life; for what has the old woman to tell us but that she was a sinful woman, whose arms once fondled kings and are now too ugly to tempt a young youth. So with what right does she complain, for isn't it always turn and turn about? She says, Tadhg, that every acorn has to drop, and here we are among dropping acorns! But why dost thou ride with thine eyes on the ground? It would seem that thou, who hast seen acorns in plenty, seest acorns for the first time. I keep my eyes on the acorns because they remind me of my pigs, and there's another reason, too. Surely the wood we are riding through is the wood of the three old women that were hanged. And what three were they? I have the story from Ann Gregan, your honour, and she has every tale that's going about Athlone at the tip of her tongue. It was a fearful crime they were hanged for, and it was Sir Roger Mandeville that gave the order for the jerking of them into the boughs above us. But I'd hear what the crime was. Well, 'twas such a crime that naught could have got them to do it but hunger itself. For the first week the hunger gnaws like a rat, but after the first week the pain dies, so it is said. But the crime, Tadhg! The Scots left nothing on the land, and Ann Gregan tells that the people lived on acorns and beech nuts, and that when there were no more—— But, Tadhg, the ground is thick with acorns! Well, I'm telling you what Ann Gregan said, that last year the people were digging up corpses and eating them; and this year, too, there's been digging for the newly-dead. Now, master, keep your eyes on the ground whilst I tell you about the three old women that were hanged; keep your eyes on the acorns, for the last ill and the worst one that can fall on a man is to see a corpse in the tree above him, unless indeed he can get a piece of the rope, for a bit of the rope that has hanged a man brings luck—— Tadhg, get on with thy story! What were the old women hanged for? For building a fire in the corner of a field to entice little children to the warmth; and when they'd got a couple, or maybe three or four, they'd kill them and eat them, and what they couldn't eat they'd sell in Athlone for joints of pork. Many's the piece of Christian child that was eaten in Athlone last year—and that's according to Ann Gregan. The crops rotted—— I have heard enough of the failure of last year's crops, Tadhg, and would like to get out of this wood, for I've no wish to see the three cannibals of Athlone. Well, we can't be far from them now, and I don't know whether we should go to the right or to the left to keep out of their way. The rooks are cawing yonder in the grove of oaks, calling on their comrades to come over to feed with them. Wouldst see the three danglers, Tadhg? No, your honour. Then let us think awhile. We have been riding now some hours, and should be nigh a ruined village. Isn't that what the sentry told us at the bridge-head? It was, your honour; we shouldn't be much out of the way of the village by now. He said we must keep by the south-east? He did, and that if there were no clouds in the sky the stars would guide us. We are too near the Shannon and would do well to seek higher ground. And it was soon after speaking these words that Tadhg said:

I think we have missed the way, for I see nothing that the sentry told us to look out for. The plain that he spoke of is missing, and why did he not tell us of that long stretch of wood? Maybe the plain is on the other side of it. And coming upon a track in the wood, they followed it in the hope that it would bring them into the open country. Tadhg was afraid to oppose his master, so neither could cast blame on the other when at midnight they found themselves in a darkness so deep that they dared not advance farther. We shall certainly be swept from our saddles by the branches! cried Ulick. The last tree nearly had me off, Tadhg answered; we must wait till the dawn. There is no dawn in October, Tadhg, till the sixth hour. Six hours from dawn! And if we were twenty-six, your honour, we must wait. If we dismount, said Ulick, our horses may escape from us. And if we ride back or forward, Tadhg answered, we may be left hanging out of a dead tree in an old wood. By what sense dost thou know the wood to be old? A smell of nettles and toadstools is a certain sign of age in a wood, master. I hear water trickling, said Ulick. Soft water, no good for drinking, Tadhg answered. At least we are out of shelter of the wind, Ulick replied. A bad scenting night, and that's lucky for us. Of what art thou thinking, Tadhg? Of wolves, master, that might leave us alone but would like to have a bit out of our horses. Was I wrong to speak of wolves? Ulick did not answer, and the misty hours of the October night went by in thoughts of how they might climb into the trees if they were attacked. The horses would stampede, of course, and some of the wolves might go after the horses. Against six wolves they might defend themselves; a bite, and a bad one, they would get, but if the wolf missed the throat he would be stabbed, and when two or three lay biting at their wounds on the ground and howling, their comrades would turn tail. If the wolves were numerous they might all be eaten, but large packs were rare and there was no wind, as Tadhg had said. A bad scenting night, Tadhg. Let's thank God for that! Tadhg answered. And thinking the best thanks he could give would be to hold his tongue, wolves having ears as well as noses, Ulick kept silence, giving ear now and then to Tadhg, who continued to mutter under his breath. He is praying, Ulick said to himself, and praying seeming to him to be a good way of passing the time, he sought to remember the prayers his mother had taught him; and getting no relief from these memories he ran over in his mind all the songs he had sung in France, till he felt he could keep silent no longer, wolves or no wolves. Tadhg, I would have thee remember that if we sit on our horses all night we shall have to spend the day in this wood resting them. If the wolves come we won't have horses, were the words on Tadhg's lips, but his teeth chattered. The cold has taken the heart out of me, he said. I know not what answer to make, master.

In the high branches of the trees above them there was a great gathering of stars, and hearing from Tadhg that the stars retired into the sky at the approach of dawn, Ulick kept on looking up, and every time he looked he thought the stars were farther away than they were half an hour before. But Tadhg could see no difference; they were to his eyes still shining brightly. Again and again Ulick asked Tadhg to consult the stars, feeling certain they were dimmer. Not yet, your honour, not yet! And when Tadhg asked Sir Ulick to look up, saying: The stars are withering, Ulick had forgotten them in the great weariness of waiting; and advancing their horses deeper into the dell, they rode round a pool whence a rill issued, to flow away into hazel and blackthorn thickets. A likely place to find a hermit, said Tadhg. Ulick did not answer, and a moment after they heard a voice crying: O Christ, O Christ, hear me! O Christ, O Christ, without sin! Tadhg began to cross himself. I cannot remain astride whilst a holy man raises his voice to Christ, he said, flinging himself out of his saddle. O Christ, O Christ, love me; sever me not from thy sweetness! I am thine and thine alone, time everlasting, world without end. And I am thine, too! cried Tadhg, on his knees; O Christ, love me! Christ, uphold me! Christ, save me!

On hearing the unexpected voice the hermit rose to his feet. We are travellers, said Tadhg, who lost ourselves in the wood before midnight. A great danger it was to both of you to cross this wood after nightfall. Because of the wolves, said Tadhg. We followed a track, said Ulick, till the track ended—— A track made by wild swine, the hermit interjected, and among rocks like these a horse might break a leg. We have no knowledge of these rocks, your holiness, but were nearly swept from our saddles by branches. And the hermit remembering Tadhg's voice as the voice that had repeated the prayer to Christ after him, said: I heard thee lift thy voice to Christ, and now I read the divine comradeship in thy face. We are friends in Christ. Whence thou hast come and whither thou goest makes no difference; we are with Christ, and to be with Christ is enough. Our horses have stood under trees all night, said Ulick, our weight pressing upon them; they are weary and we would rest them. Awakening from his ecstasy slowly, the hermit asked why they had not dismounted. Tadhg answered that they had remained in their saddles, their horses being restless, as though they smelt a wolf. We would rest our horses, Tadhg continued, feed them and water them from the rill. All these things you can do, the hermit answered as he moved away to his praying stone. We would loosen our horses' girths, Tadhg cried after him, if we were sure that none of the outcasts would descend upon them to kill and eat them.

Loosen the girths, said the hermit; and feeling themselves to be safe, Ulick and Tadhg took the bits from the horses' jaws that they might feed more easily, and tethered them to stout trees against which they could lean if they did not choose to lie. We must lead the horses to the rill if we cannot find a bucket, your holiness. Thou 'lt find a pail in my cell, said the hermit; and when each horse was watered all was silent in the glen save for the crunching of their great stony teeth in the nosebags.

And 'tis our turn now for a bite and a sup, said Tadhg, and the morning being still raw all three went searching the dell for dry leaves and sticks; and on their return with great armfuls of fuel, the hermit lent his flint and steel, saying he would show them round Glen Bolcane whilst the fire was burning. But first taste the water that bubbles down this little ascent of rocks and tell me if any wine in France be sweeter. And they told him that though they had drunk much wine in France they could not say that any draught was sweeter than the water that bubbled among the rocks of Glen Bolcane. Nor in France nor elsewhere have you ever heard sweeter songs than are sung in the springtime in these groves. A blackbird whistles from yonder bough, and he would be the best singer of all if he could finish his song. The thrush sings a more broken song in the depths of the wood, and over the wood the grey lark sings trancedly. In this sheltered holly a wren built her nest; the young have gone, but here is the nest. Now make sure that your feet are planted safely, for I would show you the hazel trees above us; a better harvest this year than last. Come, give me your hands and I will help you. Hast ever seen, he said, turning to Ulick, boughs more weighted? See how the branches hang, inviting us to gather the delicious nuts. A little higher we shall find some blackthorns grafted by me; once they bore sloes, but henceforth my thorns will bear refreshing damsons. The eyes of God are pleased to follow traces of man's hand in the wilderness, Ulick replied, and Tadhg, who was not accustomed to hear his master speak respectfully of God, asked himself why his honour did not always refrain from blasphemy. The man that does not believe in God may blaspheme, but why the one who does should curse and swear has often been a great puzzle to me. And he pondered on this problem of life till the hermit begged to be allowed to withdraw himself from the company whilst he ate his nuts and berries: All flesh being forbidden to me by my vows unless God sends it to me. But has not God sent thee flesh, good hermit? Ulick asked; he has sent us with it, and as all things come from God—— No man can speak fairer than that, cried Tadhg. God sent you to me, the hermit answered, and your purposes and his are but one, all things coming from and returning to God; and unwilling to separate us he has sent us that little toddling creature, returning doubtless to his nest after a night's hunting of snails and beetles. . . . The hermit's eyes are quicker than ours, Tadhg said: what has he gotten? I cannot tell, Ulick answered; but what he has gotten he has taken to the rill. And what can he be gathering from the pool—watercress? I saw none there. And they both wondered, their wonderment ceasing when the hermit returned plastering a hedgehog over with wet clay. He will be ready for eating in half an hour, the hermit said; and he went about the dell gathering more sticks, which sent up a merry crackling. Good hermit, if we share thy food thou must share ours, said Ulick. There are feast days in the year and we pray thee to count this as one. And coming to know each other as men do whilst partaking of food at the warmth of a fire in a wood, Ulick asked the hermit to tell why he had left the world of men to abide in Glen Bolcane. Because of the wickedness of men, which I could not stop, though

I threw myself into the middle of the battle. But it may be that I did wrong, for to escape from reality we must go to it.

A deep saying this seemed to Tadhg, and in his search after the hermit's meaning he lost some of the story, and being anxious to hear it all he had to confess that his thoughts had been away. Whereupon the hermit began his story again, saying: In the country where we are now sitting at meat two kings once strove, each desiring to put the other under him, which they could not do, they being equally matched; and so the country was wasted between them and there was little food left, and it seeming likely that there would soon be none at all, a cleric was sought and he told the kings that there would be no peace till they had gathered their forces and given battle. And the word of God being made known to me in the night, I stepped forth into the front of the battle and cried to either host: The voice of God spoke to me last night in my sleep, and his will is that the Lord's people shall come into the battle clothed in silk so that they may outshine all in pride and haughtiness. But God's words were not welcome to the hosts, and hearing myself cursed from both sides, I said: There is none in Ireland that will listen to God's voice! so I will go hence; and leaving them to God's mercy I crossed over to the land of the Saxons, where I met a man in Northumberland wandering seemingly like myself, without aim or direction. Who art thou? said I, wandering in this wild wood, knowing no direct line but straying hither and thither like a bird or beast; and he answered: I am a madman. Whereupon I said: We two are well met, for I am another madman, come from Erin; and he answered: Erin must be a good country, for the say in Ireland is that the Irish are all mad. Troth and faith! said I, thou hast heard no more than the truth, for none in Erin listens to the word of God. How then is it thou art mad? he asked, and I answered: I am mad from the curses they cast upon me when I stepped forth into the battle and told them it was God's will that his people should fight in silk. And thou didst speak well, he answered me, for when chiefs war one against the other, their wars should be proclaimed to all the world. And then the madman told me his story, which was at variance with mine, for it was not with hosts and chieftains his quarrel was but with a cleric, who put a great curse upon him and bade him wander, for he had given way to anger against the cleric and flung his psalter into a lake. An otter returned it to the cleric next morning, he said, and ever since I have been an exile from Erin and have wandered unceasingly. So now since God has sent thee to me, let us count the trees as we wander, eating the berries and watercress when the Lord gives these to us, never failing to lie down under the same tree at night. Moreover, whosoever shall hear the cry of a heron from the blue waters of the lake, or the sharp, clear call of the cormorant, or the flight of a woodcock from a thicket, or the whistle of a plover on being startled out of his sleep, or the crack of a withered branch, or see the shadow of a bird as it flies over the wood, shall cry aloud: Brother, let us run quickly! So did he speak, and for a year we lived as he had said, never departing one from the other farther than a tree's space from tree; and at the end of the year Ealldhan, for that was his name, said: It is time that we part, for the end of my life has come and I must go to the place where I am fated to meet death. And what is the death that awaits thee, friend and comrade? I asked. I am going now to Eas Dubhthaigh, he answered, and a great wind will blow under me and I shall be swept into the waterfall and drowned therein; and afterwards I shall be buried in a holy churchyard and shall go to heaven. And that will be the end of my life. And was thy comrade drowned in the waterfall? Ulick asked. He was; and after hearing of his death I returned hither and have lived here ever since, and here I shall live till a voice speaks within me and bids me go to meet my death. And what death will come to thee, hermit? I shall be killed by a cow's horn, the hermit answered. A strange death, truly! All deaths are strange, said the hermit, in our eyes, and all are simple in the eyes of God.

The hermit foretold many wars and betrayals, flights, massacres, and the overturning of all the rights of men and all the laws of God, his converse ending with these words: So I shall not be sorry when I go to the cow's horn to be killed and find the recompense of my life on earth in heaven, for of sins I am free, having repented mine. The voice in which he spoke these last words made known to Ulick that the hermit would now be left to his devotions, and he said: Good hermit, we will ask a prayer from thee. A prayer I will give thee for the success of thine errand, the hermit answered, and he turned to leave them. But, good hermit, thou hast not yet pointed out the path that leads out of this wood. We came hither in darkness, and thou wouldst not have us leave it in the same darkness, not knowing the north from the south or the east from the west? I would not have you wander without direction, said the hermit, finding your way into the very heart of the wood instead of out of it, the twilight overtaking you and after the twilight night; and lest this misfortune should befall you, we will walk together, following a path that leads to a clearing, and after that the trees grow thinner. Our way, Ulick said, is to King O'Melaghlin's court. A long ride, the hermit answered. After riding ten miles you will come upon the Abbey of Durrow in the midst of a park or chase with a great wall round it; you will pass it by and ride eight more miles, and then follow the shores of the lake.

CHAP. L.

NOW, ISN'T he the wise man and the happy man, said Tadhg, for there being no good diet in berries every one he puts into his mouth raises him higher up in heaven. Without beer or ale cask, or harp, Tadhg continued, to help the afternoons away! Tell me, Tadhg, wouldst thou lay aside thy harp for a promise that in heaven thy playing would equal the angel Gabriel's? My faith, and my troth! I would snap the harp across my knee this very minute for a promise like that. But if after playing, and thy playing being judged equal to Gabriel's, an angel should say: So well hast thou played, Tadhg, that thy reward is to hear our great harp-players, those whose craft is much above Gabriel's—wouldst thou not rue the breaking of the harp on thy back? I have always heard, master, that there is none above Gabriel in heaven. Thy mind is but clerical hearsay, Ulick answered, and fell back into thoughts of Soracha, some miles going by in silence, till suspicious that Tadhg was thinking of the Princess, he snapped out: Of what art thou thinking?

Of what you will do with the Princess Soracha if you should get her, your honour. Have I not told thee, Tadhg, that I love the Princess Soracha? Have I not heard that story many times before, master? They went back to their husbands in the end, but here there is no husband to go back to. The Princess Soracha is Christ's bride, and if she leave her convent she will leave it for ever, though she be King O'Melaghlin's daughter, for King O'Melaghlin is a holy man and will say: Her broken vows and sins undo the blood bond, and there's no telling what mischiefs may follow after. And the Abbess, too, will say: She is no spiritual daughter of mine any longer, and so the Princess—— I would have thee cease thy chatter, Tadhg, for it comes not out of any understanding of what I have told thee. But neither have you seen nor heard the Princess Soracha, Tadhg answered unabashed, saying to himself: He will not dare to strike me again, for to do so would lose him the Princess; and encouraged by this thought he added: Maybe a big surprise awaits you at the convent, master. If the Princess Soracha be such a weighty woman that the rope breaks when she is let down from the window —what then? Roudier is a skilful craftsman, Ulick answered, and would not have drawn a slender woman if she were bulky. Nor sent you to an ugly bosom, said Tadhg, nor to a woman with no bosom at all, one that you'd turn out of the bed; for the bosom, it would seem, is a great delight if I am to believe all I hear in the castle yard. But small, heavy or light, drooping or swelling—I am no judge, all bosoms being the same to me and through no fault of my own, for I was born that way by the will of God. Have I not said, Tadhg, that a man in love raises his thoughts to the beloved one as monks and nuns in the cloister—— But you said, master, that there must always be a barrier. Tadhg, thou wilt never understand, so leave me to my thoughts of the Princess Soracha and respect them as thou wouldst the exaltations of the monk in the cold moonlight, his bodily knees afflicted by the stone floor and his soul barely breathing, so pure is his ecstasy in the bosom of a saint in paradise.

What can I do to save him? Tadhg whispered, hardly able to keep his seat on his horse but keeping it for dread of his master's whip, and so they jogged on, coming at last upon the great wall of which the hermit had spoken. A great wall it is, surely, said Tadhg, and our horses not having wings we must seek a gate or a gap. The mare will take a big jump, but the other horses might not care to follow her. I'm thinking we'd do well to wait for the rising of the moon, your honour, and she looks like rising up into a fair space of sky. And the words were hardly out of his mouth when they came upon a gate; but it was chained, and whilst Ulick shook it, thinking that they ought to have foreseen the gate and brought a file with them, Tadhg cried to him that a tree had fallen across the wall, leaving behind it a grand gap, one that the horses could cross easily when the loose stones were removed. The mare faced the pile bravely, but the pack-horse hung back, and to get him over Tadhg flung the leading-rein to Ulick and applied the whip so sharply to the brute's quarters that to escape from it he stumbled over the heap, and so clumsily that he would have unseated any but a skilful rider. And nuns not being usually skilful riders Ulick kept Tadhg throwing stones aside to the right and to the left till there was a gap for the horses to gallop through if needs be. There must be no delay in getting out of this chase, Tadhg, and to find the track to the convent we would do well to seek it from the gate. I will lead the pack-horse and do thou walk slowly in front, thine eyes bent upon the ground. I will, your honour, Tadhg answered, and he followed the track till he lost it in a hollow filled with bracken. Keep your patience, he said, I'll find it again when the moon comes up. And when the moon cleared a belt of clouds her light showed a track against the brow of a hill. The same track or another? asked Ulick. The same track, Tadhg answered, for I can feel the ruts in the bracken under my feet. Since we are sure of the track, Tadhg, mount thy horse again. Will your honour hold him till I get my foot in the stirrup, for he's seventeen hands high and I am but a little man. A great wild place surely the nuns have chosen to come to live in, Tadhg continued, and we'd better keep to the left of yon thorn-tree. Which thorn-tree? Ulick asked, and Tadhg replied:

The one atop of the hillock. But which hillock? The chase is all hillocks and hollows. The nearest thorn-tree to us, your honour; and they rode on seeking the convent wall. The convent can't be much farther, Tadhg said at last; either there is or there isn't a convent in this chase. Either there is or there isn't! Ulick repeated, and he asked Tadhg what he meant. But what matters his meaning? he said to himself, and they rode on in silence up a steep acclivity, expecting to find the convent when they reached the top. But so elusive was the park or chase that they distinguished only vague forms of trees and a glint of water. We shall have to cross that belt of trees or ride round it, said Tadhg. We had better keep to the path, Ulick answered, and pushing on through the trees they found themselves in front of a crescent-shapen piece of water. We shall do well, Tadhg, to hold our tongues. The cries of the water-fowl may warn the nuns that there are strangers in the park. Your honour is right, for beyond the lake between the trees I see a long curving wall some twenty feet high, or what seems to be like one. The convent it is surely, said Ulick, and as Tadhg did not answer him he pointed to an arched doorway with two small round towers beside it. And to be certain that it is no chieftain's castle, Tadhg, raise thine eyes to the square tower of the church amid glimpses of steep roofs. We came by some old disused track; the main entrance to the convent is on the other side of the chase. And it was our luck to have come in by the gap, Tadhg answered, for had we come in by the front gate we might have met with servants and porters. We might indeed, Ulick answered, and I am glad there are no horses feeding about here, for they would set our horses neighing. There is a pear-tree reaching to her window; hold the mare whilst I seek it. I pray God, said Tadhg to himself, that we may get away from this place with our lives. . . . Yes, there is a pear-tree. I will climb to her window. But no light shows, your honour! Did I not tell thee that her words to Roudier were that she lights a taper every evening? You said that, Tadhg answered. Can it be then that she has skipped an evening or fallen asleep before lighting the taper? I will climb to her window—— Do not do that, your honour, lest she be sleeping in another room. At last thou speakest sense, Tadhg; I will be patient. Hearken—that doleful cry far away down the horizon! Only an owl hunting, your honour. Tell me if owls hunt in the dusk or in the dark. In both, your honour. If the cry be an owl's then an owl is a doleful bird indeed. Did it not sound to thee like a soul's cry, a soul lost between heaven and hell? It could not sound to me like a soul crying between heaven and hell, for I have never heard a soul cry. Then thou hast no ear for thine own, Tadhg, which is always crying. But forget thy soul and tell me if the moon coming over the park's rim is not like a great yellow owl; it is marked like an owl. Owls white and grey I have seen, master, but never a yellow owl, and the markings have always been upon the moon without any man knowing whence they came or how. What hearest thou, Tadhg? I hear a stag braying, master, which is not to be wondered at, we being in the rutting month, the hind coming to the stag and the stag going to the hind. Tadhg, my hind does not come to me. Her window is dark. Canst tell me why? I cannot, master. Then I will watch her window from the other side.

Why should I know Soracha's soul when I do not know my own, which he says is always whining? Horses' hooves sound loud in the night; we should have muffled them. Should a wandering scent come by and set the horses neighing, we are undone; all the convent will be out of bed—a hubbub-boo of women's voices, with the chaplain calling them on! The master has no thought for these dangers. I have seen him in states before now, but never in such a one as this. Up and down he goes, like the madmen in the woods, railing against me for not being able to say why Soracha has forgotten to light her taper. Of what can he be thinking, my poor master, ranging up and down the lawn, along and across, saying, no doubt, that he will drown himself in the Shannon because his love goes deeper than his senses, saying that he loves Soracha as the saints love God in the cloister. And now he crosses the lawn to ask me once more why Soracha hasn't lighted her taper, and I must find an answer somehow that will keep him quiet for a few minutes.

I have been thinking, master, and it has come to my mind that nuns confess to the Mother Abbess. Confess to the Mother Abbess! The Mother Abbess cannot shrive them. She cannot forgive sins, Tadhg answered, but she can hear confessions, and I'm thinking the Princess Soracha may have confessed to putting a lighted taper in her window. Has your honour forgotten the words of the wise woman in Dunmore, that in Ireland the weak prevail? She said that, Tadhg, but she should have said it is the weak that pray, and thou hast been praying ever since we left the hermit's glen that God might put out his hand to save his handmaiden. I charge thee to swear before God that thou hast not prayed that Soracha should be saved from love. Master, I remember no such prayer, and if she is not in her room to-night it must be a forgetfulness on her part. Thy prayers have come between me and her. Now none can help us but the Devil, so down upon thy knees, Tadhg! My good master, I cannot pray to the Devil; my good master—— By God, thou shalt pray to the Devil! On thy knees, on thy knees! I know not how to pray to the Devil; I have no prayer, master. My soul, good Devil, I will give thee, if thou 'lt bring Soracha to my master's bed—say those words and none other, else I strangle thee! I cannot sell my soul to the Devil. The Devil wouldn't take my soul; it isn't worth his trouble. Master, take thy hand from my throat else I choke. My soul, good Devil—dost hear me? Master, the taper! the taper! Then take at once the nosebags from the horses and give me the rope whereby I shall let her down from the window; coil it round me that it may not hinder me in my climbing. Speak no word, master, till thou art over the sill in the nun's room, and speak not loud when thou art with her, for the walls are thin between the cells, so I have often heard. . . . Now, what did I hear? So my trouvère has come at last! Those very words I heard; and resting his knee on the sill he clambers into the nun's room. Now they are in each other's arms, and if she drag him into her bed they may lie till the matins bell is struck. None can help them save God himself, and may his help come speedily before sleep overcomes them!

O dear Lord Christ, Tadhg continued, falling on his knees, I have turned often to thee to ask thy help that my faith in thee may increase and that when the time is by for me to come before thee for judgment I shall not be hurled by thee into everlasting torment but raised up by thy power to heaven and given a harp grander than any Donogh O'Brien has ever made, to play upon with fingers more skilful than any fleshly fingers, even those of Finn Lorcan. But this night I ask not anything for myself but that thou shalt put forth thy power and save my dear lord and master, Ulick de Burgo, a sinner, from the Devil, who will try to snare him into Soracha's bed and keep him there till the holy nuns assemble and be witnesses to the sin unknown in Ireland since the pagan Danes were driven out.

O my Lord Jesus Christ, thou that sittest in heaven by Mary, thy mother, heed my prayer and give my master time to repent the sin he is now committing. And thou, O Mary Mother, in whose womb Christ was a guest three times three months, add thy great prayer to my poor one that Christ may forgive my dear master and the virgin in yon room the sin they have committed, and that strength may be given to them both to stay from sinning a second time. Strengthen the spirit whilst the flesh is weak, for with thy strength he will be stronger than any king in Ireland, stronger than Richard de Burgo, his father, stronger than the King of France, stronger than Nebuchadnezzar in the far off time, or any king that has reigned on earth. Give him the faith in thee which he has lost, for if he have faith the sorrow of this life which he strives to quench in sin will be banished from him and he will walk joyous as the earth in the spring.

He walked between the horses and the window, lifting his soul to Christ in whatever words came to him, and it was not till he had crossed the lawn for the third time that Soracha's suddenly litten window engaged his eyes and thoughts. They'll be coming down the tree before I have the nosebags off the horses! . . . Unloose the rope from her, Tadhg, and put her on the pack-horse. And descending quickly Ulick was on the mare in a trice. Get thee on thy horse! he cried. But Tadhg had forgotten to lengthen the stirrup leather at the gate and could only touch the iron with his toe, and whilst hopping, striving to pull himself up by the mane, a stag came belling out of the shadow of the pines, causing the grey to rear. To save himself from being gored Tadhg grasped the antlers, and the horse finding himself free galloped away, leaving Tadhg to the tussle. Sometimes the stag brought Tadhg to his knees, and sometimes Tadhg brought down the stag; and being equally matched, neither gave way to the other till Tadhg loosed his hold on one antler, thinking he would get an advantage by putting both hands on to one. A mistake he soon perceived this to be, for so violently did the stag wrench his head from side to side that he almost succeeded in freeing himself from Tadhg's grasp. But Tadhg getting hold of the other antler again, it behooved the stag to try a new trick: he began backing towards the wood. I shall be killed if he gets me among the pines, said Tadhg, and it might be as well for me to shout for help whilst there is yet time, his honour and the Princess being well through the gap by now. So with the stag pulling him into the wood, he did not cease to shout till sisters Ethna and Oona came running down the sward in their night clothes, followed by Sister Muirgil.

My last strength is spent, good ladies, and if you had not come to my help I should have been gored. Take Brian by one horn, Ethna, and I'll take the other, said Oona. I thank you, ladies, for your help, and now—— Stir not, or we will loose the stag! Do not if you would hear my story; and Tadhg fell to telling everything that came into his head, never troubling to join up one story with another but just stopping now and then to say: I am afraid you won't understand, good ladies, unless I tell you that . . . And the nuns heard a great deal of France and the troubadours and about harp-playing and the making of harps, till at last Muirgil said: But all these stories do not tell us why thou 'rt here. You shall hear that, good ladies; but keep a firm hold on the stag. I am but a servant, and in coming here was doing no more than my master's bidding. We know not thy master's name, said Muirgil. My master is by this time far from here, and to give you his name, good ladies, would not help you to get back what you have lost. What we have lost! exclaimed Ethna. Our stag was able to defend himself against thee—— By the Blessed Virgin I swear to you, noble ladies, that it was not in search of a stag we came but of a hind. In search of a hind? cried Oona; now we know why Brian is so fierce.

Thy hind shall not be taken from thee—thou hast too few. So thou camest to eat Briand's hind! I did not come to eat, Tadhg answered ruefully. But thy master? No, it was not for eating he came but for love. For love? said Ethna. Look this way! cried Oona; Brian fights with us! Loose not his horns, good ladies, for he would gore me. Let us hear thy story, said Muirgil. Good ladies, I am trying to tell my story, but you do not seem to understand it; nor is it your fault, nor yet my fault, but the stag's fault, for no man can tell a story whilst a stag like your Brian with his spiked horns is fretting to be at him. Brian cannot escape from our hands, said Ethna, so tell thy story. Well, ladies, I did not seek to drive him from his hind, nor did I come to make venison of his hind or of himself. I came hither at my master's bidding, a great Irish chieftain, one who has been all the world over and come back from his travelling; and I could tell you a fine tale of his travels in France with the troubadours—— We would hear the tale of France, and the troubadours another time, interrupted Muirgil. Did you enter by the gate? But the gate is locked, cried Oona; I locked it myself. I was with Sister Oona when the gate was locked, said Ethna. A big wind cast a tree across the wall, breaking a large gap in it, and it was through the gap we came, good ladies, said Tadhg; and to save himself from further questions he asked the sisters for the names of the two nuns now running towards them from the convent. The nuns, said Muirgil, are Sister Sheela and Sister Dervorgilla. And they, too, would like to hear my story, cried Tadhg; but I warn you, ladies, no fair story can be told of all my travelling whilst the stag is striving with you; just now he was on his hind legs, and the good lady on the far side had to loosen her hold of his horn. If there be a hind anywhere about, send the stag away to her, and then I shall be able to tell you a grand story about my master and myself. We would hear of thy master's hind, said Oona, and she called out to Sheela and Dervorgilla to bring bread for the stag. A slice of bread soaked in milk will tempt Brian away from the deer-stealer, whom he would gore. A deer-stealer in our park! cried Dervorgilla. And the two nuns ran back to the convent and returned with bread. The milk jar is empty, but here is the bread; bread will tempt him. And the hind coming up from a covert close by received her share of bread and the twain trotted away together. I am no deer-stealer, said Tadhg, and now that you have your stag and your hind, let me go. We would have thy story; tell it or we will call back the stag, said Muirgil. We shall catch our death if we stand under the moon asking for stories, Sheela replied, and a little procession was formed, Sheela and Dervorgilla walking on either side of Tadhg, followed by Muirgil, Ethna and Oona. The story he tells of deer-stealing is not a true one, said Muirgil. Didn't he say that he and his master came after a hind? said Oona. But who is his master? Muirgil asked; I would know that, and why he rode away, coward-like, and I would know, too, whom he came to carry away. We are all here—— No, Soracha is not here! cried Ethna. Can he have gone away with the King's daughter? Hush! said Muirgil, lest he should hear us. And they walked towards the convent, bringing Tadhg, a prisoner, to tell his story to the Mother Abbess. . . . Mother Abbess, said Muirgil, I would tell that Sheela was awakened from her sleep by cries. I jumped out of bed, said Sheela, and running to Oona's cell knocked at the door, saying: Come quickly, for somebody is in the park crying for help. Oona did not answer—— I cried that I was out of bed, interrupted Oona, and begged thee to awaken Ethna. I was awake before either of you, said Ethna. Another time I'll hear your stories, answered the Mother Abbess. Speak, man; why art thou here? Explain!

We jumped our horses through a gap, madam, and came into the park, but not to steal the stag. For what came ye then? asked the Abbess. For one of the sisters, said Tadhg. For one of the sisters! repeated the Abbess. You asked for my story, madam, and I 'd liefer bite off the end of my tongue than tell a lie to a holy woman like yourself. The sin is the same, no matter to whom thou liest. Unless we lie to a priest in confession, Tadhg interjected. The Abbess frowned, and Tadhg continued: It was Sister Soracha. The Mother Abbess advanced towards Tadhg, her fist clenched; Tadhg retreated a step or two, and the Abbess recovering herself returned to her chair. Sister Soracha is King O'Melaghlin's daughter. Yes, said Tadhg, yes, I knew that, and begged my master to forgo his pleasure of her; but he wouldn't listen to me, and a servant has no will but his master's. And who is thy master? One of Ireland's chieftains, Tadhg answered. Thou liest! No chieftain in Ireland would come to rape a king's daughter. There was no rape, Mother Abbess. Philippe Roudier brought her portrait to France and a message, else Sir Ulick would—— Sir Ulick? repeated the Mother Abbess, Sir Ulick de Burgo? And the affrighted Tadhg stood, his head hanging on his breast. Speak, said the Abbess, and speak truly. The Princess's message was: I am weary of my convent and burn a taper every night in my window, easily reached by a pear-tree—— Sister Muirgil, go to Sister Soracha's cell. If she be there, the Abbess continued, turning to Tadhg, thou dost deserve a whipping. You never spoke a truer word in all your life! Sir Ulick and myself came from France, whither we had gone to sing love songs, to join the army mustered to give battle to Bruce on his way to Dublin. And instead you came hither to commit a rape? There was no rape at all, madam, for wasn't it by her own wish the Princess was carried away?

The door opened and Sister Muirgil announced that

Sister Soracha was not in her cell. And the rope thou carriest in thy hand? asked the Mother Abbess. Is the rope that let Sister Soracha down from the window, Muirgil answered. We know thy story now, said the Abbess, turning to Tadhg, and thou 'lt be glad to hear that no further questions will be put to thee; and there 'll be no flogging for thee; thou 'rt but a servant—— And servants serve their masters, so I have always thought and felt, good Mother Abbess. I would speak with this man alone, said the Abbess, turning to the nuns; but as they were about to leave the room she added: No, it were better that you stayed and heard what I have to say to him. A great sin has been committed in the sight of God, and King O'Melaghlin being a God-fearing man will assemble an army and wage a great war that may last as long as the ten years' war of the Greeks against Troy. It would take as long as that to capture Castle Carra! said Tadhg, but without heeding him the Abbess continued: Another war, and the country will be a desert. The English rob us and drive us into the mountains and kill us as they kill mad dogs, and there is no law to save us. Another Trojan war! said Tadhg. Thou speakest like a fool. When my master told me we were going to release Princess Soracha from her vows—— Release Princess Soracha from her vows! None but the Pope could do that—— I turned my horse's head—— And rode him back again since thou art here! said the Abbess. Let me take off my tunic and show you what the coming back cost me. Fellow, thou art in the presence of holy women! Three weeks I was in bed at Athlone—— Button thy tunic; I am thinking it were better that he had killed thee. Isn't murder, madam, the biggest of all the sins? Our thoughts go beyond thy back and thy life to the Ireland that made us all, the Abbess replied. Dost think that King O'Melaghlin will bear in silence the wrong that has been done to him and the insult to the Church? The rape of Princess Soracha will stir up a new war between Meath and Connaught, and if thou wouldst save Ireland go hence and bring the Princess back to us. Go to thy master and tell him that if Ireland is not to be destroyed utterly he must bring back Soracha—— Virgin or no? Tadhg asked. If she be returned to us within a few days, within a week, within a month, perhaps King O'Melaghlin may know nothing of this rape. And now let us say a prayer altogether in this parlour; let us pray for Ireland, that she may be saved, for Ireland has made us all. . . . Tadhg fell on his knees and all the nuns fell on theirs, and they prayed for Ireland, and at the end of the prayer Tadhg said, rising to his feet: There must be no delay; I must go at once. By to-morrow's dusk I shall be in Athlone, where they are sure to rest for a day, and if I can come upon a good horse in Athlone I shall overtake them on the road to Roscommon. The man speaks well, said the Abbess, and her nuns seeming to agree with her, they accompanied Tadhg to the convent gate, and the last words he heard were that their prayers would not cease for his return.

God grants prayers if it be for our good that he should grant them, Tadhg said to himself, and it must be surely for our good that Ireland should not be destroyed. She said that Ireland made us all; a hearty saying that is! and with Ireland in his mind always he walked like a man in a dream, finding his way better than if he were trying to recall it or asking it from shepherds. His steps paused but once, and then only for a moment; for to confide Soracha's story to the hermit would delay him, and every moment was precious. So he hastened to Athlone, to hear that Sir Ulick and the men had come into the town, rested an hour, and gone away; and having enough money upon him he hired a horse, and was riding him hard up the old timbered road when a party of ten or a dozen men, with a pack-horse and a mule, gathered round him. We are looking for the Shannon, said one.

Looking for the Shannon? Tadhg repeated. You are by the Shannon! We are by a lake and not by a river, said the man. And who may ye be and whence have ye come? Tadhg asked. We are of thine own kith and kin, and have come from the great fight at Faughart Hill. The battle we have been talking about these many days! cried Tadhg; and which of them won, Bruce or Bermingham? The Normans had six to our one, but the battle did not begin to go their way till Sir John Maupas broke through our ranks and fought and killed Bruce, his own body falling dead over the body of our great chief. But we must not delay, cried another, telling stories of the battle; we are seeking the mouth of the Shannon. Then you have a long way to go, said Tadhg, and if you don't want to be caught by the Normans, leave the town of Athlone on your left hand. That is all I can tell you. The rest of this country is as unknown to me as it is to you. What carriest thou on thy back? My harp, to be sure. So thou art a harper? Aye, and a good one, a pupil of Finn Lorcan, of whom you have heard without doubt. Not a word do we know of Finn Lorcan. Well, said Tadhg, his vanity getting the better of him, you've heard of the great Earl de Burgo, and I am his harper. The harper of the Red Earl! was muttered. If that be so we will take thee to play for us on the voyage to Scotland, if we find a ship in the harbour; and thou'lt be held to ransom if we reach Scotland. But, honest men, decent men, let me go, for I'm carrying a message from the nuns of Durrow to Sir Ulick de Burgo, and must find him before he reaches his castle. We know nothing of these things and care little, said the leader of the gang, for we are hunted men, running for our lives. Come down from thy horse, and walk between these men, and obey them if thou wouldst not feel a spear in thy side. And now, march!

As no order had been given against speech, Tadhg

said to his guards: I have come a long way; walk not so fast lest I fall. And his words coming to the ears of the captain, he said: We, too, have come a long way and are tired, but there is no time for halting till we step on board a ship. Don't blame me, captain, if I fall, Tadhg answered; and the captain, remembering that a pike cannot rouse dead men and that a guide was needed, ordered him to be placed on the mule, already heavily burdened. We have brought with us all the food we fell in with on the march, and hope to find enough in Clare to last us into Scotland, if we should find a ship. And if there be no ship in the river? Tadhg asked the soldier. The hills or the woods for us then, till somebody hangs us out of a tree. But we shall find a ship. I hope that you may find one, said Tadhg, for you are fine men, and fine men are not fruit we like to meet with on forest trees. Might I ask whence you have come? We would be puzzled indeed to tell thee, for we know no more than that we fought at Faughart Hill, and finding our retreat northward cut off we tried the south. I would not be prying into your business, Tadhg continued, but if it's no harm I'd like to know how long you have been wandering. No harm at all, said the Scot on his left hand, a week come Sunday, losing our way in woods, up and down and around, till we could no longer tell the north from the south, the east from the west. So we are by the Shannon now? You are, faith, and a fine blue stream it is. Have you got a stream the like of that in Scotland? I am sure you have, and a bigger one, Tadhg added, afraid lest his question might anger the soldier. I cannot tell. Canst say, Wallace, if we have a bigger river in Scotland? I know not all the rivers in Scotland and therefore cannot say, but this Shannon is a fine one. A grand river, said Tadhg. An order came from the captain: Silence in the ranks! and turning to Tadhg, he asked: Why didst thou not warn us of the village we are coming into?

Have I not said, captain, that I know no more of the country hereabouts than you do yourselves? And the answer seeming good to the captain, he said: Half an hour do I give for the pillage, and no more. There'll be a few more families living on cress to-morrow! said Tadhg to himself. And all the food of worth having been robbed from the village, Tadhg was ordered to step down from the mule and to walk with his guards; which he did, feigning an air of willingness to ingratiate himself with them. And with the same wish in his heart he called to the captain towards evening: Look between them trees, captain, and you'll see a big and handy ship, the very sort you are looking for; but I'm not saying that she's a Scotch ship. Whatever country she belongs to now, if she have not her share of men on board she will belong to us, for by the best of luck we have men with us here who can handle a ship. There's M'Pherson and M'Donald—— Do not forget M'Tavish, cried another, for he knows every rope, and can take in a reef and pull an oar. And these words created a merriment amongst the wayworn men. Tadhg, thou hast quick eyes, said the captain; look now and tell us if there be men aboard. I see but one man, answered Tadhg; and others of the gang affirming that Tadhg saw well, the captain continued: Where the rest of the crew are we shall never know, for the wind is blowing fair. But how shall we get on board? one of the soldiers asked, and the captain answered: Hast thou no eyes to see the ship's dinghy? and the man stood abashed.

Work for us or swim! said the captain to the man in charge; and the breeze favouring them, they were soon a mile or two out at sea, voyaging north, turning inland when their food ran short to plunder first a Galway, then a Mayo, then a Sligo, then a Donegal village, and when the wind failed the men fell to rowing. Tadhg amongst the others had to take his turn at the oar, but his rowing was so feeble that he was sent to the prow to play his harp, the captain thinking that his fingers were of more use to them than his arms. Sometimes a single voice sang, sometimes the crew sang together in thirds, but they sang so tunelessly that Tadhg tried to help them with his voice and his harp, escaping thereby from thoughts of his long imprisonment, from which there was no escape, so the captain told him. Thou 'lt be kept in prison till a messenger arrives with money, and if no messenger arrives—— The Earl will not see me languish in Scotland! Scotland is a fine country, said the captain. Maybe, said Tadhg, but in prison every country is the same. And every country is the same to a slave, the captain answered. At these words a great fear came over Tadhg, and for many a month in his Scottish prison he repeated: Every country is the same to a slave! Is it true that if no messenger comes I am to be sold? he asked his gaoler, and the gaoler answered: Better be a slave on a hill-side than within walls. And slavery being then the only comfort he could look forward to, Tadhg's despair deepened every day, and the last blow was when the master he had been sold to took his harp from him, it being judged useless to one whose labour was henceforth to tend sheep on the Rhinns.

CHAP. LI.

ON THE Rhinns! said Alec. And what might a Rhinn be? Before I tell about the Rhinns I must get a drink of water from the river; my throat is like a lime-kiln. The river water is soft, your honour; I'll run to the house, for there's a fine well at the bottom of the garden, with water as sweet as any in Connaught. I shook my head. Any water, I said, to quench this burning! And climbing down the little wall to the river's brim I tried for a place where I could kneel and get my mouth to the water without wetting myself. But the water went swirling by between big slippery stones, and when I returned to Alec my feet and trousers were wet, and he said: They 'll think you 've fallen into the river itself. And you didn't get the drink after all? Only a mouthful, I answered, and that was enough. As I told your honour, the river comes down from the mountains through bog-land and the taste never leaves it after. You would have done better to let me run to the house. Thank you, Alec; but we have told enough story for to-day, and whilst we go towards the Lodge I 'd hear if you like the story or if the convent disappoints you. We had some stories about convents a week ago, but no such convent as this one. And the stag, Alec? The stag is a rare bit, and you were lucky to get it from Timothy Moran. But why do you think that it was from Timothy Moran I got the fight? Isn't it just the thing that I 'd make a story about myself? he answered. But I 'm wondering what became of the two in Castle Carra, and I 'm fairly bet, for now you are on the Rhinns and likely to stay there awhile, for all I can see, for you have got that misfortunate Tadhg into a sad mess, surely. All the same, you 'll get back to the Castle Carra people, won't you? Tadhg 'll meet Sir Ulick again? for without that meeting the story won't do at all. They must come face to face, and should it be that you tell the story another way—— You won't want to hear any more of the story, Alec, is that it? That would be a harsh way of putting it, your honour. This much I 'll tell you, Alec, that they do meet face to face. And Soracha—what becomes of the girl? You have asked me one question and I have answered it; ask me no more. Then to-morrow, your honour, we 'll start off again, at the same time and under these same beech-trees.

CHAP. LII.

YESTERDAY, ALEC, I was telling that Tadhg followed his sheep up and down the great cliffs of the Rhinns. And if I should say my say about the same Tadhg, said Alec, I'd put it that he was one the dogs would pay little heed to; those wild sheep dogs will only work for a stern and knowledgeable master. And there must have been eagles building in the cliffs; terrible birds they are, fierce birds and right hungry for lambs; and if they can't get a lamb, often enough they'll drive a sheep over the cliffs, knowing well that they'll find him on the beach broken up ready for picking. So they have done many times in Achill Isle till powder and shot got rid of them. It is easy to see, Alec, that you are a story-teller; you see into the heart of Tadhg as well as I do myself, and better, for what you knew in a single instant I took months to learn: that Tadhg was but an indifferent shepherd. What would he know of that trade? Alec answered. You will never make a handy shepherd out of a swineherd; if a man has the instinct of one animal he hasn't of the other. And you'll understand, Alec, that a great longing for Ireland being always in Tadhg's heart, his thoughts wandered often to the cliffs over the water and beyond them into the pleasing county of Galway, to the palace of the Earl, where he had played the harp to great companies assembled; or his thoughts would return to the long winding roads and the poplar avenues of Normandy. Rare moments of delight these were, to see himself in his thoughts riding by his master's side to a castle where a lady and her court awaited them. For a moment the past was reality; he was in the minstrels' gallery and his master sitting by the great lady's side in the banqueting hall, till the scream of an eagle awoke him. A sheep is over the cliff! he said, and to-night I'll get no sleep thinking of the lashing waiting for me in the morning, unless indeed the master's humour be changed from what it was last time; and the day was spent weaving excuses that might mitigate his punishment. But waste of time were his thinkings, for when the master heard that another sheep had been lost he was not in the harsh, flogging humour that Tadhg feared, and looking down on the pleading, grey-faced man the thought came into his mind that it would be better to give him a harp than to send him back to his sheep—a thought that was quickly put out of his mind by another thought: that Tadhg might be sent to follow a flock of geese inland into quiet cloughs less frequented by eagles than the cliffs.

A good thought this was, for the geese proved more obedient to Tadhg's call than the dogs or the sheep, one goose indeed giving herself wholly up to him, separating herself from the flock, posting herself as a sentry on a hillock and whenever an eagle came sailing overhead calling to Tadhg to drive away the bird with his staff. After six months' service with his geese he earned some words of approbation from his master and returned to his flock determined that no eagle should get one of them; but he reckoned without his faithful ally. His goose died after two years, and after her death goose after goose was raped away to feed young birds on the rocks, and again the master became incensed against Tadhg. Thou hast worked well for two years and art now dropping back into dreams of a country that thou 'lt never see again, of friends—if those who will not pay a ransom for a servant can be called friends! It was on Tadhg's lips to tell the master that his friends had not forgotten him, but it is better for a servant never to say nay to his master; so he hung his head and was bidden to return to his flock, with the warning that if another goose was lost he would be tied up again. And his back still bearing remembrances of floggings, he sat in his coign of rock so deep in his prayers that had an eagle come at that moment the bird would have gotten a goose for her young easily. Good Jesus, thou that knowest well the pain of a flogging, give me death instead. And as if God had heard his prayer, a goose separated herself from the flock and came to him, seeking caresses from his hand, uttering all the while such affectionate sounds that Tadhg believed the bird was sent to save him from lashes; nor was he mistaken in this, for Maria posted herself on a hillock just as Annie had done. A bird's eyes are keener it would seem than a man's, and before the eagle was overhead Tadhg had time to gather the flock into safety and to tuck Maria under his arm; a beautiful white goose, to whom Tadhg became more attached than he was to Annie. Every day he owed his luck to Maria, and soon after he found on the beach a boat abandoned, or one that had drifted from some wrecked ship, and whilst making it watertight he often stopped in his work to think of what would happen to Maria if he left without her. Maria had saved him from many lashes, and he had saved her many times from having her throat cut, saying to his master: She is the sentry of the flock; choose another for the spit, but leave me Maria. All the same, he couldn't remain away from Sir Ulick and from Ireland, and he couldn't carry her down the steep rocks in the dusk. I should miss my footing, and we both would perish. It will be hard to steal away unbeknownst to her; she is always the first to awaken.

He continued his work on the boat, thinking always of Maria, eluding her at last by starting before the first stime of light. Maria has overslept herself, he said as he stumbled down the rocks in the dusk, bruising his shins, till about midway the descent became so perilous that he paused, daring no farther till the light strengthened.

There's not a wind of any sort about, he said, and if the master should be up early and find me gone, he'll come down to the cliffs and send a boat with strong rowers after me and I shall be overtaken. And his back remembering the pain of the lashes it had received he was moved to begin the ascent again. But he lacked power to return, nor could he go forward, and the great fear that was upon him was dispelled only by the thought that it were better to be drowned in the sea than to be taken back and flogged. On a sudden resolve never to hear or feel the lash again, he climbed through the last rocks, and barely had he pushed off from the beach when a wind curling from the Scotch coast filled his sail, and a bird flying heavily overhead fell exhausted into the water near to the boat. Maria, come after me! he muttered, and to save his beloved goose he dropped the sail, and Maria having enough strength to swim a little, he was able to lift her out of the water. Had she words she would tell me if the master is about; not much good would it do me to know whether he is or not—much better to raise the mainsail and get out to sea. With both sails set the boat made good progress towards the Irish shore, tilting over the ruffled sea, with Tadhg in the stern steering with one hand and with the other fondling the affectionate goose. If this wind lasts we shall be in Ireland in six hours, or two drowned corpses in the sea. Thou didst well not to delay thy flight longer, Maria, for it needed all the strength that love gave thee to reach my boat. No food have I, nor fresh water to give thee, but in a few hours thou'lt eat Irish grass, a riper green than any that grows on the Rhinns. And whilst the tired bird slept he was able to steer the boat out of sight of the watchers posted on the Scotch cliffs. But he did not reach the Irish coast without an adventure. He was suddenly caught in a swirl of waters, his boat bumping so roughly that he said to Maria: We shall drown together; and it was only by putting all his strength into the oars that he managed to pull the boat out of the great turbulence. Once out of it the sailing was pleasant and safe, and two or three hours afterwards he steered the boat into the quiet waters of a deep inlet. Above him the rocks were high and steep, and he had not the heart to leave Maria behind, though by doing so he would make sure of his own life.

On reaching the top he said: Maria, our way lies west for several days; afterwards we shall turn south. And he trudged on, carrying Maria, who was still too tired to walk, too tired to pluck the sparse grass that grew in the desolate plains through which they were going. The spangled sun-rise above them betokened rain, and its early promise was fulfilled about noon, a sharp, slanting rain falling on the still distant traveller coming towards them rapidly. In a few minutes Tadhg knew him to be a harper from his pack, and the man's first words were: Canst tell me, traveller, how far we are from the coast? No more than half-a-mile, Tadhg answered, and foreseeing some lengthy talk with the harper he let down Maria into what seemed to him a succulent patch, saying: Some slugs thou'lt find in this wet herbage; seek them whilst I talk with this honest man. A tame goose thou hast with thee! the stranger said, for every time Tadhg whistled to her she raised her head. Tame as a dog, said Tadhg, and he began Maria's story; but he had not got far into it when he saw that to end it he would need at least half an hour, and moreover it could have but little interest for a stranger hurrying to the coast. So he broke off abruptly. Thy gait coming up yon field told me that thy need was pressing. Great need I have, said the stranger, to get out of this country. And to tell that need would take as long as to tell the story of how I came to bring Maria with me across the strait. So thou hast come across the strait? Yes, and have left the boat that brought me over lying in an inlet, drawn up on the beach, with a sail and oars in it. So if thou 'rt anything of a sailor and can bide for a fair wind, embark when the wind blows from the south, not before, for the tides are dangerous and a west wind would sweep thee into the great sea. So thou hast no further need of the boat? said the harper. None; I have been in Scotland for seven years and have returned to my own country, to leave her no more, if God bless me! Is it the truth thou 'rt telling me? Why should a man trouble to tell anything but the truth about a country that he left in a boat that came to him by chance? If that be so, thou wouldst not return to Scotland, where there may be moments of quiet for men to listen to harp-playing and poetry? For seven long years, Tadhg answered, I have been following flocks yonder over the wild moorlands and have not touched a harp. So thou, too, art a harper? In days gone by I was known for one. Then return with me, said the harper; put Ireland behind thee, the best country in the world to leave behind. Faith, Tadhg answered, thou 'rt asking me more than I can do, for however bad Ireland may be in these times, my master is there; it is of him I have been thinking these seven years, and it is him that I have been seeking and shall go on seeking him till I find him or God takes me. I honour a man that can love his master as much as I honour a man that can love his servant, said the harper, so go thy way; and an hundred thanks to thee for the boat. A hundred welcomes, said Tadhg; but before leaving me, tell me what road will take me quickest to Mayo, for being a harper thou knowest the country, and I 'd liefer put myself under thy guidance than another; for——

Say no more; thou 'st given me the boat that will carry me out of Ireland, and I 'll give thee the road that will take thee into it. Now, there be two roads thou mayest go to Mayo, by the north or the south of Lough Neagh, and though the north will take thee through a hard, rough country, I 'd have thee travel by it rather than by the southern road, for that would lead thee through woods where wolves are plentiful, the shes outside the dens playing with the cubs and all eyes and ears for food. And if thou camest to no harm by the wolves, there would be lakes and marshes and mountains to cross, with only one ford, the one that Cuchulain fought by and killed Ferdia—being a harper thou knowest the story. So I would have thee take the northern road, for by this road thou wilt be walking nearly due west, the sun always guiding thee. There will be the Bann to cross, a deep, swift current into which thou must not trust thyself. A ford thou wilt not find, but at this season the salmon are coming up from the sea and there will be men with nets and boats to take thee across. Belike, we may never meet again, but I wish thee a great discovery of thy master, wherever he be. And I wish thee, harper, a great discovery of glory in Scotland for thy harp-playing. Were we not so pressed for time, and were not the clouds again gathering for rain, I 'd hear thee play, for the sound of a harp I have not heard for seven years. We shall never see each other's faces again, said the harper, nor hear the sound of each other's harps. I have no harp, Tadhg answered ; and if I had, this is no time for music. Keep to the right of the trees yonder and descend the rocks, but trust not thyself to the boat till the wind changes. On these words the men turned their backs one upon the other, but Tadhg had not taken many steps before he heard the harper crying : Thou 'rt forgetting thy goose ! Tadhg answered back : A goose is a clever bird and no hindrance to a man on a journey. She feeds herself and has wings to make up the distance if a patch of grass to her taste delays her. A waving of hands and they were swept apart. Tadhg plodded on, hoping that Maria had her eye upon him, nor was he disappointed.

Not five hundred yards had he walked when he heard wings and Maria was beside him. But though Maria's wings bore her quickly to her master, thought is quicker, and Tadhg having in mind the onrush of a fox said: Naughty girl! naughty girl! thou shouldst not leave five hundred yards between me and thee. A fox might have taken thee by the neck and then I should have been alone in this world. And just as if the bird understood the reproof addressed to her, she followed close at his heels like a dog whilst they struggled through a landscape drenched with winter rains in which a few old thorns were beginning to catch green. The wind moaned and the shower was blown aslant, and Tadhg thought of the harper, who in a little while would be finding the boat on the beach. If he puts forth, he said to himself, a gust of wind like this will fill the boat and he'll drown within a hundred yards of the shore. And it may be days before the weather changes; the longest winter, the bitterest I have ever known. Now, what did he tell me about Lough Neagh? That I was to walk due west, and due west I am walking, for the sun is coming down in front of me through a tangle of clouds.

A shepherd told him he was within a few days' journey of Lough Neagh, and allowed him to sleep in his sheeling that night, he and Maria together on a truss of straw, and next day they started again for Mayo. But webbed toes swim better than they walk, and the bird was heavy to carry. And thou 'lt be a heavier load before we are in Mayo, said Tadhg; yet I would not be without thee. And he trudged on through a country of great bogs and high hills till he came to Lough Neagh, vanishing southward out of sight like a sea. A great lough, surely, and were it drained dry the waters of Lough Corrib, Lough Mask, and Lough Carra might be poured into it without filling it up again. But it's weary walking through bogs and hills with thee under my arm. Thou 'rt hungry, my treasure; I'll wet a little of the bread that the shepherd gave me. The bird ate it from his hand, and having fed bethought herself that a bath would be welcome, and slid into the lough, drawing upon herself a flight of wild geese, bringing grief to Tadhg's heart. She'll find a gander, he said, and he'll beguile her; for the female creature, human kind or beast kind or bird kind, is easily deluded. I know them well! The wild geese will get the smell of my hands upon her and will leave her alone (or chase her away); and he was sorry for Maria, who would be deprived for evermore of her kin. Belike thou wouldst be happier with me, and belike not. His thoughts seemed to be fighting one with the other, and unable to control them or to put any order or reason into them, he watched them flowing. Now, for what am I crying? he asked. For a goose that has gone after a gander? No, not altogether—for the way life had come to him; cruelly it had come, yet he had borne it and might have borne it a little longer on the Rhinns. But in his own country, by the side of a lake, with his strength failing, and far from his master, he felt that it would be better for him to lie down and die on this beach. All his strength was gone; he could bear his life no longer, and prayed that it might not be the will of God that he should go any farther. Why was he like this, and why was life so hard? he asked, and the storm that raged within him passed away as storms pass into the upper air, and he began to ask himself how it was that his life, that had begun so well, should have finished so badly. He had liked feeding his pigs in Ardrahan, and he was the happiest boy in Ireland when whistling to the great big fellow that had an ear for a tune and would put up his hooves on a rail of the sty to ask that it might be whistled for him all over again. He was sorry to leave his pigs when his mother sent a message saying that he was to come to the castle to wash dishes in the scullery. I shall be back in a few days, he had said to the big pig; thou 'lt hear no more whistling till then. Little had he thought as he spoke these words of the good fortune that waited him in the Earl's palace; and a smile came into his sad grey face when he remembered that, whilst whistling in the scullery, all the servants had crowded round to hear him, angering his mother, who said: I have to get on with my dinner and thou art wasting my time and thine own with whistlings. Tadhg, thou shalt go back to the pigs! I will and willingly, mother, for the creatures like my whistling. And I might have gone back on the morrow if the Earl, who was walking with his steward on the terrace, hadn't heard me. Now, who is that boy whistling? said the Earl to the steward, and the steward answered: The boy is Tadhg O'Dorachy, the cook's son, who came from Ardrahan to wash dishes in the scullery. He has an ear for music, said the Earl. I would speak with the boy.

At the remembrance of the moment when the steward clapped his hand on his shoulder and said: Come thou to the Earl, Tadhg forgot Maria and the lake before him and was again near to fainting, but through the dimness he heard the steward's voice saying: It 's no lie I am telling thee; the Earl thinks thy whistling good. . . . And though I was next to naked, I came before the Earl, who said: Put clothes on him and clean him and bring him to me. I was told to whistle, but not a whistle was in me and I stood trembling, unable even to speak a word. Thou 'rt frightened, said the Earl. Here is a harp; try to pick out on these strings the tune that I heard thee whistling. The harp took all fear out of my heart, and the sound of the strings as I touched them led me into the tune; and when I had found it out on the harp, he said: Thou shalt learn harp-playing, my boy, from Finn Lorcan, my harper, who is too old now to play but not too old to teach. And six months afterwards I was playing in the minstrels' gallery and a great assembly listening to me. Didn't the Red Hand of Ulster offer a great sum of money to the Earl for me? But the Earl wouldn't take money for his harper, for I was to teach his son, Ulick de Burgo. And when the good lady his mother died another great day was in store for me, for wasn't I chosen to take the young Earl, or him who should be the young Earl, to France and look after him? Now, isn't it the wonderful thing that a poor boy should be taken from the pigs at Ardrahan for no reason at all but to be left stranded on the shores of this lake without strength or hope that he might ever see his dear master again? There's no sense, no reason, no anything, in this world. We are all unhappy, and perhaps my master is as unhappy as I am. Maria is still sporting with a gander, and if she will waste her time thus, let her waste it. I shall journey easier without her. He rose from the stone on which he was seated, but he had not walked far before Maria overtook him; and after travelling with her for a mile or more, he said: This must be the river the harper told me to look out for, the Bann and none other, and I might do worse than ask for a day's work from the fishers. Come, Maria, thou'rt tired, and wouldst rest a while in the lap of my arm. . . . If you should want a man to drag a net or pull an oar—— Canst pull an oar? I can pull an oar as well as another, Tadhg answered. If thy work be as good as thy promises, thou shalt have a ten-pound fish for two days' work. But my goose, said Tadhg. She never lets me out of her sight, following me like a dog. Well, shut her in yon sheeling. She'll cry all day—— There'll be none to hear her crying, the man answered. And when Tadhg had shut Maria into the sheeling he was told to take the bow oar and keep the boat steady in the current so that the spearmen might not miss the fish. And at the end of the next day Tadhg asked: Have I earned my fish? The fishers would have had him stop another day with them, but he went to the sheeling, and bringing back Maria with him he asked for his fish and a loaf of bread for Maria, which they gave him, saying: Thou wouldst do well to leave Maria with us; a goose is no companion for a long journey. A month of soft foods, the man continued, feeling Maria's breast—— No, said Tadhg, I will not leave my goose to be eaten; she has followed me so far and she shall follow me to the end. I have come from Scotland in search of my master away in Connaught, and she has come with me. She flew over the cliffs after my boat, and a bad day it would be when I'd leave her to be eaten by you. Well, it would not be good for us to come between a man and his luck, and if the bird be thy luck, care for her, for a man without his luck is a poor thing in this world. And that is the difference between this world and the next, said Tadhg; in the next world there's all the luck, and in this world there's little of it, if there's any at all. At which they laughed and returned to their fishing, leaving Tadhg and his goose to continue their journey, Tadhg searching amid his disjointed memories and the goose quacking from time to time to be carried.

So thou wouldst have me carry thee? Tadhg said at last, picking up the bird, and with his sleepy Maria tucked under his arm he pursued his way through the sullen end of a March day towards a grim wood that he had been told at the Bann to keep outside of, wolves and foxes abounding therein. Worse enemies to thee than to me, he said to Maria. And whilst walking towards the wood he remembered that the weather had favoured him from the day he had set out from Scotland, a sunny sea and fine winds; and on land, too, he had enjoyed some fine days when the wind was southerly and the sky blue, veiled with transparent vapours drifting to the north. But those fine days were followed by harsh winds and cold rains; snow had fallen; and remembering the wet winter they had passed through, when it had rained all day and begun to rain again in the middle of the night, he said a rainy winter truly—and one not over yet. A winter of floods, rivers overflowing their banks, torrents, rills, runnels, and no sound in the country from bird or beast, only the cold sound of water. Can it be that God is once more minded to drown the world for its sins? Up above he is making ready for another big downpour. A wet night for us, Maria; thou in thy feathers will not heed it, but in these rags I will come on my death if I find not a dry ditch. Not one is to be seen, nor even a hawthorn. So into the wood we go, though we lose our lives in it. But I can carry thee no farther, asthore; thou must trust to thine own legs. Maria's webbed claws were ill suited to clambering through bushes and tall tangled grasses, but she reached her master at last at the edge of the wood, which she seemed to recognise as dangerous for her, for she kept to his heels closely whilst he sought for a holly bush under which to pass the night, never finding one, only forest pools which Maria would have liked to voyage about in. There's no finer shelter in a forest than a holly-tree, shelter from the rain and the wind. We have come upon one, my pulse, that will suit us as well as a house; and sleeping together, side by side, we won't feel the night passing.

So tired were the travellers that sleep came to them without their seeking it, and they slept for many hours, the darkness of the holly deceiving Maria as to the time of day; she had never overslept herself before, not as she did that night; and Tadhg, too, might have slept for another hour if Maria had not clapped her wings and screamed, a fear of the wood having awakened in her. And Tadhg, rising, said: Well, then, keep close to my heels, and we'll try to find the other side of the forest; and be saved many a mile of tramping. And with lighter hearts the two of them set out, but after walking through the trees for an hour the thought came to Tadhg that he ought to return to the holly where he had slept, for from the holly he knew his way out of the wood. But he could not find the holly and began to think he was lost. A hateful place to be lost in is this same wood, he said, tall trees straining to get a glimpse of the sky; elms I think they must be, but so thick is the ivy on them that there is no telling. An evil-smelling place it is; not much better than a swamp, he added, looking into a hollow overgrown with briars. Water is in the bottom, and it stinking water; and he wondered that so white and beautiful a goose as Maria should scramble down to it. After the frogs, he said; and he waited on the bank for her, taking note of the trees, not having anything better to do. At a little distance from him was a decaying pine, and he remembered the beautiful pine-trees of Galway near Ardrahan and the beech wood whither he used to lead his swine, and wondered why no word of endearment or reproof could persuade Maria to relinquish her divings in the dirty pool below him. After all, there is not much to complain of when a man is free, he said, and his thoughts returned once more to Ardrahan and the pigs running before him, knowing well the delicious mast they would find. Beyond the beech wood was Tirconnel's oak wood, littered in October with acorns. How the swine crunched, and how fat they were towards Christmas when their term of life began to close. Poor swine, he thought, they live only to get their throats stuck! And to escape from his memories of their squeals, he remembered that he had never liked an oak-tree. A squat, harsh tree, not much shelter for man or beast beneath it, but good for acorns; fine food there is in acorns for pigs. And there are no other trees here but tall elms swathed in swart ivy; the ivy loves the elm better than any other tree. No larches are there; larches thrive not in a wood but on the fringe of a wood. Is Maria never coming out of that bog-hole?

He was wronging Maria, for as he spoke the words she clambered up the steep bank, and they went on together through the mud about the roots of the trees. No secure foothold is there for the trees, but they grow so closely, he said, that each protects the other against the big winds that blow up from the sea. An evil-smelling wood, he said again, but the smell that comes up is not of rotten leaves. A fox has been by here. Maria, keep to my heels. Thou hast had a fine feed of frogs, and thou hast drunk thy fill of a water that would poison any human belly, but does no harm to a goose's, so it would seem. But there must be an issue out of this wood. And wandering on they came to many blackthorns covered with little white flowers. Like roses, he said, only smaller. To escape from the thought that he was lost in the forest he climbed a tree, and the hen-hawk waited till he was within a few feet of the nest and then flew away with a scream that roused other hawks, and he said: Maybe I did wrong to disturb the bird, for if they catch a glimpse of Maria they might come down through the branches to be at her with beaks and talons. But no hawk came down, and the man and the goose plodded on, the man eating the salmon the fishers had given him on the Bann, offering a piece now and then to Maria. Salmon puts a great thirst into a man, he said, and it may be that it is of thirst I shall die in this wood. But we must surely come upon a brook or a well, for the whole wood cannot be a bog; in every wood there are hills. And sooner than he hoped for they came upon some rocks, and in the rocks was a trickle of water, at which he drank his fill. And after eating, he said: The day is no time for finding a way out of a lonesome wood. The nights are fine and the north star will show between the branches. Let us rest now, Maria, and travel during the night.

In this spirit of hope Tadhg and Maria dozed by the rill, but he had not been long asleep when Maria woke him with loud cries and clapping of wings, and he said: She has got the smell of a fox; we had better move on. Maria cried to be carried and he took her under his arm for safety, and walked on till fatigue again overcame him. Now, he said, I know which is the west and which is the east, for the sun is setting yonder, so I am headed for the west. And it cannot be more than a day's walk out of this wood. We'll both be better for a good sleep, for to-morrow will be long travelling; and once more Tadhg and Maria lay down to sleep, for the last time, for at the deepest darkness, about midnight, Tadhg was awakened by Maria's screams. A fox has her! he said, and seized his staff; but he knew not where to seek her, and as he stumbled he heard her ever-weakening screams and guessed the fox had got her by the throat. The screams ceased, and he picked her up bleeding in his arms. Maria's eyes closed, and he carried her a long way, seeking a big stone under which he could hide her, for he could not bear to think that a fox would feed upon her. But to stand with one's back against a tree, nursing a dead goose, and waiting for the dawn, is lonely and is tedious, and a stout heart is needed to bear the length of the slow hours. But Tadhg's heart was still stout and at daybreak he started again, and coming soon after to a hill-side covered with rocks and stones of all sorts, he said: A great place for the dead; every kind of tomb is here. And choosing a cleft where the fox would not be able to dig her out, he put a stone over her. I am not the man that I was, he said, for it is surely a foolish thing to mourn a goose. But there was never a goose like Maria, the one good soul in this world. And if God is willing to take me I am willing to go, for I am tired of this bleak, sorrowful world, as evil for the rich as for the poor, evil for all, I am thinking. He thought of his master, whom everybody loved, and of his master's father, the greatest man in Ireland, though some of his own were against him, saying that he was for the Scots. But if the world is evil for the great, there is but one good thing in it for the little: the hope of getting into heaven. And it may be that it was God's own will that kept me from the love of women, making me different from those that love and are loved. All the same, he might have left me Maria, for hers was a sinless love. The poor creature, like myself, never cared for one of her own kind; no gander ever tempted her, no woman me. We were alike and lonely and we were good to each other. And his grief became so intense that he thought he must die of it, and leaning over the rocks among which he had found a seat he wept upon them for his goose and for himself until he could weep no more. And then he wandered without heed or care whither he was going, not awakening out of the stupor of his grief till the sound of rooks in the branches caught on his ear and he said: Wherever there are rooks there is a house, for like poor Maria they are lonely away from the homes of men. And wandering round the rookery he asked himself how it was that so many of the creatures of the earth had given up their freedom to dwell with men. Mayhap, he said, it is because we have souls and they have not; maybe it is our souls that draw them to us.

The rookery was among the last trees of the wood, and beyond it in a scoop of the land was a cottage; and going round it Tadhg said: There are people here, for I can hear them snoring. But to awaken them out of a good sleep would bring me no welcome; an outhouse with a lock of straw in it will suit me well. He lay down, and the sun was shining brightly through the chinks in the roof when he awoke. He slept again, and hours passed before anybody came to the outhouse. A child's voice! he said, struggling to his feet, and leaving the outhouse he came upon the child's mother. Back to the wood, rapparee! she cried, brandishing a weapon, for she had mistaken Tadhg for one of the outlaws or the madmen that roamed the woods in the times I am telling, and it needed Tadhg's quiet, winning voice to reassure the woman that he was merely a traveller come from Scotland and on his way to Mayo. And the woman hearing fair words, answered: Look at thyself and say if any child wouldn't scream to see thee. And Tadhg looking down saw that in clambering over rocks and through bushes he had left few clothes upon himself, some rags that hardly covered him, and these all foul with the mud and filth of many days' travelling through wet and sleet, and the droppings of Maria, too, were all over him. I am ashamed of myself, he said: my clothes are worse than I thought for, though I knew them to be bad enough, and thou 'lt be indeed a kind woman to give me a needle and thread and let me rest myself for a few hours more, a rest that I need surely, and during these hours I'll sew my rags. I might give thee a few clothes, she answered, and Tadhg said: Troth they 'd be welcome. I'll seek them, she said; and if they are not much to look at, they will be better than those on thy back. My husband is away burning a castle for his lord or driving somebody's sheep and cattle, but if he came himself it wouldn't matter, for he is a kind man; so make thyself at home. And she brought the clothes she had promised to the stable, thinking it would be unpleasant to have him in the house. A dip in the river would do thee no harm, and there is one at Strule, not many hours from here. Be not in a hurry; when thou art rested. 'Tis the kind soul that is in thee; another night on the straw in the stable will give me back my strength. It was next morning, after having thanked the woman, that he took his direction from her. At the ford of Omagh he stripped and waded waist deep through the river, saying to himself when he reached the top: I am cleaner now than I was before. But how cold I am! A little run will get the ice out of me.

He trotted out of Strule wrapt in thoughts of the first meeting—the first sight of Sir Ulick's face, the first sound of Sir Ulick's voice. If he died on the journey or from the fatigue of it when he reached Castle Carra—well, he would have died whilst in search of his master or after having found him. And so intense were his thoughts that he walked almost consumed by them, the reality about him shadowy and confused, the dream all real within him, Castle Carra and Sir Ulick all clear and distinct; and when he met a wayfarer he listened to the story of the burning of O'Rourke's castle at Dromahaire and of O'Gara's castle at Coolavin, interested vaguely, saying to himself: Whoever is up to-day will be down to-morrow. To give a willing ear to all he heard, to take it all in as if he were listening to a story, saved him from suspicion, and on parting from his travelling companion he would ask that which really concerned him, if he were right in making for the northern shore of Lough Erne and if a path was there that would bring him to Ballyshannon. He had a few coins among his rags and these he hoped would pay for the two days' rest he had promised himself at Ballyshannon, if he should be unable to find somebody charitable enough to give him a truss of straw in a stable to lie upon. His fish was now all eaten, but it was in the genius of Tadhg to discover charitable people. The truss of straw was given to him to lie upon, and he said: It is a great thing to sleep under a roof and to meet kind folk. Often kinder they were than he expected them to be, for on the day of his departure they would take nothing from him, and fish being plentiful that year he went away with one on his back.

Well, it's hard travelling, he said, as he started out on a dim grey morning; if the weather would only brighten a bit I wouldn't fail to get home. And no doubt God wills me to get home, or he wouldn't have sent all these people to help me. At that moment his thoughts of God and God's providence were interrupted by a sudden scent. The smell of the sea, he said, coming over the hills; I got it first after leaving Ballyshannon; and if the sun would light up those hills in front of me I'd have better courage to face a night under the stars, for it is the bleak night that is before me. But there have been worse nights in Armagh, wet fields and no more than a scraggy hawthorn to keep the wind off, and why should I be frightened now of a night on a dry hill with this good cloak to wrap me, unless it was the two nights spent in a warm stable that have disheartened me. Or is it that we can suffer for a while and no longer? He continued walking without eyes or ears for the country he was walking through, till the steep of a hill-side obliged him to stop to take breath; and it was whilst wiping the sweat from his forehead that he noticed that the sky was blue—— Sunny clouds hanging in the wind, he said. And away he went again, faring without a pause till he stood by a lake atop of the last peak. Deep as the earth itself, he continued, filled with big pike, and maybe an eel in it that on certain nights is allowed by God to be a fairy again and speed over the lake to the stone where she sat with her mortal lover and then dragged him down into the depths with her, though she knew he would lose his breath under the water. His thoughts drifted into melodies, melody linking into melody, and the music in his mind did not cease till he came to a rich green plain with woods. A lovely country Ireland is surely and a pleasant country to live in if we had sense enough to leave off fighting. Again he lost his wits in dreams and many miles passed behind him without his seeing or hearing them or anything, but finding the way always as if an instinct guided him; and so strange was the instinct in him that at last it put the words into his mouth: The feeling of home is strong upon me and Sir Ulick; I can see him in my mind plainly—— The sound of harp-strings interrupted his seeing, and whilst walking and peering he came upon three harpers tuning their instruments under a hedge breaking into leaf.

The poor, wayworn fellow listened like one enchanted, and when the little rehearsal was over the harpers began to tell of a great cattle-spoiling and the slaying of a chieftain within a mile of his own castle: and a mournful shout broke from them all, for the chieftain was a friend of harpers, and Tadhg learnt from the leader of the band that he was perhaps the last chieftain of whom it might be said that a harper was never turned from his doors. There are now few among the kings with ear enough to tell the difference between a harper whose fingers move through the thirty-two strings as smoothly as a breeze through wheat stalks, keeping his own part in an assemblage of six or a dozen harpers, never dropping into the tune but playing the chords allotted to him, and an old strummer of strings such as Pat Phelan; and the speaker caught up his harp and imitated Pat's notion of a tune, causing great laughter thereby. My faith, said Tadhg, it's a sad story that's coming and going through my ears, and I listening to you; and it's the first story I heard from a harper on landing in Ireland after being carried off by a party of Scots that had lost their way after the battle of Faughart Hill. Why, that's seven years ago, said one of the harpers. Seven long years, said Tadhg, and ever since I have been minding sheep on the Rhinns. But what of the harper met on thy landing? Well, I'd come over in a boat with my goose—— With thy goose! And diverging from the story he had set out to tell, Tadhg told that Maria was taken by a fox. Tears came into his eyes and he sobbed, saying: None loved me but a goose, and she was taken from me. The only goose? There was another, Annie, and a fine watcher she was, cocking herself up on a hillock and letting a great cackle out of her when an eagle appeared in the sky. Thou must be something of a goose to have been loved by two geese! That may be, said Tadhg, for no man knows how much goose he is or how much man; no man knows more than this: that we are all God's creatures. And this appearing to the harpers like madness, they whispered among themselves till one of their number said: Thou wast about to tell of a harper met after landing in Ireland. He was in as big a hurry to get out of Ireland as I was to get into Ireland, and I told him of the boat that had brought me over from Scotland. So that he might take it, said one of the harpers, and go over to Scotland? And why wouldn't he be in a hurry to leave a country in which, as you tell me, the harp is played by strummers and raspers? And Tadhg was asked if the harper to whom he had given his boat hoped to find a welcome for his harp in Scotland. And thou, said the leader of the band, hast thou an ear for harp-playing? The ear is left, but the hand is stiff on me after following sheep and geese for seven years on the Rhinns. Pass him on thy harp, Morgan, for I'd prove him. Tadhg took the harp, and though he had lost much of his skill enough was left to astonish the harpers, who after hearing him, said: There is Dennis O'Carroll of Sligo who gives a great welcome to harpers, and thou wouldst do well to come with us. He plays well, said the others, and after a few days' practice will play better. Lord O'Carroll will give thee a bed and a bite and praise thy playing, for thou hast a touch on the strings that he's been looking for this many a day. Tadhg said: So be it, and he walked with the harpers till a cloud of smoke rose over the tree-tops. Now, what can that smoke be, coming out of O'Carroll's country? Their steps quickened and none dared to speak the words on his lips: Was his castle burnt last night? It was, faith, said a peasant they met on the road. Burnt it was whilst he and his men were cattle-spoiling in Leitrim;

and there being no more between you and the castle than half-a-mile, step it out and you'll see the roof fall in. It will be a fine sight, said one of the harpers; we would save his roof if we could. But not being able to save it, said another, we will play about the burning, for he was a good man to harpers. And the same phrase was repeated: He never sent a harper away without a sup and a bite and a coin in his pocket. He may have been that with harpers, the peasant answered, but he was a hard man with us. And whilst the castle burnt stories of whippings were told: a whipping for the stealing of a dead branch, two strokes of the whip for faggoting, four for snaring rabbits and hares, and death under the whip for the killing of a deer. The harpers played and the castle burnt, and when the roof fell in the leader said to Tadhg: Thou'lt never play under that roof; it's gone for ever. But we haven't taken thee out of thy way if it's to Mayo thou'rt going. Faith, thou hast guessed it, Tadhg answered, and then the thought coming to him suddenly, he asked among the crowd of peasants come to witness the burning if any of them could give him news of Richard, Earl de Burgo.

He died last year, said a peasant. Of what sickness? Tadhg asked. The doctors couldn't tell him, which didn't matter, for a man knows better than doctors when he is among his last days. My last Parliament! he said at Kilkenny when he locked the door, and he called all the county together for the biggest feast ever given in Ireland, after which he forgave everybody; and vowing that he would sin no more in this world if he got well, he died in the monastery at Athassel. Well, said Tadhg, it's a great thing to die among holy men that have in their keeping the forgiveness of sin and God's sacraments. But since you've told me about the Earl himself and his end, you may be able to give me news of his son. Whereupon a babble began in the crowd about William, his grandson, their heir, and Tadhg cried: It's not him that I want to hear of but the bastard Sir Ulick that went with me to France. Whereat they stared at him. Went with thee to France! Yes, for I'm Tadhg O'Dorachy that was the harper of the Earl himself, and many a time I've played behind his chair. At these words they all wondered, and Tadhg had to tell how he had been taken to Scotland by the Scots and kept prisoner till he found a boat and escaped. We would hear how the strait was crossed; God was in charge of thee, else thou wouldst have been drowned. I would have news from you, if you have any to tell, of my dear master, Sir Ulick de Burgo. He is gone where his father went, said a man. Dead? cried Tadhg. Not dead, but in a monastery. Sir Ulick de Burgo in a monastery! You are asking me to believe more than I can. Sir Ulick de Burgo a monk! I cannot believe that, for why should he, who never had a thought of God but to laugh at him, turn suddenly to God? And at once everybody began to talk of the grace of God, one man telling a story how grace came to a sinner between the saddle and the ground; but despite the miracle Tadhg continued to hold to his belief that one loved God from the beginning or not at all, and he held to this opinion till a priest that had just come from his chapel after saying Mass told him he mustn't say such things as that to his parishioners. For we are all sinful men, he said, in this world. And he turns a deaf ear, cried a man, to the miracle of the man that received God's grace between the saddle and the ground. Sure, said the priest, every man knows that that miracle is a true one. Now, who can this man be? An Irishman, come from France—— Ah! that makes a difference. But even in France they should have known of the miracle. And he continued to exhort Tadhg as if he were an unbelieving man, Tadhg answering: Sure, father, I never heard the story before; it came sudden upon me. But can you tell me, since you are a cleric and should be informed, if it be true that Sir Ulick de Burgo is a monk? No news has come to me, answered the priest, of his having entered an Order, but he has given much money to the monks of Ballintober in Mayo; more than that we do not know. Well then, said Tadhg, I must bid you good-bye, for I must hear the story out, and nowhere shall I hear the whole of it except in Ballintober Abbey. And the crowd watched him stumbling down the road, and had any one of the crowd been behind him he would have heard the old man muttering to himself: A monk! And what did he do that for? His father was old, but he is still a young man, and Soracha with him. But maybe it was Soracha herself that got grace to say: Ulick, we are living in sin. I vowed myself to God, and if the nuns will take me, I'll go back and pray for thee. With Soracha gone from him he had nothing to live for and wandered about the castle and into the forest, unable to put his thoughts to any purpose but thinking of the nun he had lost with no breasts at all, the way he liked them, for surely when she came down the rope from the window into my arms she was as slender and supple as a ferret. He got what he wanted, but she has been taken away from him by the grace of God, and very soon now grace will be given to him.

He could think no further, nor could he see much in front of him, a mist being in his eyes. He stumbled on, and fell upon a green bank by the road-side hard by a cabin—— A great piece of luck, Alec, for there weren't many cabins in Ireland at the time I'm speaking of. Where did the people live then, your honour, if not in cabins? In the woods and in the hills, and not many there, for in the time I'm telling there weren't a million people in all Ireland, and Ireland being a big place there must have been long stretches of road between one cabin and another. Tadhg wasn't long on the bank-side when the woman that lived in the cabin caught sight of him from her gate, and going to his help she lifted him up and took him into the cabin, saying: Here is a sup of milk, honest man. There are children about that want it? he asked. No, she answered, my children have gone from me. After drinking he asked if he might lie down. Is it a harp I see by the dresser? he said. Faith, it is, and my dead husband's—a great harper, the greatest in Ireland. As much has been said about myself; but it 's a long time since I 've seen a harp, and longer still since I have touched one. And though he had barely strength to take the harp from her hands, she knew he was a harper and pitied him. I will string it for thee, he said, when I am rested. He fell back upon the straw and awoke after several hours' sleep more tired than he was when he lay down, and the woman could tell that not much life remained in him, just a thread, which might strengthen by degrees or might snap at any moment. There were always eggs and milk, and he was fed with these whenever Catherine could escape from her work in the garden and the few fields about her cabin, and when she left him he slept, to awaken two or three hours later, or less—time having ceased for him. For many days he barely distinguished morning from evening or day from night; he ate when food was given to him, slept, and awoke to find himself alone in the cabin, the fire burning on the hearth and himself without strength to pile on a few more sods. The fire died into white ashes, and he was sorry that he could not rouse himself, for when Catherine returned she would have to seek faggots and re-light her fire. But so it was. He dreamed a little; images came and went; and it was not till the end of the second week that he began to speak of Scotland and the seven years he had spent on the Rhinns shepherding a flock of sheep, following geese, beaten and starved. When thou art stronger thou 'lt tell me of thy travelling from

Larne hither. He smiled, a weak, happy smile, and answered: Next week. She said he must have some chicken broth, and a long-legged, headless fowl walked about for a while, nearly falling into the fire, but was rescued at the last moment, drawn and plucked by Catherine, and plunged into the boiling pot that hung from an iron bar by a chain. The soup revived Tadhg, and she said: To-morrow thou shalt eat the meat of the chicken.

I remember, he said, a harp that needs stringing; I'd like to string it if thou hast strings. She went to the bed-side and sought amid the shelves, and finding what she was seeking came back, saying: My husband was a harper; here is his harp and here are his strings. And the day being fine, the sun shining in the garden (summer has returned whilst thou wert gathering strength on this pallet), come with me to the seat under the lilac bushes, and there thou shalt string the harp. And being no mean judge of harp-playing, my husband being a harper, I can tell which of you be the greater player, the man that God took from me or the man that he sent to be cared for and nursed. I have done my best with thee. Lean on me, she added, and Tadhg was led into the garden; and falling into the seat under the lilac bushes, he said: Now, give the harp into my hands. To-day I have two boys working for me, said Catherine, and must be about cooking their food. The harp will be strung, Tadhg answered, before they have had their dinner. But the garden being just behind the house, the strains reached Catherine's ears whilst she cooked, and she marvelled and said: Never did my husband play as this man plays. She came and listened to him, forgetful of the food, and returned to it in a hurry and gave it to her workmen, asking them to eat. Listen, she said, to his harp-playing and you'll forget that the porridge is burnt; and she put a big jug of buttermilk before them and went out again to hear Tadhg, who when he saw her ceased playing. Do not stop playing, she said. I am tired, he answered. I will play better to-morrow. And the two sat watching the birds coming down in great numbers from the poplars beyond the garden. The bees, too, are busy; the lilac will soon be in bloom, he said, and the quiet day died, leaving them sitting together; and the next day opening on a sunny morning, Tadhg was out again with the harp. And whilst listening to him it seemed to Catherine that happiness might be in her cabin if she could keep him and hear him play the harp every evening whilst she spun. But her foot forgot the pedal and her ear the music, for the thought came to her that in a few days he would go, for he had told her all his tale and how he must find Sir Ulick de Burgo, who was in the Abbey of Ballintober at the head of Lough Carra, not more than thirty miles from the spot on which they were now standing. But thirty miles is a long way for a man to travel on foot, and he without money or a harp on his back to earn a bite or a sup. Didn't they take the harp from me in Scotland, he answered, saying I'd be wasting my time with it instead of looking after the sheep. The Devil take him who took the harp from thee! she said, and the blessing of God be upon the harp that I'll give thee, for it was my husband's. But I wouldn't be taking thy husband's harp. Why not? for it's he would be glad, however he may be changed or wherever he may be, to know that his harp has come into the hands of one who can play it. So it's been hanging on a nail unplayed ever since he died? said Tadhg. It will bring thee food and lodging, and if thou shouldst ever come this way again 'tis I will be glad to hear thee play it.

Faith, I shall not forget that the first time I played it was in thy garden, Tadhg answered, and he passed down the road thinking that there would be no more lonesomeness for him now he had a harp on his back, and he remembered that if it had not been for Maria's company he would not have been able to travel from Larne down into Sligo. And good company she was, he said, none better, asking to be carried when we were passing rocks and bushes where a fox might be lying in wait, and asking to be let down when we were within sight of a plain where she could look after herself; and knowing that her waddle was delaying me, she'd fly three or four hundred yards ahead to feed till I caught her up. She knew as much, that bird did, as a Christian, and the fox wouldn't have got her if I hadn't been sunk in sleep out of hearing of her cackling, for she must have squawked her insides nearly out when she got the smell of the fox and she must have got as tight up to me as she could, the poor creature! A daring fox, to be sure; if I had wakened then I'd have dealt him a blow with my stick that he wouldn't have forgotten in a hurry.

I'd like to tell you, said Alec, about a duck that left all the other ducks and followed my sister like a dog, as clever a bird as your Tadhg's goose, and it wasn't so strange after all, for geese and ducks are of the same kind, the brainiest of the birds that walk, fly, or swim, and perhaps the most apt to make pets of men and women. Even the wildest of them all, the hawks and the eagles, can be trained to hunt game, and jackdaws ask for nothing better than to be tamed; and he told a story of a jackdaw in Westport that would fly after a carriage and come in by the window. The rooks, too, he continued, like to build round men's houses, and pigeons are as tame as fowls. Foxes and wolves, I said, are as dogs if you give them a chance; and I told him of a tame wolf I had known, more affectionate than any dog. For all the domestic animals were wild once, Alec. And he asked me what there was in man that should tempt animals to leave their kin. Horses will follow men about, but they won't follow bulls or cows, deer or swine. It must be, said Alec, that they worship man as we worship God.

Faith, a dog will outdo any priest in this part of the country in worship of his master. And wishing to stay his tongue and get on with my story, I answered: It may be that animals have an instinct for the soul that is in man more than we have ourselves. If a ghost comes into a room a dog has knowledge of it before we have; he is guided by other instincts and perceptions than ours. We know as little of his life as he does of ours, and perhaps his life is as incomprehensible to him as our lives are to us. But I have told a good deal of my story to-day, and on our way back to the Lodge I would hear how it strikes you. You have heard a great deal about ancient Ireland from your uncle, and should be able to point out some mistakes; there must be some.

My uncle was always reading and thinking about Ireland and was knowledgeable about the country, about customs and ways, how they ate and drank, how they rode and behaved themselves. The Fianna always walked, for there were no horses then in Ireland, and there wasn't even an ass in Ireland for many centuries later; asses came into Ireland with the potatoes about three hundred years ago. The two big social events in Ireland, Alec, were the ass and the potatoes; and there 's an ass in my story at Dunmore! He had better come out, your honour, for those who are up in Irish history will be saying—— Maybe they will, Alec, but if they aren't saying that they 'll be saying something else, and I 'm thinking now on what the Irish lived before the potatoes came. They lived a great deal upon beans, I am thinking; and though you don't say much about Catherine's holding, it wasn't out of keeping with what I 've heard from my uncle. In the ancient times a man with twenty acres of land and a strip of bog, or a bit of wood for firewood, was in paradise. For your honour knows that grass grows a month longer in Ireland than it does in any other country on the ridge of the world, and there were few people in Ireland at the time, most of them having been killed in the wars. I think you said yourself not up to a million, and that I'd judge to be about the right figure; so there was often a mile between a cabin and the next, and perhaps twenty between villages, and all through your story I've been thinking that Tadhg wasn't out of his luck when the fox took the goose, for he never could have crossed Ireland with Maria. He lost her at the right time, and he met the widow, too, when he needed her most. Every journey is lucky or unlucky, and Tadhg was a lucky man all the way to Sligo, to the mearing between Sligo and Mayo, and it isn't far from the mearing that we are leaving him now.

CHAP. LIII.

IT WAS about thirty miles or five-and-thirty from Castlebar that we left Tadhg, meeting with kindness from everybody; all the same, these last miles were perhaps as hard as any he had known, and more than once he sank into a dry ditch feeling there was no strength in him to walk another mile. But after a long sleep in the ditch he went on as a dog does in search of his master, and there was a great joy in him when he came within sight of the county of Mayo, the cone of Croagh Patrick nearly always in front of him and the great ugly mountain of Nephin dropping into rich grass-lands with Castlebar nearly at the end of them. The weather favoured him and he walked admiring a girl carrying a pail of pigs' food through the blossoming trees, followed by a great sow and a dozen squealing bonhams that reminded him of his days in Ardrahan. A little farther on he stopped to admire a herd of cows collected round a spring-head, and clucking hens leading their broods through the hedges delighted him, and he was sorry when he left the last orchard behind him and came within sight of a stretch of forest. The trees began in the marshes, for in the days when Tadhg O'Dorachy walked from Castlebar to Ballintober Abbey in search of his master the county which is now cut away bog was fen and forest; but on the other side, as you know as well as I do, Alec, there are some pleasant green hills, and it is over against green hills that the Abbey was built on a knoll by Roderick O'Conor, last King of Connaught. But your honour hasn't said why Tadhg turned aside to Ballintober instead of going straight on to Castle Carra, where he 'd find his master. You have forgotten, Alec, that the news in Sligo was that Sir Ulick was a monk in the monastery of Ballintober; and Tadhg as he walked out of Sligo into Mayo was a disappointed man and vexed by the thought that the soft climate had put a monk's habit on Sir Ulick and shaved his pate. Your honour thinks that the soft climate has a lot to do with the making of us? My uncle thought the same. And I wouldn't be saying, Alec, that Tadhg as he walked wasn't troubled in his conscience for wishing for the same Sir Ulick as he had known in France rather than a monk; and maybe he had walked a couple of miles before he got the two ideas that were badgering him to agree, saying to himself: It isn't every man that 's suited to be a monk, and Sir Ulick isn't half the age that his father was when he left the world. A good confession would have been enough and a vow never to give a thought to women again, bad or good, for didn't he tell me himself that he never could talk to a woman without thinking—now, what were his words? He had not discovered in his memory the words that Sir Ulick had spoken whilst riding from Dunmore to Athlone when the porter opened the door, saying as soon as his eyes fell on the grey, ragged figure, with the weariness and dirt of long travel upon him: From thy knock I 'd have thought I was going to see the Archbishop himself! Did I knock loud, brother? Three times. I didn't know I knocked three times; I was thinking of what my master said to me seven years ago. But thou hast not come knocking three times to ask me what thy master said to thee seven years ago? I have come here in search of Sir Ulick de Burgo, my master, a monk—— We have no monk of that name. Maybe he is not a monk but a guest, and if that be so go and tell the Abbot that Tadhg O'Dorachy has come from Galloway and would see him. Did I hear thee rightly—thy master was Sir Ulick de Burgo? My master is Sir Ulick de Burgo. Whereupon he was asked to step inside and a few minutes after the surly porter returned. The Abbot will see thee.

Tadhg followed the lay brother up some stone stairs built amid clammy limestone walls till they came to an ogive door; and there being no landing (the door opened on the stairway), the monk ascended two steps and Tadhg passed into a low-ceilinged room lighted by two lattice windows. A low musical voice with an affectionate ring in it, speaking from a high-backed chair, asked Tadhg if he were the messenger from Galloway. Yes, my lord Abbot, I have come from Galloway. Round this way, please, so that I may see thee. And when Tadhg had come round and stood in front of the high-backed chair, he found in it a little man quiet as a rabbit, long-bodied and short-legged, pleasantly rotund. Thou wast with him in France? Yes, my lord Abbot. And on thy return from France thou wast with him in Castle Carra, and rode with him to West Meath, to Durrow? There were deer in the park, and being a little man, my lord Abbot, it was hard for me to reach the stirrup, the horse being seventeen hands high; and whilst trying for the stirrup a stag attacked me and it was a great wrestling match between us. I threw the stag and he threw me, and so it went on, turn and turn about, till I had to cry for help. I know that part of the story, said the Abbot, but afterwards? I was taken prisoner by a party of Scots that missed their way and for the last seven years have worked as a shepherd round the moorlands over against Larne. But I'll be better able to tell you of my escape in the boat when I hear from you that Sir Ulick de Burgo still lives. My lord Abbot, I beseech you to speak at once. Sir Ulick is not dead, the Abbot answered. Thanks be to God! and a good God he is, for I knew he would not have brought me all this long journey for nothing. I'd say a prayer, my lord Abbot, but I wouldn't be delaying you. Sir Ulick is not dead, the Abbot said, but he is not to be found in Castle Carra nor in the Abbey, but on an island in the lake praying that the Princess Soracha may be returned to him. Has she left him, my lord Abbot? Or has King O'Melaghlin waged war and carried her away from Castle Carra and put her back into a convent? None of these things happened; but before going to see Sir Ulick on his island it would be well for thee to hear his story. Is it a long one, my lord Abbot? I will not keep thee from thy master longer than I can help, but to save thee from putting questions to him—— To save me from putting questions to my master! Even so, said the Abbot, and the reasons thou 'lt apprehend easily in the course of the story.

After waiting for thee by the gap in the park wall, Sir Ulick de Burgo and the Princess Soracha rode on, reaching Athlone soon after midnight; and when their horses were rested they rode on again, stopping at Roscommon, Dunmore, and Ballinrobe, and from Ballinrobe they rode to Castle Carra. But I am thinking that they would have done better to have ridden from Ballinrobe to Cong, whence one of the Earl's barges would have taken them to Galway; at Galway they would not have had long to wait for a ship bound for Honfleur, and in France they might have lived in plausible happiness till the

Arch-fiend abandoned them to their consciences and they were constrained to make their peace with God. But they rode to Castle Carra. I am not saying, Tadhg, that they might not have lived in peace in Castle Carra for a week or a month, or maybe till the new year. News travels slowly through an empty country, and Bruce's head being sent to Edward of England in salt, Ireland had little thought for anything else but ridding the country of the remnant of Bruce's army in hiding in the woods and hills. The Normans were busy killing them all the winter and in the spring of 1319, and I am afraid that many Irishmen were killed in the different skirmishes; for it is not easy for Normans to distinguish between the Irish and Scotch, and the lust of killing being upon them they killed indiscriminately. King O'Melaghlin's grief at hearing that his daughter had left her convent with Sir Ulick de Burgo is not to be described in words, at least in no words that I can find, but the twain had nothing to fear from him. Ireland desired peace above all things, and King O'Melaghlin may have said to himself: My duty is to consider Ireland's welfare, and it is for the clerics to tell me if her spiritual welfare would be served by my gathering an army to avenge the wrong that has been done to me. Or again it may have been that King O'Melaghlin had not the great number of soldiers needed to lay siege to Castle Carra. We may indulge in many conjectures without getting nearer the truth, so I'll say no more than that King O'Melaghlin did not leave Lough Ennel at the head of an army in 1319, and Sir Ulick and the Princess Soracha might have lived undisturbed, enjoying whatever happiness their sins brought to them, if Sir Ulick had been content to live in the castle as he found it; he sought to make it worthy of the Princess Soracha, and to do that he summoned his father's builders and ordered them to transform the old Irish fortress into the likeness of a French castle. But it was not the rebuilding of the castle that roused the people, clerics and laity together, nor the furnishing of it; tapestries, carved bedsteads, chests and polished tables, might have continued to come in waggons from Cong without a word of protest, for it was not yet known that the Princess was an escaped nun. Even an escaped nun would not have been enough to rouse Ireland out of her war weariness, and it was not till statues of Venus and Apollo and many other Gods and Goddesses were brought from France that the Irish people began to murmur, asking if the Paganism that St. Patrick had put out of Ireland was going to be brought back by Sir Ulick de Burgo. I cannot cast blame upon the clerics; they brought no charge against Sir Ulick; it was the people themselves who spoke about the statues without a stitch on them. The clergy may have added: Without loin linen or vine leaves, no more than that. It was not till the Princess Soracha, dressed in a scarlet habit and carrying a bow and quiver, led the chase through the forest, that somebody cried: Diana of the Ephesians is among us! I have said that the people were weary and desired peace more than anything else, but the human mind is ingenious and will not be gainsaid, and a story arose, whether in moot-house or chapel I know not, that Pagan worship was practised in Castle Carra by Sir Ulick de Burgo and the Princess Soracha; worse still, that those among their dependents who consented to genuflect before Apollo and Venus were rewarded by presents of money and grants of pasturage. Then the gorse began to blaze, the fire running hither and thither, and it was not the clerics that sent a petition to the Earl asking him to protect them from Sir Ulick de Burgo, who would force upon them the Paganism of ancient Greece, but the people themselves. The petition was written by a layman and brought from Mayo to Galway by a layman, and the Earl being advanced in years, was much concerned that his Mayo subjects should be asked to worship Pagan Gods and sent a messenger with letters to his son and to me. And I said to Sir Ulick, who came to me for advice: I do not believe that you wish to restore the worship of Apollo and Bel, but the best way of proving your good faith will be to leave the country for a time. That I would do and willingly, he said, but there is Soracha, who will not leave Castle Carra. When you leave Castle Carra, I answered, she will return to her father or to the convent. And it was whilst wrangling over this point with him that the thought came to me that it would be well for him to go to Rome and lay his case before the Holy Father. But, said Tadhg, wasn't it to God himself that she vowed her virginity? The Pope is God's vicar on earth, the Abbot answered, and has not God himself said: Whatsoever thou shalt bind on earth shall be bound in heaven, and whatsoever thou shalt loose on earth shall be loosed in heaven—words that proceeded out of a divine foreseeing, for ever since God died for us on the cross the Church has been menaced by infidel powers. The Arabs made themselves masters of the greater part of western Asia, of the north of Africa, of Spain, and now the Turks, another Mahommedan power, are causing great disquiet. The ultimate aim of Turkish ambition is Constantinople, and if we lose Constantinople many Christians will be forced to trample upon the cross or die for their faith. To save the Church much money is needed, and were Earl de Burgo to help with money or with an army to resist the Turks, the Holy Father might be moved to release the Princess Soracha from her vows. So did I write to the Earl and so did I speak to Sir Ulick when he came here, and he left me in the belief that the case of the Princess Soracha might be referred to the judgment of the Pope. But delay followed delay, and when the news of the revival of Paganism in Castle Carra reached the ears of King O'Melaghlin he began to preach a crusade to save Connaught and his daughter from Paganism; and the Earl foreseeing that a cry like this would unite all Ireland against him, sent for his son. And it was whilst waiting for her lover to return to her that the news reached Princess Soracha that her father had left Lough Ennel with an army. She came here to ask my advice, and sitting in that chair she said: The siege of Castle Carra will be but the beginning of a war that will last for years. She asked me how this war might be stopped and I told her I had given Sir Ulick a letter for his father in which I derided the story that Pagan worship was being established in Castle Carra. Truth compelled me to add that the story was believed and that I could see no way of making an end of it except by Sir Ulick leaving Castle Carra; and I spoke of his return to France. Sir Ulick approved of the letter, I said, and every day I thought to hear of your departure. My lord Abbot, he tried to persuade me to leave Castle Carra. If you are right, and I should have left Ireland with him, the fault is mine. To which I answered: Is your liking then for Castle Carra so deep that you would prefer to plunge Ireland into a war that would last for years rather than leave it? There is no love for the castle in me, she answered, but he could not persuade me, and I cannot tell you, my lord Abbot, why he could not persuade me. I am like a chained prisoner. We sought the chains that bind me to Castle Carra but we found none; yet there are chains, for I feel them heavy upon me, invisible chains. I am bound to Castle Carra, I know not how or why, only that it is so.

At these words Tadhg dared to interrupt the Abbot in his story. May it not be, my lord Abbot, that her good angel was without strength to lead her out of Castle Carra, he having been routed so badly by the bad angel at Durrow? It may have been something like that; but to continue my story: I turned to the Princess Soracha and taking her hand I said: My dear daughter, confession is a great help. True, my lord Abbot, she answered, confession would be a great help if I could promise to leave my lover, but that I cannot do. You have come, my child, to ask my help? My lord Abbot, I have come to tell you that I would give my life willingly if by doing so I might save Ireland, and to ask you to look into St. Paul's words; he says that he would hold himself accursed from Christ if by this means his brethren according to the flesh, meaning the Jews, might be gathered into Christianity. But it may be that I have put the meaning that I wish to find on the Apostle's words. My brother Peter is famed in this monastery for his interpretations of Scripture, I answered, and I beg you to put yourself under his guidance whilst I ride to the Shannon, where I shall meet your father and his army nearing the ford at Roscommon. If not, he will take the shores of Lough Allen, and enter Mayo by the southern shore of Lough Gill—words spoken whilst thinking of my journey and of the haste I should make, of the different villages at which I should change horses and many other things; so for some seconds I lost sight of Princess Soracha, and when I turned my eyes to her I saw she was taking no heed of me or of my words. The spell of martyrdom is upon her! I said to myself, and once more I begged her to put herself under the guidance of Peter; and to Peter I addressed myself afterwards, saying: Be gentle with her, else she will escape from us. Speak no harsh words; detain her with promises; tell her that I shall succeed in persuading the King her father to return to Lough Ennel, which I shall do. And Peter seeming to apprehend the danger, I rode away to Ballinrobe, where I changed horses, and then on to Dunmore, and so tired was I during the last miles that I had to be lifted from my horse. A day's rest and then on again, and it was after passing the Suck that I got news of

King O'Melaghlin from the Abbot of Ballintober in Roscommon. Thou hast great need to meet him, brother, said the Abbot. The greatest need on earth, to save a soul from hell, I answered; but ask me no more; and barely able to sit upon my horse I rode on. At Roscommon I crossed in a boat and coming to the encampment of the King, I said: I have come from Mayo, riding by day and by night, hoping to reach you in time, for I bring news of your daughter. Then speak, my lord Abbot, he said, and when he had heard the whole story, I said: Now, in the name of the Church I beg your majesty to withdraw your army; I beseech you to return to Lough Ennel, or as sure as you live your daughter will throw herself from the battlements of the castle or drown herself in the lake. Has it come that a daughter of mine will defy God? he said. She came to ask me if there was salvation for her who takes her own life, and I put her under the guidance of my brother Peter, who is famed for his interpretations of Scripture; but he will not be able to keep her from what she looks upon as a martyrdom when the news reaches Mayo that you have crossed the Shannon. I put my faith in you, cleric, he said, my hand upon it; and he ordered the withdrawal of his host. And my horse being exhausted he gave me a fresh horse to take me back to Mayo. I bought or hired horses when I could get them, and at Ballinrobe my heart misgave me when the inn-keeper said: My lord Abbot, all my horses are out on hire. After looking into my face, he said: My lord Abbot, if all my horses were in the stables I'd sooner they remained in their stables for the next six months than give you one to ride to-day, so tired is your face. I have been riding for nearly six days in great anxiety of mind, I said, and I'll stay with thee for a day, Colman, but a longer stay I dare not. You will be sore to-morrow morning, my lord Abbot, and the day after and the day after; six days it takes to rid the bones of the weariness of a six days' ride. No matter, Colman; to-morrow I must go. And the next day I stumbled to my horse and clung to the saddle as a drunken man might, and all the while a great misgiving was upon me, for I could not put back the thought that had I been able to ride without stopping at Ballinrobe I might have come in time to avert a great calamity. Every mile from Ballinrobe right into the village of Carnacun my heart smote me, for I could not put out of my mind the look of dark ecstasy I'd seen on her face. She is in the lake or in pieces under the battlements, I said, and turning out of my way I rode into the forest. A wood-cutter gave me the news in his simple language: She flung herself over the walls two nights ago, and this morning Sir Ulick, who came from Galway, walked over her and is now like a man demented. If he is only like a man demented it will be well enough, I said, and I rode to my Abbey like one in a dream, now and again awakening to the remembrance of what had happened, her young life dashed out on the stones to save Ireland from another war. Her martyrdom will be remembered, I said; it will go forth all over Ireland; it will cross the sea.

CHAP. LIV.

'TIS A terrible tale you're telling, my lord Abbot, said Tadhg. He covered his face with his hands and speaking through sobs and tears he said: A terrible tale, surely, the worst ever heard in Ireland. My poor master, my poor master! He coming home thinking of the sweet face of his Princess, of the delight it would be to him to see her again, and finding only bruised pulp in pools of blood. O, my lord Abbot, if I had known of this in Scotland I think I would never have come out of Scotland. My poor master, alone in Castle Carra—alas! not alone but with black grief to keep him company up on the ramparts and round the rocks, wherever he went; by day time and night time he'd be wandering with his grief. My lord Abbot, I must go to him. Have I not said, Tadhg, that he is a hermit living on an island in the lake? Yes, my lord. And I say, too, that I must tell the end of the story, which is not far off now. You, my lord Abbot—did you never go to Castle Carra? The news from Castle Carra was that he saw nobody and never passed the drawbridge except at night to walk in the forest. Ah, if I'd been there! said Tadhg. Thy presence would not have soothed his grief; grief heals like a wound, leaving a scar. And looking back upon the year that I kept myself from Castle Carra, I think that I did well to keep away. A sudden intrusion on his solitude would open the wound again, I said to myself, and again and again I resisted the temptation to go to him, saying: We had better meet by chance; and the answer was, thought answering thought: We may live for years within three miles of each other without meeting. But I was confident that some chance would bring us together; I did not know how or when, but I put my faith in chance, and when I heard that he had built little huts in the forest into which he might escape from the curious and the passer-by, I said: I will ride in the forest, my eyes away from the huts. One day he'll catch sight of me and run to hide himself in one of the huts, and this he'll do perhaps twice or three times; but sooner or later he will call me back. My patience was rewarded, for one day I heard a voice saying: My lord Abbot! I drew rein and Sir Ulick said: You have taken to riding, my lord Abbot, in the forest, and I answered: If it is your will, Sir Ulick, that I should keep to the hills I will do so. On these words we drifted into casual talk, myself watchful to say nothing that would betray my thoughts to him, for of course I was thinking of Soracha all the time; and he, too, was thinking of Soracha. But her name was not spoken that day, nor the next nor the next. Sometimes our talks were short and sometimes longer, till at last he said: My lord Abbot, I have missed you from the forest; you have not ridden by for nearly a week; and I answered briefly that business had detained me. But you will be riding this way again before long? Sir Ulick asked, and in the hope of bringing him to speak his mind to me, I said that I was going away for a long holiday to the sea. And reading disappointment in his face, I added: You, too, Sir Ulick, would do well to go away for a holiday, to your own country, to Normandy; what say you? And he answered sadly that if he left Castle Carra the Princess Soracha would not know where to find him. Spirits are not weighted with bodies as we are, I replied, but as if he had not heard me he said, looking into my face steadfastly: If she be not withheld by some great power she will come to tell me that she is waiting for me. I hear her cry every night, the wail of a spirit that would speak to one on earth and is given but a short time between night and day to speak. Tell me, my lord Abbot, if your learning and piety reveal to you the secret whether the Princess Soracha is in heaven, in hell, or in purgatory. If she were in hell, I answered, it would be no help to you to know that she was there. Pardon me, my lord Abbot, I would welcome the news that Soracha was in hell, for I could go to hell easier than I could get to heaven. How so? said I. I have but to worship other Gods to make sure of damnation, he answered. But I do not know that Soracha is in hell, and if I earned a place in hell by worshipping statues and did not find her there, then indeed I should be a lost soul. Hell is hell always, with or without the Princess Soracha, I said. Avaunt theology! he cried. But tell me if the suicide is debarred from heaven always; answer me that, cleric. The Princess put the same question to my brother, and he read to her from St. Augustine the story of three holy women who threw themselves into a river to escape violation. These women were afterwards held in reverence by the Church, and there are many cases in Scripture that cause the Saint to doubt whether he should condemn or condone. All that seems certain is that the suicide debarred from heaven is he who would escape from the trouble with which his life is beset. God involves man in much trouble that he may be purified, and whoever bears the troubles that God has put upon him becomes pure in God's sight even as Job. Come to Ballintober and I will read you what St. Augustine says about suicide.

O my Lord Christ, I thank thee for having let me live to this day! A happy day it is for me, his sins being forgiven to my master and he ready to take his place amid the choirs of angels and arch-angels, seraphs and cherubims. Tadhg buried his face in his hands, and so moved was the Abbot that he could not do else than unite with Tadhg in a prayer of thanksgiving to the High King for his power and goodness in bringing a sinner back to grace. At the end of the prayer Tadhg rose from his knees and was about to depart, but was called back by the Abbot. There is still a story to tell that thou must hear before going to the island to see thy master, and Tadhg murmured in answer: I am in no hurry, for 'tis a delight indeed to hear how my dear master came to repent his sins. Did he confess, my lord? Tadhg, thy question surprises me, for how could he pray whilst he was in mortal sin? I had forgotten that; sure I'm wandering, said Tadhg. We could not withdraw him from his prayers—— Withdraw him from his prayers, my lord Abbot! A sinner comes to the Church and to prayer like a hurt child to his mother. In such wise did Sir Ulick de Burgo come to the Abbey of Ballintober, and none too soon; for I feel now that I was sent by God to Castle Carra to save him from the plans that he was laying to make sure of his damnation. O Lord! O Lord! O Lord! was he planning that devilment? said Tadhg. Have I not told thee, Tadhg, that he was willing to set up a worship of Pagan Gods to make certain of damnation? And isn't God a good God that he should bring a sinner from such a depth of sin right up into heaven, into his love and his sacraments? All life is the work of God, said the Abbot, and all is wonderful; from the angels above the stars to the worms under the earth, all is wonderful. He must be the holiest man now on the top of this earth! said Tadhg. At these words the Abbot frowned a little, and to escape from uttering a reproof that might betray him he began to tell how the desire of prayer for the release of Soracha's soul from purgatory kept Sir Ulick in the chapel at all hours. One more prayer, he would cry to the tired sacristan, one more prayer, I beseech thee, and I will leave the church. But however long the sacristan waited Sir Ulick would want him to wait for still another prayer, till at last Moling would take him by the hand and lead him out.

His father's death in the monastery of Athassel affected him so deeply that he gave all the money he had inherited by his father's will to us for masses for the repose of the soul of Soracha and of his father, and these masses were said daily. But the more masses he got for his money the more he asked for, and every mass he would have a high mass, so all our time was spent in offering up masses. Every monk in the Abbey spoke of him with kindness and bore with him till he dared to interrupt the mass—— Interrupt the mass! said Tadhg. Now, why should he do that? It is true, the Abbot answered, that Brother Ambrose often dozes in the choir and forgets to sing; I have reprimanded him myself for his idleness; and it is true, too, that Brother Michael is often a little flat. He was flat in the *Gloria* on the day Sir Ulick cried out: I am paying for singing that will not wound the ear of God! He would have had us live on water-cress and dry bread for Soracha's sake, and he looked on butter, curds and whey as regrettable indulgences of the flesh. At last feeling that nothing we could do would satisfy him, I begged of him to leave us, and to persuade him to do so we offered him the island in the bay as a retreat. Brigit Lonn rows over daily to milk the goats and to see that he wants for nothing. I will take Brigit's place, said Tadhg. Sit thee down, Tadhg, sit thee down; for if we give him into thy charge thou must know what answers to make to him should he question thee regarding us and regarding Soracha. Let there never be any hesitation in thy answers; let them be always: Soracha is in heaven, if not in heaven at least in purgatory. And if he should ask: How can any man on earth know the justice of God, which is said to be unsearchable? answer quickly that only those who would escape through death from the toils and troubles of life are debarred from heaven. Tell him that St. Augustine has examined the question carefully. I will do that, said Tadhg. But thou hast not heard what St. Augustine has said. And mounting a small ladder slowly step by step, the Abbot reached out his hand to a large folio, Tadhg coming to his help. I see impatience in thy face, Tadhg; I know that thou wouldst run away to see thy master, but a few minutes more will not hurt thee; have patience.

The Abbot placed *The City of God* upon the lectern and was turning over the leaves when the door opened and a small, thin man entered whose dark, pinched face awoke a feeling of antipathy in Tadhg as soon as it was turned upon him. My brother Peter, said the Abbot, and Tadhg rose from the chair that had just been given to him and offered it to Brother Peter, who thanked him stiffly. Tadhg O'Dorachy, the harper, has come to see us. He reached Ireland some time ago from Scotland. From Scotland? repeated Brother Peter. Yes, from Scotland;

he was taken prisoner by a party of Scots—where was it, O'Dorachy? A few miles from Athlone, my lord Abbot. I was carried off to row in a galley, and have been tending sheep on the moors of Galloway ever since. A strange and adventurous story! answered Brother Peter; and thine errand is . . .? Tadhg O'Dorachy is a great harper, brother, said the Abbot, and thou, who art fond of music—— Tadhg thought he had never seen a more unmusical countenance than Peter's, and the Abbot, feeling that he could not conceal Tadhg's story from his brother, related all of it. Hast told him, brother, that the Princess Soracha threw herself from the battlements and that Sir Ulick lost his wits in his grief for her? I have told him the story, Peter. And art reading to him St. Augustine's judgment of the suicide? I would remind thee, Peter, that God alone is judge. And I would remind thee, Tom, Peter replied with a faint hilarity which ill suited his sour face, that we may gather from Christ's teachings what God's judgments are; else for what purpose, for what end, did the son of God live on earth and suffer crucifixion? That we might know him, surely! Quite surely, Peter, Jesus died that we might know him, but man's knowledge is necessarily imperfect, and we submit to the interpretation of the Church as better than our own. The book is before thee, brother, and I had hoped that we were in agreement regarding the interpretation that should be given to, shall we say, the suicide of Jonah and of Samson.

And going over to the lectern on which the book lay, Peter read for a little while, and then raising his eyes from the text he looked from his brother to Tadhg and again from Tadhg to his brother, as if he desired to claim their entire attention for the words he was about to read. St. Augustine's words are precise. Let him, he says, who would take his own life be sure that he does so under God's command. Jonah, the Abbot remarked, was not a Christian, nor was Samson. We must not put aside the Old Testament, not entirely, Peter answered. And then returning to the text he read: No man shall take his own life on account of the sins of another. The Princess Soracha took her life to save Ireland, said the Abbot. No Christian, said Peter, shall take his own life because the world in which God has placed him seems to be unworthy of him, or because he hopes for a better world on the other side of the grave, as Cleombrotus did. What did he do? asked Tadhg. The Abbot turned aside, but his back revealed to Peter the sad fact that he was laughing, and in a doubled exasperation against Tadhg, doubled for he had to repress his anger and give a reply in as calm and even a voice as he could command, Peter told that Cleombrotus having read Plato on the immortality of the soul, threw himself from the top of a wall because he believed that he would thus leave this life for an infinitely better one. No man knoweth what is in man save the spirit of man which is in him, said the Abbot turning from the window. I would not seem unmindful that thou art Abbot of Ballintober, but every man's conscience is his own. A strange doctrine, Peter, to hear from thee. I have heard thee maintain that every man's conscienee is the possession of the universal Church. The Church, Peter answered, does not inquire into any man's thoughts.

And Tadhg, feeling that the moment had come for him to leave the theologians to settle the matter between them, summoned all his courage. I have come a long way in search of my master, and if you have no more need of me I will go to my master on the island. I think I understand St. Augustine very well from you both, and if Sir Ulick should speak of drowning himself or any other way of quitting this life, I 'll remind him of the fate of Cleombrotus. The Abbot cried after Tadhg: Call from the shore and Brigit Lonn will come forth from the island and take thee across.

CHAP. LV.

NOW, which will get the better of the argument, and how long will they be sitting over it, and in which of the regions, hell, or heaven, or purgatory, will they put the Princess? Tadhg asked himself on the way to the lake. Wasn't it the fearfullest thing ever done in life to go to an Abbot and bid him search in theology books for the sin that would be the quickest and the surest to bring a man to the gate of hell, with the angels of God and the troops of the damned all pushing him in from behind? And it was a woman put that daring into his heart! I have travelled the world, but never in all my travelling did I hear of such black daring and never will again. First he'd set up the ancient Gods in Castle Carra, it being the surest thing a man could do to get into hell, and then he'd kill himself, dying an unrepentant sinner that God himself could not forgive without going back on his own laws. But the Abbot was able to withstand him, and it was a great thought to tell him to beware of setting up Pagan Gods lest he might be looking up out of the red pit of hell at Soracha sitting amid the angels, and God himself not far off her in a heaven dewy and sweet as a May morning. It was his luck that the talking fell to Tom; the master would have taken such a hatred for Peter that he'd have said: I'll choose hell if only to be out of sight and hearing of you! But it is no ways sure that you won't be there yourself! The master has his own tongue, and would dare the Devil's self at times. Faith, I'd like to have seen the little prig's face, a scowl on it as black as the Devil's worst, when the master began to shout out: Sing up, Brother Ambrose, sing up! I am not getting my money's worth. I don't know how I'd have kept a straight face upon me! Now there are but a few more rocks to climb and I shall see the island in which my dear master is praying for his lost lady; and I shall pray for her, too, if he thinks that a prayer from me—but are not all prayers equal up above? Yonder is the island standing out of the water like a great bunch of feathers. And seeing a flat rock with the rays of the sun upon it, he seated himself thereon. She may be on the other side; it looks a fair-sized island, and my whistle may have been lost in the trees between us. It is pleasant sitting here in the sun, and if I wasn't wild to see the master I 'd let her take her own time. He whistled again, and was thinking of stripping for a swim when a boat put out from the cove opposite.

After a few strokes of the oars ripples began to appear in the still water. A strong wench, said Tadhg, and as handy as she is strong, one I 'd bet that knows how to kill a kid, to quarter it, to hang it, to roast it, and to eat it, one that has a hard palm from the quern and will show me how to grind the corn and milk the goats and make butter and cheese. A fine stroke! He waited to see her jerk one of the oars out of the rowlock into the boat and with the other shoot the boat up the beach, which she did so well that he began to think that she might be kept on to ferry them to and fro. Her strength put him in mind of his years and his sinking strength; he wouldn't be able to do everything, and he made up his mind to say nothing that might lead her to think he had come to replace her. Thou canst whistle if thou canst do nothing else, she said, and thine errand here is Sir Ulick de Burgo? It is, faith, he answered, and I have come from Scotland. A journey indeed, so perhaps I did well to row over to fetch thee, a thing that I don't do always. They whistle, and they whistle again, and then they go their road. Is that so? said Tadhg. Now, don't keep me here talking; step into the boat if thou wouldst talk with the master, and speak to the point, or I shall be told to take thee back again before he has heard half thy say. He was always a bit like that, said Tadhg. So thou knowest the master? Ah! am I not Tadhg O'Dorachy, his harper, who was sold as a slave in Scotland after the battle of Faughart Hill? Then I did right well to fetch thee without going to the master for an order. It was beginning to be lonesome this evening, and I couldn't put off the feel that I'd like to have a talk with somebody. That's women all over, always wanting to talk to somebody, Tadhg said to himself, and aloud: The island seems a fine place. There's no finer island on any lake in Ireland, Brigit answered. The others, said Tadhg, are but brushwood; here there are fine trees—— Keep thine eyes for the master! she interjected, and Tadhg stepped out of the boat. I thank thee, good woman, for pulling me over the water. No thanks to me for rowing over the master's own harper. And now wilt thou find him for me? Have I nothing to do but look for the master? Hast thou not a pair of legs to go and find him? Keep walking and thou'lt come upon him at his prayers in the oratory, or among the trees, or among the rocks beyond over against Castle Carra. On afternoons like this he lies there asleep like an otter, or he plays his harp to the Princess in paradise. Thou hast heard the story? From the Abbot himself, said Tadhg, and he walked up the beach wondering if there was a trick in all this. There could be no trick; yet why did she come over to fetch him and she without an order to do so? And as he couldn't find an answer to this question his thoughts flitted from Brigit to the island itself, and he admired the limestone shingle. No stone bigger, he said, than a man might put into a sling, save a rock here and there, and these not greater than the Normans shoot against each other's castles. He hearkened to lake water lapping, and his eyes wandered over reaches of white sand, thickly studded with tussocked rushes. Above these hard, wiry grass grew in and out of patches of juniper bushes, whins and blackthorns, forming a sort of thicket round the wood, so dense and thorny that Tadhg did not dare to push his way through lest he should leave the clothes that remained to him on the branches. At last he came to a space free from thorn bushes leading into a meadow in which rich grass was springing up. Fine feeding for half a dozen cows, wasted on goats, he said.

As he walked the island seemed to grow bigger, opening out in every direction, with sinuous paths leading round tall groups of trees, elms seeking the sky and not finding it till they had overgrown the crowding beeches. Here and there were hollies and in all their berries; the winter having been soft, the birds were able to find slugs and worms. Of oaks the island had not many to show, which Tadhg did not regret, for he did not love that tree, saying to himself as he wandered: The young larch in April, and the sixty foot larch in May, loveliest of trees! and he recalled how he had seen in his boyhood larches of that height swinging their branches in the May breeze, so surely rejoicing in the sun that he could scarcely believe they were not living as he was. The birch, too, was coming into bloom, and he was sorry for the pine, dead and stark amid its live brethren. In the branches swarms of bees were going hither and thither among the buds, following the various scents, their droning sounding pleasant as church bells heard from afar. At the foot of the elms primroses were everywhere, and in the meadows cowslips, and the flowers of the ground ivy were hard to distinguish from the dog violets—the very island, Alec, that Marban tells of in his poem written in the tenth century on the occasion of King Guare's visit to him, an island whose birds and flowers and the peaceful life that his brother lived amongst them set the King thinking that perhaps he had lost something in his palace that Marban enjoyed in his lake. I would give my glorious kingship, with the share of my father's heritage—— To the hour of my death I would forfeit it to be in thy company, O Marban! are the words with which he takes leave of his brother. And with Guare's words of farewell on his lips it is pleasant to think of Tadhg O'Dorachy seeking his master from interspace to interspace, marvelling the while at the comely trees and the songs of the birds and the colour of the flowers. Marban's island he would compare with the gardens and the parks he had seen in France, thinking as he wandered how much better was this simple retreat than the hills and the dales the French craftsmen would have moulded, the balustrades and the marble-rimmed fountains and the Pagan Gods that they would place under every tree. All the same, he would have liked some rising ground as the site for Marban's oratory, and his heart quickened when he came to the acclivity on which the hermit had built his chapel. A rowan-tree grew by the oratory in Marban's time, for he mentions it in his poem, and a rowan-tree was covered with berries when we picnicked there in the 'sixties; so it is pleasant, Alec, to think that a rowan-tree flourished when Tadhg O'Dorachy wandered seeking his master. Dreams you will say, but is not a dream the only reality? From generation to generation, the dream outlasts the rocks and the hills. After this little exordium I will return to my story of Tadhg's wanderings on the island till he came to a small pine wood sloping down to the rocky point where, he was told, Sir Ulick often lay when the rocks were warm, looking towards Castle Carra. Now the pines were thick enough to cover his approach and there were thorn bushes near to the rocks, and when he reached them Tadhg hesitated, uncertain if he should rush forward, crying: Master, master, I have come back! or if he should play the harp. The sound of the strings will bring him out of his rocks, he said. And then a remembrance of the master's own tunes coming into

Tadhg's mind, he played them, and it was not long before a tall, gaunt figure rose from the rocks. Ulick stood listening, a look of rapture on his face. Thinking, said Tadhg, that Soracha has come down from heaven and is playing the harp, calling him to her! that is his hope; and I must break the spell at once that my harp has laid upon him, else his joy will turn to grief and kill him. Master, master, 'tis I, 'tis Tadhg! he cried, and, his rags fluttering in the wind of his jumps, Tadhg bounded over the tussocked grass and threw himself at Ulick's feet. Master, I have come! Tadhg O'Dorachy, is it thou? It is I, surely, and none other, Tadhg answered. I have escaped to thee from Scotland. He babbled the story of the stag and the nuns, his capture by Scotsmen seeking a ship to take them back to Scotland; he rambled from incident to incident, and when he came to the story of Maria, Ulick said: It is Tadhg and none other, Tadhg reft of his senses! Not reft of my senses at all, master. All I am telling is the truth, but the joy of seeing you again is so great that I cannot tell the whole of my story at once; it gets confused, but think not ill of me for that. Who told thee of the island? The monks of Ballintober, Tadhg answered. Get thee to thy feet, Tadhg, and talk quietly. Thou hast heard my story and have come here, rowed over by Brigit Lonn? God bless her good, strong arms that rowed me! said Tadhg. Thou wert in Scotland, in slavery? Yes, master, over yonder a slave. And Tadhg began to tell of the Rhinns and the mending of the boat which took him across, and of the harper he had met with; but he put no shape on his story, and seeing that he wearied Sir Ulick, he said: I am getting it mixed again, so I will come back to Brigit Lonn, who rowed me over and told me that I'd find you on the rocks looking out towards Castle Carra. But why didst thou play the old tunes that we wrote together in Normandy years ago? I thought none knew them but me, Tadhg answered; I was forgetting the Princess who must have heard them from you, but she is dead, so they told me in the Abbey. The dead are not always dead, Tadhg; they pass from our sight, and to find them we need a second sight. We 'll speak no more of this; play the tunes to me that I composed in Normandy long, long ago. That is the tune that Rambaud d'Orange wrote in praise of the Comtesse d'Urgel, whom he never saw and who never saw him. Thou hast not lost thy skill in slavery and wanderings. We must have some harp-music together, and for that we must seek Brigit Lonn, who will row to Castle Carra and bring back a harp. Come, let us find her.

Thou 'rt in need of a bath, Tadhg, and of new clothing; get to the other side of me. Faith, your honour never spoke a truer word, and I 'd have been bathing in the lake before I came to you, but was afraid that if I took off my clothes I 'd never fit them on again. Brigit will bring thee clothes to-morrow from the Abbey; and here we are now within the quiet wood in which I live, glad to be out of hearing of the babble of the monastery. And kneeling down they said a prayer together, Tadhg's heart overflowing with joy, for he had never dared believe that the time would come when his master would kneel with him before God's altar. And here, Ulick said, rising to his feet, is the paved path down which Marban walked to his cell, where I sleep at night and where thou shalt sleep too. Whilst speaking their eyes sought Brigit by the cove where the boat lay, and found her in it about to start forth. Brigit, said Sir Ulick, is there strength in thine arms to row the boat to Castle Carra? She answered: Though it be a mile from here and a mile back, there is, faith; and the lake is so still that I won't feel the miles going by. Well, then, take this script to the captain of the guard and ask him to give thee two harps. The harp that Tadhg O'Dorachy plays here is one of seventeen strings; tell him to give thee one of thirty-two.

And standing side by side they watched the boat gliding through the crystal waters, the rhythmical beat of the oars not dying till the reflection of the Partry hills left the lake.

A lovely evening, said Ulick. The blackbird still sings from the end of the bough; his mate is in the bush hard by and the bird is satisfied; his note tells all that is in his heart. Since you know the birds so well, master, what bird is that little one? A robin? Tadhg, thou hast ears but no eyes. The bird has a red breast, but is a chaffinch; see how he flies, the glint of his wings very white in the dun evening. In another hour the stars will be out. Tadhg unslung his harp and played, and Ulick listened, and when Tadhg ceased playing there was silence on the island. Soon after the bees were asleep and the bats were out, zig-zagging round the shores in pursuit of their prey, and shortly the kestrels came and took birds out of the ivy-trees; disconsolate cries were heard; and through the hushed woods the two hermits found their way down the paved path that Marban had trodden long ago. In a very few minutes their lives passed into dreams, and on their awaking in the morning they found two harps hung upon the tree beside them. Brigit had no thought to awaken us, Ulick said. I wish that she had thought, Tadhg answered; it is like a woman to leave harps out all night in the dew-fall. Do you hear this? And he ran his fingers over the strings. A silence fell, and Tadhg felt himself divided from his master, farther from him than he had ever been in all his wanderings. Divided by a chance word, he said to himself, for he lives in the Princess Soracha, in memories of her words and ways; and every moment he expected a blow or to hear his master call to Brigit Lonn: There's a man here, Brigit, who would like to be taken over to the other side, and take him quickly, for I'd be rid of him. But the storm he had expected passed over, and he said: The harp is now in tune; I'll take the other one, master. And he bent over it in great ease of mind, for there was now no danger of the upspringing of a quarrel, of blows or hard words, and soon they would be sitting side by side in the sun, playing the harp just as in old times, as if not a day and no marvellous adventures had passed over them.

So it fell out; and repairing to the rocks where the sun was warm, Ulick sang songs that he had not sung for many years, leaving out the lines that referred too plainly to other women, and at every one of these omissions in the poems Tadhg said to himself: He would believe that he had loved none before Soracha, which after all is but the truth. And Tadhg's thought passing wordless into Ulick's mind, bade Ulick say: The many were but my daily bread, as easily forgotten; she was the bread of my salvation. His love of her is a great grief to him, said Tadhg to himself; yet he would not be without his grief for all the world. And he watched his master pass into the woods, remaining on the rocks till evening, afraid to leave them lest he should intrude upon his master, who was with Soracha, kneeling, no doubt, by the shrine, praying that he might meet her in heaven. He would meet her in hell rather than not at all; but that was long ago and the sins the priest has forgiven must never be thought of again. And to keep his mind unimpaired by theology he played and strummed and dreamed of Maria, and wept a little when he remembered his dear goose, and the fox that had bitten her long neck through; and remembering the Rhinns and the boat, he fell to wondering once again by the side of Lough Carra at the mystery of man's passage through life, his meditation differing very little from the meditation that Maria had inspired when a gander had lured her for a moment from him. Another day wanes, he said; once more the cormorant flies with rapid wing-beats down the crystal surface of the lake to some ruin, to Castle Island, maybe, or to the ruin opposite the Brownstone shore; and it was not until the evening darkened that he heard footsteps and saw Sir Ulick coming towards him; and once more they sat together and watched the lake, and once more the moon rose and they slept in the sheeling above Marban's cell.

The next day was Sunday, and the bells of the Abbey were wafted by pleasant breezes over the great marshes. So faintly were they heard that the sound was not much more than the murmur of bees in the ivy blooms and the bluebells and the wild anemones. Thou wouldst not let the Sunday pass without hearing mass, Tadhg? I would not, faith; but, master, you 'll be coming with me? No, Ulick answered; I will never hear mass again in that Abbey, not as long as Peter is in it. 'Tis not the priest but the mass that matters, master! Away with thee; I have no heart to argue thy points. Brigit will take thee across. Go to thy mass, Tadhg, and tell me on thy return if Brother Ambrose sleeps over his singing, and if Brother Michael is a quarter of a tone flat, as he is usually. And you, master? Do not think of me, Ulick answered. I am accustomed to the songs of the birds, to the flowers, and the murmuring of summer in the boughs, and when I am tired of these the lapping of lake water round the shores is enough; and I have my thoughts. Go. Tadhg lingered, loth to leave his master, but driven fiercely away he stepped into the boat. Brigit, too, disliked Brother Peter, and during the journey Tadhg questioned her as to her dislike of the peaky-nosed little prelate learned in theology. But she could not tell more than that she disliked him. I wouldn't confess to him, she said, not for all the money that he 'll ever earn for the saying of masses and the like. And Brigit's dislike for Brother Peter awakened a liking for her in Tadhg. She was no longer as uncomely in his sight as she had been the day before, and there was much good sense in her, he thought. And after landing, whilst walking towards the Abbey, they talked of the master on the island who had given so much treasure in masses and was not getting his money's worth, attributing the sleepy singing and the flat singing to Brother Peter. And they returned together to the island with the news that Brother Ambrose had kept awake in his stall and that Brother Michael had either not sung at all or had sung in tune. Sir Ulick did not answer, but a sad smile gathered on his lips and he bade Brigit prepare the food they were to eat that day. The third day thou hast been on the island this is, Tadhg, and henceforth every day will be like these days. We shall pray and play our harps together, and as the sun goes westward the shadows will fall from the Partry hills into the lake. Winds will sweep across the lake, said Tadhg, raising waves out of the depths, and there will be foam along the shore and dead reeds will come drifting in. Yes, all that will happen, Tadhg, yet it will always be the same day on the island, happy or tedious as we like to think it; but I am glad thou hast come. Then indeed the island will be a happy home for me, Tadhg answered. And they played together that Sunday afternoon and all the next week, and for many weeks day passed over day without bringing any change, each day more melodious than the last. We cannot play the same tunes always, said Ulick; we must compose some more songs. How is that to be? asked Tadhg, for I am like a dry well; and I'm thinking that it isn't new songs that we need but a wider hearing for our harp-playing. Amn't I enough for you? said Brigit, and they laughed and walked together up the island strand.

Of what plan art thou thinking, Tadhg? I can read a story in thy face. There is one in my mind, surely, and it is this: that we might leave the island and travel the country playing our harps. As we did in Normandy?

Ulick interjected. Why not in Ireland as in Normandy, your honour? The summertime is all over the country, and will be, with the help of God, till the last sheaf of corn is gathered in, and when the ache for travel is in the feet it 's time to tighten the shoe-strings. So thou wouldst away, Tadhg? But I may not leave the island. We will always come back to the island, Tadhg answered, and they sat together on the warm rocks over against Castle Carra so that they might think the better. No, said Ulick, I cannot go. Is it the priests up at the monastery that would be stopping you? asked Tadhg. Not they; and a look of cunning came into Ulick's face that Tadhg had never seen in it before and which he did not like. But to ask a question would be to check the answer. Better to put my trust in silence, Tadhg said to himself, and he sent stones skimming into the lake as if the number of jumps they made was all that interested him. The fellows up at the Abbey think that they are keeping me from my Princess, but I am getting my own way in spite of them. Now, how could that be? said Tadhg, for I thought she was dead. Have I not told thee, Tadhg, that the dead are not always dead; they change their forms and return to us? So I have heard, Tadhg answered, and he sent some more stones into the water. Leave off throwing stones, Tadhg. I said that I 'd get my own way in spite of the Abbey and I have. Soracha comes to see me every night. Does she now, in faith? Nor is it surprising, for when two have loved as ye have loved—— Tadhg, thou art beginning to understand. When two have loved as we two they cannot be separated, and it won't be long now. . . . It is always between the day and the night that she comes, and in an hour's time she will be there, floating between the trees. Meanwhile, we 'd do well to go to Marban's tomb and say a prayer together. And the prayer finished, they watched. But Soracha did not come; and so many nights passed without them seeing her that Tadhg gave up hope.

Now, Tadhg, Ulick said one night, we may be missing her, and they walked through the woods again, their eyes on the opening in the trees; and it was not long before a whiteness floated by, and Ulick said: Thou art seeing Soracha; she will come again this way. A strange flying whiteness it is! said Tadhg, not daring to speak his mind, that mayhap the whiteness was no more than a snowy owl come to roost in Marban's oratory. An owl or the ghost of a goose, he said to himself, for if a bird can have a ghost surely Maria would find me out. She would be happy on this island, walking after me, eating the rich grass and swimming along the shores, keeping an eye upon me. Of what art thou thinking? Ulick asked. Of the Princess coming to your honour in the shape of a bird. No bird, but a Princess, Tadhg; and they walked through the evening woods, Sir Ulick on the watch for Soracha to show herself again to him, Tadhg with the thought of Maria in his mind, and they had not walked the length and breadth of the island before a white form came through the trees making for the lake so it seemed, but they were not sure. We will see her to-morrow night, Ulick said, and they lay down. A night will come when she will speak to me, Tadhg. . . . How long he had slept Tadhg could not tell, but he was roused suddenly, he knew not by what, and sat up searching his memory. He stretched out his hand but nobody was beside him, and with thoughts curdling and terror shaping in his mind he ran through the woods, reaching the rocks over against Castle Carra in time to see a whiteness passing down the lake. Master! he cried, but the swimmer did not or would not hear. Tadhg cried to him again, but the swimmer swam on through the grey moonlight. Gone out of my sight, gone to Soracha! And Tadhg remained on the rock till the night waned and the dawn began.

Now, is that how the story finishes? said Alec. There is a little more, I answered. That misfortunate Tadhg doesn't stretch out on the rocks and die of grief? I hadn't thought of Tadhg's end, Alec. But you've been telling Tadhg's story and not Sir Ulick's. Maybe you're right, said I. And how do you think Tadhg should end? Married on the island, Alec replied without a moment's hesitation. But how we are to get him married I don't know. You've set me a hard nut to crack. Your honour has cracked so many nuts that you'll crack this last one. I'm not sure. I shall be back in Westport next year, and the end of Tadhg will not be my story but yours, Alec. Alec replied: I'll do my endeavours, and if I pick up a notion I'll keep it in stock for you.

CHAP. LVI.

ON MY return to London letters began to come from America asking for the new books that I had spoken of writing to replace certain old books which I could not honestly include in the canon. The suppression of the volume entitled *Celibates* necessitated a new set of stories about bachelors and spinsters; *Conversations in Ebury Street* seemed to me a suitable title for a volume to fill the niche left vacant by the withdrawal of *Impressions and Opinions*. But no sooner were these books finished than a letter came demanding revised texts and the translation of *Daphnis and Chloe*, a Greek story, and a perfect pleasure my translation would have been to me had I been able to put out of my mind Alec Trusselby and his desire to see Tadhg O'Dorachy married, and of all, his desire to see Tadhg die. But an old man of eighty dying under the trees or on the strand of a desert island is no wise dramatic or pathetic; an eagle cannot carry him off; a pike cannot drag him down.

losing the longed for anecdote could not persuade me. Now, put that idea out of your head, said he. Believe you me, this pot was never put under a bed. It was broken in the shop while the children were chasing a cat, and I happened to step in, just to see what the row was about, and the mother gave it to me. But I understand you well enough; the thought of the way pots like that are used morning and evening would put any one off his tea and off his feed. If you hadn't seen me bringing the water up from the brook in it there'd be something to say for you—— I wouldn't say you've guessed wrong, Alec. The imagination makes great cowards of us all. That 's a great saying, it is sure, and one out of your own writings, I 'll be bound. As I was about to reward Alec's acumen by an acknowledgment of the plagiarism, he said: A fine, warm wind from the south-west is coming through the trees; my shirt ought to be as dry as a bone by now. He picked it from the branch, and I could not but think of the picture in the National Gallery when he pulled it over his head. Whilst he stood in front of me buttoning it down the front he put an almost dreaded question: Has your honour made up a good story about Tadhg's marriage? No, Alec, I can think of nothing, and have come all the way to Westport to ask you if you have been able to arrange the marriage for me. I won't say that the story I 've made is up to what your honour could do—— But you have got a story, Alec? Good story or bad story, you have got something? Well, I have got something, he answered, but it may not be pleasing to you. Let me hear it, let me hear it! As soon as we get to our old seat under the trees yonder, he said, I 'll begin it. . . . Begin, Alec, begin!

Out of sight, out of mind, he said, and Soracha is now forgotten. But she was a great saint while her memory lasted, and not all that the clergy said could stop the processions and the pilgrimages to Castle Carra to do her honour; the people guided the blind and toted the lame to her grave for a curing. But Brother Peter (you remember him!) didn't believe in miracles, and he kept harping away at it that the one who takes her own life can't get to heaven, and he went so far as to say that if miracles were done at Soracha's grave it was the Devil's self did them. This last bit of Peter's talk put the monks of Ballintober into the wrong box; for to tell the people that a woman who had killed herself to save Ireland was stewing in hell one minute, and trotting from hell to Connaught the next minute, to work miracles by the aid of the Devil, got their backs up, so that there was a hump in the county of Mayo as big as a camel's, and if it hadn't been for the Abbot the people might have risen up against Ballintober and shoved the monks into the lake. But the same Abbot was a cleverer lad than Brother Peter, and he decided that it would be the best of the Church's play to take over the grave and the miracles, and to shut up about the suicide and the broken vows, and about Sir Ulick de Burgo hopping and trotting a nun out of a nunnery. A bad crime, God bless us! and one that the least said about it the better! Sir Ulick hadn't had the chance to do much for Ireland, having been thwarted at the last moment when he wanted to join Bermingham's army. All the same, it is hard to get two lovers out of people's heads, for love has that firm a root in the heart that people honour it, and nowhere more than in Ireland; so Sir Ulick came in for his share of the glory that was going round. That peaky little man Peter was half out of his wits, and there was a deal of ill feeling between himself and his brother, who, it was said, had offered him a hermitage on the island. But Peter wasn't the man to go live on an island; 'twould be too lonely like, for he always had to be scratching and nagging at somebody, and never did he want to scratch and to tear more than he did now; small blame to him, and the way it was! for nobody likes to find himself bested. He tried to work up a party against the Abbot, but that failed on him, too, and at last he had to take the hint from his brother not to say another word about Soracha and the breaking of her vows, nor to put in his spade against the miracles that were performed at her grave, for the pilgrimages and the miracles were bringing cash into the Abbey, a thing that annoyed Peter more perhaps than anything else, for no man can turn his face against money; and so Peter was fairly bet for a while anyway. But he was thinking hard and tight, scratching his head, thinking always, and peeping round every corner of his skull to find a way out of the corner he was in. At last a sight of Biddy Lonn put a thought into his head. That will bring the whole country over to my side, said he. Now, said he in his sermon, and he giving it all out from the altar—now, said he, an unmarried couple living alone on an island is a disgrace and a scandal, and if we let it go on the parish of Ballintober will be a disgrace and a scandal in Ireland. The likes of it has never been known in holy Ireland before, and it has got to stop, if I have to walk to Rome on my two feet and tell the whole story to the Pope himself. And that I'll do, he said; even if my brother Tom were to hold me by my habit, I'd leave it in his hand and be off with me to Rome.

Now, Peter, said Tom, you'll soon be seeing the mischief you've been at, for Tadhg, whom I know well, will never marry Biddy Lonn, nor any other Biddy; and if you get him out of the island, even if the Pope himself is on your side, there'll be a great falling off in the pilgrims, and the funds aren't too healthy at the present time, that I can tell you. At this the giggling faces of the monks became sad as men's faces do when they find they haven't got the money they expected in their pockets. But Peter had his answer. Tom, said he, you've heard tell of the faithfulness of a dog, haven't you? Yes, Peter,

I have. And every brother of the brothers here knows that a dog is true to the death? There 's no going against it, said the monks, and they began to tell stories about faithful dogs, and there isn't a thing will put a man into a good humour as quickly as the telling of a story. Well, now—— When the last story was told Peter ups again and says: What is O'Dorachy after all but a dog? He has the dog's nature; and the nature of a dog, which I see you all understand, is not to leave his master's grave, and I am only telling the truth when I tell you that he 'd marry the Devil's dam rather than leave the island. We have Tadhg properly chained up, and after a talk with me he 'll marry Biddy Lonn, or I 'll know why. Now, have I got my lord Abbot's leave to get O'Dorachy's consent to the marriage? The Abbot kept a stiff face on him, and then Peter turned to the monks and he said: You know that a stop must be put to these pilgrimages, for the pilgrims will spread the story of Tadhg O'Dorachy and Biddy Lonn living in sin and we not lifting a hand to stop it, winking at it, indeed. And seeing that Peter had the crowd with him, the Abbot said: Go to the island, Peter, and do what you can. There 's no time like the present, as the clock said when it was going to strike. Off on the minute went my bold Peter to the shore, and he hadn't whistled three whistles out of him when the bow of Biddy Lonn's boat shot out of the cove. A fine, strong girl she is too, he said to himself. She 'll make a strapping wife for O'Dorachy, and look after his sick bed better than any other she in Ireland. When the boat ran up on the gravel he put out his hand to Biddy and said: Now, the stern of the boat is the place for a lady. I will row you over to the island myself; which he did. And when the boat reached the island, out of it he hopped and offered his hand to Biddy as if she needed his help, for he knew it would cock her up to be handed out of the boat by a priest.

Now, where is himself? On the other side of the island chopping sticks, she answered. So much the better, said Peter. This is a fine strand for a little talk, and we'll walk up and down together. And to make a long story short, I have come to tell you that I am for putting an end to the stories that are going around about you and Tadhg O'Dorachy. Sure your reverence can do that same without turning me out on the lake side without a man to be with me spearing eels, or cutting me a raft of sticks in the wood. We have found a way to put an end to the scandal, myself and my brother, but the greater part is owing to myself. And listen to me: all we ask is that the talk shall stop, and to do that is easy. As his wife—— What is it you are saying, Brother Peter? Me to be married to Tadhg, and he as little a marrying man as yourself! Sure he wouldn't know me for a woman at all unless somebody told him, not even if he met me without my petticoat on, which God forbid! The young marry because they are hot, and the old marry to get hot, said Peter. But what I say is, that no better reason for this marriage could be found than to stop bad talk. Bad talk about me and Tadhg is it? If it wasn't yourself that said it I'd say . . . What would you say, Biddy Lonn? I don't think I'd be saying much; I'd spit in somebody's face. But it being myself that is talking—— I'll say nothing and I'll save my spits. But you'll remember, Biddy, that as soon as we make one flesh of you both the talkers will stop as if a pitch plaster was clapped over their mouths. The Devil is always roaming, Biddy, and as nobody can tell when she will meet him we should always be prepared, and I hope to put the ring on your finger this day week. This day week! Is it my ears that I'm listening with? or what is it? This day week I'm to be the wife of that old ancient, and he nearer to eighty than he is to seventy. What sort of good would marriage be to me or to him? Now listen to me, father!

Sure, the turf will be green over him in another few years. None of us can foresee the day of our death, and the younger may go before the elder. If you think that I 'll peg out before Tadhg, father—— I would not say who may go first. We may all be dead before the sun dips yonder behind the Partry hills, and if Tadhg should die before you, Biddy, you 'll be free to take a younger man. . . . But here comes your future husband, and I 'll ask you to leave us, for I 'm going to talk with him about your marriage. I do believe that he 's in earnest after all, Biddy muttered as she looked back.

O'Dorachy, said Peter, I 've been talking to Biddy about her marriage. Biddy's marriage! And who is she marrying? And what in this and that does Biddy Lonn want to get married for? I see you 'd be sorry to lose her, Tadhg. Faith and troth, I would! A firmer hand never pulled an oar or got the thread of milk out of a goat's tit easier than she. By my word, I won't know how to manage without her, and I more than ever at the beck and call of the new lots of pilgrims, and every lot more wishful than the last for stories of the days in Normandy when we went walking the world with our harps on our backs, singing, from castle to castle, songs that were the cause of many a woman making a fool of her husband. But the sins of those days, I 'm thinking, have been forgiven. I beg you to believe, Brother Peter, that if I sinned it was by following his voice on my harp. There was the rape of Soracha—— Rape, indeed! Sorra a rape was in it! Didn't it all come from her? Didn't she send her picture to him and he in France out of harm's way? Out of harm's way—in France! He was out of her way anyhow! But the carrying a nun out of her convent—— Speak no more of it, for the night we went to that convent is eating the heart out of me, preying upon it, waking me out of my sleep, and springing upon me like a weasel on a rabbit as I go about my work among the trees yonder.

But you have been to confession, Tadhg. Aye, faith, and many times. But it is still on my conscience and will be for ever more till I go before my God and himself releases me from memory of sin and death and the world. You have forgotten, Tadhg, that the words of our Sovereign Lord and Master are: Whose sins ye shall remit shall be remitted. True for your reverence! The whole of the Scripture isn't in the mind of the laity, but the clergy is like a keg with the spigot driven in, always on tap. Sure 'tis they can give you a text with the froth on it. . . . I 've come to talk to you about your marriage. Biddy's marriage you said a minute ago, Tadhg interjected. Of your marriage and hers. Am I listening to you, father, or am I dreaming? Or are you making fun of me? No fun at all, Tadhg. But, Brother Peter, what would I be doing with a wench and I eighty years of age? You mayn't know it, but in the days gone by Father Carabine was my confessor, and I told him that having heard much of the trussing of women I thought I 'd have a try at it myself, but I made a bad hand of it, I can tell you. 'Tis no lie I 'm telling; let you ask Father Carabine, for he knows my story, and you wouldn't go thinking that after coming off the ship I 'd make a bad confession to the priest? I know that what is said in confession is sacred trust, but I 'll give you a brief that will open Father Carabine's lips. Tadhg, you are talking rubbish. Much scandal has been caused by you two living alone upon the island. The angels in heaven are not purer than we! cried Tadhg, in deed and in thought, too. I doubt it not, said the priest, but the scandal must be ended. If it weren't that my master's tomb is on the island I 'd start to-morrow for Jerusalem and die fighting the Saracen. But your master's tomb is on the island, and now I want you and Biddy to talk this matter over together. Does she know about it, father? I was talking of the marriage when you came out of the trees, Tadhg.

And I 'll bet she was as flabbergasted as I was! She was. Next week—— Your reverence doesn't mean that we are to be man and wife in a week? I mean just that, Tadhg. But your reverence has left this out—that a man of eighty is like an old goat; he can't jump, and he won't jump! Isn 't it Scripture that if the man can't go in to the woman there is no marriage in the sight of God? Then the woman can appeal to Rome to have her marriage broken? But Biddy won't do that; do you and Biddy talk it over together. And fetch her from the goats, for I must be returning to the Abbey. She 'll row you over in a few minutes, your reverence. . . . And sitting on a rock Tadhg watched the boat dwindle to a black spot in the distance, and when the priest stepped ashore, he said: Every minute of our lives God's greatness is being shown to us and we understand it a bit better. No two lives are the same. Many 's the time I 've wondered what my end would be, and faith, it took the Church herself to root up a married man in me. A queer sort of a married man I 'll be, but I 'll be a married man all the same. . . . Making a fine show she is, said Tadhg while watching the boat returning to the island. A fine back she has; fine arms she has, and no mistake. A decent upstanding woman it is that God is marrying me to, and I have no fault to find with anything except myself, that wasn't up to a wife when I was young, and amn't up to one now for certain.

Well, Biddy, said he, so it would seem that we are to be man and wife in a week, if you 'll do the priest's bidding and if you won't be expecting too much. I won't expect a thing at all, for at your age, and twenty years before your age, a man has more thoughts for a dinner than for a wife. And how do you know that, Biddy? How do I know that! How do I know anything? Amn't I following a herd of goats since I was a slip of a girl? We 're Christians, Biddy; we 're not goats. And clasping her hips Biddy stood looking at him, putting the fear of

God into old Tadhg, so brazen like was she. I 'm not to expect too much, you said! I 'll sleep in the draughty hen-house no more, my good man, picking the filth from the pullets out of my eyes; so between this and our marriage let you be nailing up the boards lying about so that we may take our clothes off and pull our clothes on in decency. Now I 'll go to draw the milk for our porridge. Yes, and indeed! she cried back, bending over the goats, I 've slept long enough and too long in the filth in the wet of the hen-house. I 'll sleep snug from this day out! And he thinking of decency before all else, began to wonder which of the two beds he 'd plant her into. I 'll sleep in Sir Ulick's bed, he said to himself, and then a change of mind coming upon him without his knowing the meaning of it, if it had a meaning, he said: No, I 'll stick to my own bed, and she can have Sir Ulick's. And he set to building a screen out of loose planks, working so hard that the house was divided in halves when Biddy came back with two noggins of milk in her hands. You 're the kind man surely! she said. Well, isn't a bed to yourself the least I could do for you? The least, surely, she answered, and he watched her stirring the porridge, till her voice bidding him good-night startled him. And soon after, hearing her kicking off her clogs, he said: 'Tis I should be stretching back on the bed, for the chopping of them sticks has tired me out. Time was when I 'd chop twice over what I did to-day without feeling it, but I am an old man now and there 's no denying it. There was silence in the hut, and after listening to the silence for a while he began to listen to the other side of the planks he had raised up between himself and herself. Is she asleep or awake? And what would she be at now? And thinking he 'd like a peep at her in her bed, he rose up, and putting his eye to a chink in the boards he took a peep, and she sitting on the bed combing her hair, like a woman in a story-book.

CHAP. LVII.

ALEC, I like your story very much so far as it's gone, and my hope is that the end will not fall short of the beginning. I'm only at the beginning, and it will give me great heart when I hear that your honour begins to think I am making a neat job of it. Old men, I answered, are often more indecent than young, and old men that have resisted temptation for a long time are apt to fall into the very sin they have successfully resisted all their lives; for we never get away from nature, not altogether. And I can imagine Tadhg dreaming over the smoothness and the whiteness of the shoulder he had seen, his enjoyment not lasting very long, for on turning over I'm sure he'd start up a little scared, remembering that Biddy wasn't his wife yet and that he had been guilty of a sin in watching her. Not a mortal sin, but some venial sins are very near to mortal sins, no doubt, and need long years of purification in purgatory before the sinner can be admitted into heaven. You seem to know him, Alec, as intimately as I do myself, and if I know Tadhg at all, it is not the sin he had committed that would frighten him most, but the conviction deep in himself that he would certainly yield to the temptation to look through the chink again. For it is not the sin committed, Alec, that alarms the sinner, but the knowledge that he will not be able to withstand the Devil when he is by again, and of all, that he cannot pray for grace to resist sin, so ardently does he desire it. I can see my Tadhg—forgive me, Alec, I should have said our Tadhg—gloomy and distressed all the next day, in the midst of a trouble so great that he could not do else but refuse Biddy's offer to row him over to the monastery when he began to speak to her about the confession that a man was expected to make before his marriage. I am sure he would suspect

Biddy of having caught sight of his eye at the chink, and would answer her: No, Biddy, I'll keep my confession till the day before the wedding. And when Biddy returned from Ballinrobe with a new petticoat and a shawl, the old curiosity would awaken in him again, and he'd hear a voice within him which he couldn't shut down, saying: I'd like to see that fine smock dropping from her shoulders. He would dread and desire the night, and drop back on his pillow racked with disappointment, there being no stime of light for him to see the dropping of the smock. And next day his conscience would worry him so that he would begin to lose his health and to think that he might die before he was married to Biddy. But I am saying too much, Alec; it may be that you are taking quite a different line. Not a bit different at all, said Alec heartily; my Tadhg and your Tadhg is the selfsame lad, whichever of us is telling about him. Then away with you, Alec, and let me hear the end, for I suppose he sees the lank woman sooner or later? Bide a bit, your honour, and let me get the story out in my own way.

Tadhg was feeling weak, and out of sorts, and out of humour, and when Biddy spoke of rowing over to the Abbey for a priest, he said that he wouldn't confess to anybody else but the Abbot. Very well then, I'll fetch you the Abbot. He'll come to confess me if there's a breath in him, or a kick in him, said Tadhg; and these words seeming good to Biddy, she repeated them as she had heard them, raising a smile of satisfaction into the Abbot's face. Off then with the two of them for the island, and when they got within twenty perches of the beach Tadhg rose from behind a rock to greet them. You said that you wouldn't leave the bed, said Biddy. Never mind the bed, Tadhg answered. Be off with you, for my business this day is with his lordship. Are you taking me for a listener! said Biddy. What do I care about your confession? Full sure I am, all the same, that the stories you've got to tell are enough to make a goat blush, let alone a priest. Do you hear that, O'Dorachy? said the Abbot. I do, faith! She's giving it to me as if I was her husband already. The Abbot and Tadhg walked up the path till they came to a pleasant seat under some tall trees, with a fine piece of meadow land spreading in front of them. Now, said the Abbot, I was sorry to hear that you weren't well; but you're looking better than I expected. 'Tis the old mind is sick and sad, my lord. An uneasy conscience? said the Abbot; well, we all of us suffer from that at times, saints as well as sinners. Do they now? said Tadhg. And I wouldn't say but that the angels get a twinge or two when the anniversary of the great revolt comes round, the ones that sat on the fence, that weren't for God and weren't against him either. A man with a sick conscience sees sin in everything, till at last there isn't a thing but sin in the world, and hell at the heel of the hunt. But you, O'Dorachy, shouldn't be suffering from conscience on this healthy island, where there isn't a chance for any sin of them all to get going. Ah, sin is everywhere, my lord, and last night itself I was a sinner! Now, tell me how you were a sinner; and the Abbot pulled his stole out of his pocket. Well, my lord Abbot, all of yesterday I was building a screen so that Biddy and I should have a room to ourselves and a bed to ourselves; and we both lay down in our beds, she on that side of the screen and me on this one. When I heard her kicking off her clogs I said to myself: 'Tis a fine upstanding woman I'm going to be married to, it is indeed. And I'd like well to have a peep at her, I said to myself. Up I sat in the bed and put my eye to the chink, and I saw her combing her hair. There's no great harm in that, Tadhg. But, you see, my lord Abbot, I was thinking, if I wasn't hoping, that I might see more of her than one arm and the tip of her shoulder. Well, it was but a venial sin at the worst, and I don't think God will treat you badly for it; and you'll get such a shriving from me that the peep you had at Biddy combing her hair won't cost you ten minutes in purgatory. All the same. . . .! What is it, my lord Abbot? What you tell surprises me, O'Dorachy, for 'tis late starting you are, at eighty years of age! You said once, my lord Abbot, that a sick conscience was a conscience with the Devil inside of it, and in a sinner's old age the Devil bests the guardian angel easily. But what was it set you peeping through a hole to see what Biddy was like? Well, I've been thinking of that, my lord Abbot, and I hope to tell you the truth. You know, ever since the pilgrims got their way with Brother Peter, and got their rights to bring the sick and the halt and the blind to Soracha's grave to be cured, some of them row over to the island to visit Marban's tomb, and some come over to see myself, and to hear about Sir Ulick de Burgo, who loved the Princess and was loved by French women. Now, I have never told this to a soul before, but a lot of them come . . . To hear you play the harp, Tadhg? Why shouldn't they come to hear the greatest harper in Ireland, Finn Lorcan's best scholar! I am all that, said Tadhg, and they like well to hear me on the harp; but what they like better is the stories I tell of the women that used to trip down the castle stairs to sit with Sir Ulick, kissing him and being kissed by him, by the marble-rimmed fountains in their gardens. That's what they like! And if I can throw in a bit of sinfulness they like it twice as well, and tell their friends that I am a better story-teller than I am a harper. Nothing loosens the purse strings like a good story. You never knew it before but let you know it now, that a deal, and a good deal, of the money that comes to Ballintober comes out of the stories I tell the pilgrims. But I'm getting to be an old man now—indeed, I am an old man all out, and I can't put stories together the way I used to. Sure, the more I tell of the bits of sinfulness the greedier they are for them; and now there isn't a bit of sinfulness I can make up and they are complaining. You can't get out of the head what never was in it, and as I 've never seen a naked woman in my life I thought it would be a chance now to see one. The anniversary of Princess Soracha's death is coming round, and they 'll all be here in a month's time looking for stories. But all you saw through the chink was Biddy combing her hair, said the Abbot, a bit of shoulder, a bit of a lifted arm; and you could see nearly as much when she is rowing you in a boat. But her arms and she rowing the boat, aren't the same thing as her arms and she getting into bed, my lord Abbot. I 'm telling you, too, that it would have pleased me greatly to see the smock drop off her shoulders, and I have been waiting to see that same all the week. Well, she 's going to be your wife soon. I 'm afraid you are too easy on me, my lord Abbot; not that I 'm instructing you. In telling me your sins you 're not instructing me. It 's hard to reveal it all to a priest, who knows no more than a babe about the wickedness of those that haven't got the sacraments, or only one in a blue moon. It 's a wicked thing to look at a woman the way I looked at Biddy, for mind you, she 's not my wife yet. She will be to-morrow, said the Abbot; and I 'll give in to you this much, that you might have waited a week or two. It would have done no harm; it would perhaps have been better. Now, when I am married to her, will it be a sin for me to ask her to drop her smock before me? That 's what I want to know, for if I got one eyeful of her, and she naked, I think it would be a real help to the stories I do be telling the pilgrims. My brother Peter is more learned in theology than I am, said the Abbot, and I think that this is what he would say. He would say: A man may kiss his wife whenever he likes, and he may clasp her if he is minded to put her in child. But if he doesn't want to put her in child, or if he couldn't put her in child if he tried? said Tadhg. I 'll look the case up when I go back, but you may take it from me before I get down the tome which all the theology is in, that for a man to take pleasure in his wife's nakedness when he has no thought of begetting a child is a venial sin at the most. That 's what I 've been anxious about, my lord Abbot. But you couldn't give me a hint about what stretch of purgatory a venial sin will land me in for? Not long at all, Tadhg; not a year itself. And Biddy won't refuse to drop her smock if you tell her that a sight of her figure will help you to tell a great story to the pilgrims. So far I think I can answer for her and for yourself. Now you 're not to say a word of this to her till you are married, and married more than a day! At the end of the month will be time enough. And here comes Biddy, who will take me back to Ballintober. Biddy, said Tadhg, you will take my lord Abbot back. And right glad I am to be able to do so! she answered. And once more Tadhg watched the boat pulling through the still lake till it reached the opposite shore. Biddy was first out of it, and she gave her hand to the Abbot to save him from the shock of too big a jump, and they stood talking together in view of Tadhg, who wondered what they might be saying.

A great good thing it is to have the clergy, for life isn't all eating and drinking, and lifting the neighbour's cattle, and digging a spear into the neighbour's ribs if he started to defend his wife against a spoiler. Without the clergy we wouldn't be more than the brutes of the field. I suppose the Abbot over yonder is instructing Biddy what our lives are to be when we are married, and sure it was a good, clean thought he had telling me not to ask her to get into her pelt before me the very night of our marriage, nor for a while after. But to prepare her for it I 'd better let her know that I am in trouble about the story to be told when the pilgrims come over in the big boat to do honour to Marban's tomb, the tomb of a poet, a hermit and a holy man, for he was all three, and brother to a king as well—and to hear my stories about Sir Ulick and the French women. I 'm thinking he was sweetest on the Comtesse d'Artois, saying always that she was shaped in the mould of old Greece. But what do I know of the mould of old Greece, or old anywhere? and Biddy not a bit wiser than I am, less indeed; for the Abbot himself could not make her understand that a man has to see the story if he 's to be telling it. When it comes to the night that the Comtesse goes down to the fountain to bathe herself, I am no better than a blind man trying to tell how the sun lights up the crests of the hills. There she was in her pelt, I 'd say, and there I 'd stick, like an eel in the mud. A poet must see, as well as the painter and the sculptor, and I thank my stars that I 'm going to see one whole woman the way God made her before I leave this earth. What man is there, barring the clergy themselves, that wouldn't want to? And there are no clothes in heaven; the saints and the angels, every saint and every angel of them, are mother-naked so far as we know, and to see Biddy stripped will be just the same as the peep you might have of the world to come and you in a dream. But I 'll have to make a great bother about this story. And he fell to cudgelling his brains as to how he might fool Biddy about the troubles he was in with the story, asking her questions about the look of her body, whether she was like this or that or the other; and when she told him that her skin and her bones were very like his own except for certain parts, he would have to put on a booby face and say that it was a great misfortune to a story-teller never to have seen the same parts. So day after day he made up talks that he meant to have with her, and after about three weeks of that he was fairly worn out.

Biddy darling, said he, there's no getting on with this story at all. What's wrong with it, honey? she asked. Sure, 'tis all about a naked woman, and I never saw one, said he. What is to be done at all, at all? And they looked at each other inquiringly. Would it be asking too much of you, now that we're properly married—— Now that we're properly married you'd be asking me to strip myself so that you may be telling what a woman is like to the pilgrims who come here? Well, if you like to spoil the story, Biddy—— What have your stories about rampy women got to do with me? she said, and on that she turned into the house, leaving Tadhg a bit scared, saying to himself: I ought to have told her what my lord Abbot said, that every husband had a right to look on his wife any way he likes; she'd hardly put herself above the lord Abbot. Peter himself even—but nobody knows what that bitter little priesteen would say. While he was thinking about Peter he heard a step and his face flushed, for a thought goes as quick as lightning, and the thought that came to him was that maybe Biddy had gone into the house to strip. But her clothes were all on her, and she had only come back, as he soon learnt, for the sake of the argument, saying: Is it you, learned and all in the history of the heroes and the Gods and Goddesses of Ireland (and let me tell you that not an Irish God, let alone a Goddess, was ever seen out of their clothes), is it you that is asking me—— If what you are telling me is true, Biddy, the Abbot of Ballintober doesn't know what he is talking about. He is a good priest, said she, and it is his business to know the story of Fial, daughter of Mil, who, when she saw Lugaid looking down at her from the top of a high rock, got a cramp and sank to the bottom of the lake; and though he dived in after her and brought her up, she struggled away from him, saying: Let me die! Let me die! for I'm not the one to live after seeing a naked man. That's one story, but one story isn't enough, and I can match every story you tell with another. And I'd hear the story you'd match against Lugaid and Fial, she said. I'm thinking of Adam and Eve in the garden, said Tadhg. And weren't they driven from the garden by an angel? But not for being naked, Biddy; nakedness is not sin, and now I'd be listening to another story from you. Gilĕ wouldn't marry Omra because he said to her he'd never know a minute's happiness till he saw her naked, and for these words she turned on him. You are no better than a Pagan, she said, for none but the Pagans see each other naked. And Omra went away hungry, chewing his desire, like Connla eating into his apple, it never growing less. You know that story? Yes, I know the story, Biddy; get you on with the one you're telling me. Gilĕ lived in a great fear of Omra, but great as her fear of him was she had to strip when she wanted a bath. Now there was a well near by that she thought nobody knew about, and nobody did know about this well except Omra himself. He followed her to the well, and when she looked up and saw Omra looking at her, she found her death in the well. But that's no new story, Biddy, but the story you told me before. Fial drowned herself in a lake and Gilĕ in a well, and I bar this last one, so will you be trying again. Everything in Ireland goes by threes, but you'll be hard put to it to find three stories of women that died rather than be seen naked by their husbands. You'll hardly let on to me that you never heard of Sabia, the daughter of Ailill Find? One day she was washing herself in the spray by the clear sand-strewn spring, and she saw out beyond her on the plain tall Cahir coming towards her, and he hasty and rude as an oak. He is coming to enjoy the sight of me in my skin, she cried, but he'll never see me naked and alive! the last words that came out of her mouth, for she held her head under the water till she had no strength to lift it up. You've heard enough now about the modesty of the women of Ireland and about the courage of the women of Ireland not to ask your own wife to strip herself before you, for you to concoct her into a story for the long ears, and they dirty, of the pilgrims. What is a pilgrim after all, Tadhg honey, more than anyone else that you'd show them your wife? Forget about the story, said Tadhg, and remember an old, old man that has never seen a woman naked in his life; and if his own wife don't give him as much as a look, or the half of a look itself, he'll find himself in heaven one day, where the angels and archangels and the seraphs and the cherubs are as naked as the sole of your foot, and that poor old man will be the same silly innocent in heaven that he was on earth. What in the world do you expect to see? said Biddy. Do you think that my legs, or my anything else, will be different from any other woman's? There's none that would look so near to Mother Eve as yourself. I can see you in my thoughts, Biddy, long and lank—— Long I am, and lank too, said Biddy. Let you do now what I am asking you to do, Biddy honey, for when I'm gone from you you'll be sorry that you refused me. It is better to please your husband than to be telling him old stories that have not as much sense in them as a whistle of wind. Well, then, said Biddy, I wouldn't be refusing my husband anything lest I might be regretting it afterwards. Is there a finer place for a woman to walk about in naked than this island, nobody looking on except the birds, and every one of them thinking that Paradise is back again, blackbirds and thrushes, willow wrens and warblers of all kinds, just as it was in the days when Marban spoke of the birds as the little musicians of the world to his brother, King Guare, who came to see him. Well now, if you won't be looking at me stripping, I'll give you a sight of me. And when she comes out of the thicket she's gone behind, he said, it will be like one of the days in Paradise long ago!

And troth and faith, Tadhg wasn't far wrong, for when she appeared the words that slipped from him were: Biddy, you 're just Mother Eve herself, come out of the word of God. Now, if you start talking of the Bible I 'll run away and put on my clothes. You won't mind me saying, Biddy, that you 're round as a gossoon, with sloping shoulders and great big breasts. You don't think them too large? No, he said; I like the breasts because the hips are thin. I wouldn't have any part of you changed, and none of the sculptors of old Greece could have mended you. My master Sir Ulick would have bowed his knee to you, for before a naked woman such as you are, Biddy, her loveliness wouldn't leave a bit of pride in him. Well, it 's good to think I am pleasing somebody! Pleasing me! said Tadhg. I shall leave this world happy now, for though I have never sinned with a woman I have seen God's creation. And is it my back or my front that you like the best? I wouldn't separate the back from the front, but perhaps you are more willowy down the spine. And now you have seen your fill of me, and I can put my things on. Another minute, Biddy, just a minute more. And Tadhg stared his eyes out at her. If you look at me any longer you 'll be sick of seeing me! and she took herself back into the thicket. When she came out again in her smock, Tadhg said: You are the finest woman in the county of Mayo, and there isn't a man wouldn't say the same as I do if he saw you without the smock. I like this smock, she said; I paid a good penny for it in Ballinrobe before our marriage. I don't know what you 've got against it, or against the petticoat either, and it embroidered. I never heard of a man that hated clothes as much as you do, Tadhg honey. And now that 's nonsense enough for one day, and the supper to be got. She threw some sticks on the fire, but the sticks were small and couldn't bring the pot to the boil, and while she was getting bigger ones she found Tadhg sitting where she had left him, with his head on his chest and his eyes turned in, and he all down and out. You 'll be better lying a bit, honey. And taking hold of him she pulled him to his feet and kept him on them till they reached the hut, where she stretched him back with a pillow under his head. The pot 's boiling, said she, and she got to thinking about her man, and that he wasn't well at all, at all.

The poor old man, said she; I don't think he 's long for this world; and doubtful if he would have much appetite for the bowl of porridge, she added some spoonfuls of honeycomb. A little sup of the milk is all I want, he said, and having drunk he dropped back into a doze. It 's a strong weakness is on him, she said, and not healthy sleep. The sun was up before he stirred, and after a little walk she brought him back to his bed, and he slept till nearly midday, when he woke up refreshed, and she said: That was a fine fright you gave me last night. I am tougher than you think, he said. Now, are you hungry? I have some nice eels hanging up. Tadhg shook his head. And I got a trout while you were sleeping. A taste of the trout wouldn't hurt me, said he. He is very weak surely, she said, turning from the pan, and she made up her mind that she 'd go to the Abbey for help. He 'd like to see the Abbot anyhow; 'twill cheer him up. . . . But the Abbot was in his own bed and wouldn't leave it for the next three days, for he was trying to cure himself of a bad cold on the chest; but still, coughing or not, he was worried when he heard about Tadhg, and he sent Biddy back with one of the brethren who was said to know what a sick man wanted almost before he looked at him. Now, O'Dorachy, said he, I 've brought you a bottle of wine, and you can have a sup out of it from time to time; and keep still between the sups—rest is what you need. And when he went back to the boat he warned Biddy that she must keep him quiet, which she promised to do. Although, said she, he 's a restless man, and the minute he feels a little better he 'll be about, trotting the glades and thinking of the story he 'll be telling the pilgrims, or tuning his harp, or thinking up new tunes to amuse them; for he 's bent on making the next pilgrimage a great success, if it kills him. Well, he 'll see no pilgrims if you don't keep him quiet! Biddy promised to do her best, and was finely scared on finding Tadhg by the little quay waiting to meet her. You 're doing just what Brother Luke said you weren't to do; come you back to the bed at once, and I 'll make you a nice warm drink.

Next day Tadhg seemed almost as well as ever he was, and feeling his strength returning, he said he must be at his story. Can't you make the story just as well lying down? To which he made no answer, but bade her be off. He came back very tired that evening, and finding him weak the next day and with a dawny look on his face, she said: I have business over at the monastery, and you 'll be taking care of yourself till I return. Don't leave me now, Biddy, he said. Brother Luke can't help me. I am not long for this world. Now, let you not be talking like that! And after drinking some wine and eating, he seemed again to get his strength. And one day, speaking queer and not like a man at all but the way a prophet might, maybe, he said: When a man gets into the eighties there isn't much of the world left in him and not much wish to live; there does be a secret hankering in old men for a good rest, a thing there 's very little of in this world. But what do you want to talk like that for? said Biddy. You aren't thinking of dying on me? You 'll get into the nineties before you stop. Well, he said, I may live a few years more. I am feeling better this day than I have done for a long time. But all the same, Biddy, I won't be long in it, and there's one thing now that I'd like you to do for me. I'd see you once more the way I saw you before, so that I may finish the story. Now, of all the men! said Biddy. Can't you be asking me anything else at all rather than that? You wouldn't let me die, Biddy, without finishing the story that I set out to do? I'm going to heaven, Biddy, where there are no clothes at all, and if that be so I'll be all the better for another look at you. Why can't you wait till I join you in heaven, where we'll be looking at each other always without wearying of each other, so it is said. Well, the argument went on, and Biddy felt no wise inclined to consent, but in the end, when she saw that the old man would come to more harm by her not doing it than by her doing it, she went behind the blackthorns and came out the same as before. Hardly any hips at all on you, Biddy. Ah, that's the great disfigurement in women—the same hips. But I have a big bosom. The bosom goes in well with the rest of you, and it's as you are that I like you. Now, turn a little the other way. He was a long time admiring the willowy curve of her back. Built like a weasel you are, he said, with a dip in the middle. Biddy wasn't altogether pleased at being compared with a weasel, but she didn't like to say a thing that would contrary the old man, so she stood in the way that he seemed to care most for till she got a cramp in one of her legs; and she was about to ask him to let her shift them when she heard a faint cry. Now, what is that? she said, and turning round she went over and had a look at Tadhg. He's gone at last! and she closed his eyes, wondering if he'd know her the next time they met. I must go over to the Abbey, for the funeral will be to-morrow. They'll bury him beside his master, where he'll be happier than he was with me. He wasn't unhappy with me either.

A great story, Alec. I can see and hear it all, the

Abbot coming over to the island to get a true account of Tadhg's death from Biddy; and I can hear her answering him: Not a story I 'd like to be telling your reverence. Biddy, I would have the truth from you plainly. Since your reverence is willing to listen to how my poor man came to his death, I 'd say it was through the odd fancy that took him to make a grand story. . . . About what, Biddy? Saving your reverence's presence, about my rump. About your rump, Biddy! My poor Tadhg set great store on seeing me naked, and every right he had, your reverence, to seeing me whatever way he wanted, we being husband and wife. He had it from yourself, else I 'd never have stripped before him. But you haven't told me how he died, Biddy. He died saying that my back was like a willow branch and the round of my rump as fine as anything ever dug up in Greece. A strange death surely, Alec, and a noble death, for shouldn't every man die in love with his wife? You have exceeded me in invention. The Ballinrobe cock is outdone, and the crow is to the Westport rooster!

CHAP. LVIII.

A VERY few days after Alec's telling of Tadhg O'Dorachy's marriage and death on a lake island, I met him in the high wood, and sitting by him under the beech-trees by the old mill within hearing of the tumbling brook, I said: Whenever I hear a sound of water falling over high cliffs or purling over big stones I remember the stories you told me, and better than any French or English or Italian stories. Hadn't they a great story-teller in Italy by the name of Boccaccio? Alec asked. Yes, Alec; but his stories ramble over a great number of years and about too many people, and no sooner read than they float out of our heads like thistledown. Now, if you aren't making game of me, your honour, putting me above Homer and Boccaccio, I'd like to hear the stories you do be chewing when you're away in London. I often think of the story of Liadin and Curithir, Alec—never were lovers suited with such lovely names before. But his face did not light up with pleasure, and after watching him for a while I began to tell of a young man that came over from the Pyrenees with wolf-hounds. I remember it well, the young man and the wolf-hounds; but the rest of the story belongs to your honour more than it does to me. We wrangled a while, and then Alec came out with the truth, saying: I told your honour stories to amuse you on your holiday, but I'd be glad to know that you aren't given to telling them in London to newspaper boys and their like, for a great harm might come to me. I'm not thinking now of the story of Tadhg's death, for there's no clergy in it to speak of. All the same, I might have left the clergy out of it altogether. I don't see how you could have done that, Alec, great story-teller though you are. Alec looked round nervously: Would you be speaking a bit lower? There might be somebody hiding behind the old mill. Even so, Alec, he wouldn't hear our talk across all that bubbling water. Isn't it an old saying, your honour, that stones have ears? And isn't it an old saying, too, Alec, that no story means the same to every man that hears it? Isn't it in the story of Bran, or in Briciu's Feast, or in Maine Morgor, or in some other great story, that two men shade their eyes with their hands so that they may see better; all the same, one beholds a boat sailing over the sea with a man in it, whilst the other beholds a man driving a chariot over forest boughs. And the words of the old Irish poet, Alec, are but the telling of a great truth: that the world is a different world to every man that looks upon it. For what sets one man holding his sides with laughter fills the next man's eyes with tears of pity, and all the newspaper boys in London have got hold of the cry that the genius of the Celtic race is to mingle tears with laughter. And there is plenty of both in your stories.

Even this praise did not remove the gloom from Alec's face, and I continued: You are tormented with scruples, Alec, about your stories of spiritual wives. A spiritual wife, I grant you, will not be understood by the ignorant and the stupid, but all men are not stupid and ignorant, and no story can capture the sympathies of the whole world. Every one must be content with its own circle, and I think there are many who will understand that there is great beauty in the story that came to me between sleeping and waking last night, one that I heard years ago in my childhood from Timothy Moran. A story of two children, Dinoll and Crede, who grew up side by side in the north of Ireland by a lake overhung with great woods, through which they wandered on long summer days, returning home tired, the girl's thoughts on the flowers she had gathered, the boy's on the bees' nest they had found, and the honey they had brought back; and of such adventures they would talk as they lay together in the same bed, too tired for sleep, till in a happy weariness they fell asleep, sinless, to awaken without thoughts of sin. And innocent as our first parents before the fall, they passed out of their childhood into their teens, when Dinoll came under the spell of Christ without Crede having any thought for the change, till one Sunday morning on their way to Mass she began to wonder why he did not speak of the great host of blackberries they had discovered—for the summer was drawing to a close and they were now at Samhain—nor did he speak of the bird they had caught and put into a cage and hung above the cottage door. A girl is quicker than a boy to notice any change in their relationship, and it was a sorrow to her that his eyes were not fixed upon her but upon the lighted candles shining on the white scriptures.

Why is he like this? she asked herself; cannot he love Christ and me at the same time? Do those who love Christ put aside all other things? She was afraid this was so, and walked nearly in tears by his side, till she could bear the silence no longer and said: Are we going to rob the wild bees' nest to-day of its honey? No, he answered, we are not, for during Mass I have been praying for strength to waste no more days in the woods. It is not to wander in woods and to watch the bees and the birds and the foxes and the badgers, and all the other wild things, that we were born into this world. You know what I mean, Crede? I do faith, the girl answered. And it almost broke the boy's heart to say: We shall never wander in the woods again; and the girl felt that her heart was broken.

So much I can say without trying to separate their loves telling which was greater than the other. They loved, but they loved God more than each other, so it is hard to say whether it was in joy or sorrow that they parted. You won't be delaying at home, Crede, after I am gone to the monastery? You'll be off to the convent the day after or the same day? And among the nuns, singing the holy offices of the Church, you'll be gaining a high place in heaven, and I, too, among the monks, may be as lucky as yourself. But you won't deceive me? For though I can live apart from you on earth, it is only because I would be living with you in heaven. You understand me, don't you? And the girl said she did, and her promise was given readily that she would not delay at home but would be on her way to the convent as soon as they parted at the cross roads. But after their parting she broke down crying, finding that she loved the boy more than she thought for; and sitting down she gathered a few blackberries, but she could not eat them, and though she was thirsty she could not bend down to the spring of water. Of what use, she said, to drink?

Of what use to eat? Of what use to do anything now that he is taken from me? The only useful thing that I can do is to go into a convent, for when he hears that I am not in it he will know that I have broken my promise and will love me no more.

All the same, though there was great reason for her going to the convent and asking to be admitted among the holy nuns, she did not go, though she found no pleasure in life and was miserable for more than three years, till at length she could bear her misery no longer, and when that happened the thought came to her that she might go to his monastery and take counsel with him. After speaking to him, she said to herself, I may get strength to shut myself up with the good sisters and forget this world and hope that the next world will be better than this one, for it's this that has been a sad world to me and I so young. A sad world! she walked repeating, for though the spring was singing about her, in the runnel and in the branches, the world was very sad and dark, without beauty in the clouds above the lake or in the blue between them, and the monastery itself was an ugly place on a hill-side, ugly, no doubt, inside as well as out, for as she walked she could see no more than his shaven head, his brown beard and his fresh face, and a cord round his waist.

And wondering whether his eyes would be glad to see her or if they would be scornful, she toiled till she came to the door of the monastery, and might not have had the courage to knock, but the door opened and she was face to face with the porter. It is Brother Dinoll I have come to see—my foster-brother. Foster-brother? We know no such things here! said the porter. But if you are talking of Brother Dinoll I can give you news of him, and strange news it will be to you; for no more than two years was he here when he said that there was too much chattering and talk, too many quarrels and bickerings and things he did not like, and that he'd find time for his own thoughts and prayers better in a forest dell. Now, where may the dell be? Crede asked. I do not know; and if I knew I wouldn't dare to say it, for I can tell by your eyes that you are hungering for him. Hungering I am, said Crede, but it's the spirit hunger and not the flesh. Ah, you all begin in the same way; I've heard that tale too often! said the porter, and he slammed the door upon Crede.

Never, said she, shall I see Dinoll again! But wandering on in the woods, where she hoped to die, for there was no joy at all in anything for her now, she came into Glen Bolcane, and it seeming a happy place to her, she said: I will stay here, for there is a fine spring of water and nuts, too, and these will keep me alive till God in his mercy calls me out of the life of this earth into the life that is in heaven, which must be better than the life of the world; for no woman can suffer the same pains twice unless in hell itself, where pain goes on forever, and I have done nothing that I know to deserve hell; so once I am dead my sufferings will cease. As she made her moan she heard a voice praying: May God grant us peace and happiness; may the countenance of the King shine brightly upon us when we leave behind us our withered bodies. . . . So, said she to herself, he is thinking of me still. And rising up from the ground she walked and found him praying, and his back being turned upon her she touched him on the shoulder and said: Dinoll! So thou hast come from thy convent, Crede? From thy monastery, whither I went to get tidings of thee. And who in the monastery told thee to come to Glen Bolcane? None told me, for none knew of thy hermitage; but the porter said that the babble of voices in the monastery and the many quarrels of the monks brought thoughts to thee of some quiet dell where thou wouldst be nearer to God. And he spoke truly, said Dinoll, for whosoever would hear God must close his ears to the tongues of men; God speaks very gently, and His voice is heard under these boughs. Beautiful are the boughs, she said, of Glen Bolcane, and the glades were full of flowers as I came along, and the birds were singing so blithely that I thought I was back in the woods we have left. Ah, the woods that we have left! said Dinoll. Thy voice tells me, Dinoll, that thou dost keep a tender corner in thy heart—— For the memories of our youth are all that we have except God, he answered. It pleases me to hear that thou hast not forgotten our woods, our quest for wild honey, and our grief at the loss of the blackbird; and thou rememberest, Dinoll, our house in the woods, the dry ditch overgrown with briars in which we ate our bread and drank goat's milk together and wove a cage out of osier bands for the bird, thinking that we had a song bird. We waited for the brown fledgling to turn black, but no black came, for it was but the brown mate of the bird whose wings are blue-black and whose beak and claws are yellow as gold, and who whistles as no other bird whistles, catching very nearly the strain of a human melody. We set the dusky bird free to find her mate in the woods—ah, thou hast forgotten! No, Crede, I have forgotten nothing—nor the day we were pursued, or thought we were, by the boar and climbed the great fir-tree together hand in hand and remained in it till evening, nor thy words as we touched ground. My words? Crede asked. Hast forgotten thy words?—— We shall be thinking of this night that we spent in the fir-tree till the end of our lives. There are nut bushes in Glen Bolcane, said Crede, and blackberries over the ridge of the hill at Samhain. And good water, too, said Dinoll; but thou hast not told me why thy promise to me was broken. The most I can tell thee is that I had sense that thy life would not be spent among chattering monks; more than this I do not know. And when the porter, Brother

Murchad, told thee that I was gone in search of a quiet dell, thy feet led thee hither? Yes, it was so seemingly, for I thought not of seeing thee; my feet led me, or it pleases me to think that they did. And what wouldst thou here? I would, said Crede, live with thee as thy sister and helpmate, joining with thee in thy prayers and talking with thee over the doings of the day as we lie side by side. Thinkest that this can be again, Crede? Why not? For all things return to the point from which they started. We began our lives together and will end them together, though I do not know how it will all come about.

Crede, thou speakest vain words, for thou art a woman. Glen Bolcane is beautiful in the spring when the lark sings trancedly—we hear him now in the blue between the branches of the trees, but Glen Bolcane is not always as it is to-day; after spring comes summer, and after summer autumn, and winter nights are cold in this dell. The owl comes here and hoots, so cold is he, and hungry too, all the mice being in their holes. But lying together we shall not be cold, Dinoll. Wouldst thou turn me away? and will it be counted a good deed to do this? And art thou without knowledge that a sister and helpmate is permitted to every hermit? And to be near thee I will take one end of the dell and thou shalt take the other. But then, Crede, there will be no temptation, and we are here—— Ah, that is true; but we were not tempted before, so why should we be tempted now one by the other? We will think of the good Christ that whispers in lonely places to those who would hear him and promises a great recompense for those who live according to his law. If thy thoughts be so, Crede, and thy mind be set upon earning in this life a high place in heaven, let us earn it together, for two souls praying reach God's ear easier than a single prayer. Now come, and I'll show thee the hut that I live in, shapen like a beehive.

They walked a little way together, and leading her

under the thatch he showed her his bed and outside the hut the hearth whereon he built his fire. Here I boil my beans and lentils when I have them, he said, and thou shalt share them. And from that day on they lived together, sharing beans and lentils and living on wild fruits and the hedgehogs that God often sent them in times of scarcity, till one morning putting out his hand to touch his companion he found her share of the bed empty. And rising up a great gloom came into his face, and he went forth to seek her; and finding her gathering acorns, for it was autumn time, he said: Thou art preparing for a journey. Whither goest thou? I know not the path that will lead me to a dwelling, she answered, but we live in great Banva, where dwellings are met with outside of the woods, and at some dwelling or from a friendly shepherd I shall hear the way to the convent, where I shall be safe from sin for evermore. Alas, we were too near to sin last night, Dinoll, to trust ourselves together again. But we are free from sin, Crede, by Christ's help we are free; we are sinless still as we were in the old days in the woods that crowned Lough Riach. We were near to sin truly, and if Christ had not been watchful we would have sinned; and then if death had come—— Think not of it, Dinoll. We are still pure and can come before God without shame on our faces or doubt in our hearts. Was it thy fault, Crede, or mine? There was no fault, Dinoll, either on thy side or on mine, no sin; and to keep ourselves sinless we part. But when my hair is grey I will return to thee, and sinless, as I leave thee. So she knows that no man in the great world of Banva can tempt her but I! said Dinoll, and he returned to his praying stone to thank God that it was so, and to pray to God that he might forget the love that had almost overwhelmed them in the night and divided them from each other till they were grey-headed, lest they should be divided for eternity.

On rising from his knees he wondered at the sight of the trees growing among the rocks on the hill-side, and the rocks, too, and the torrent bursting over them; for Glen Bolcane was no longer a familiar spirit to him but alien shapes, he having no thought for what he saw or touched, nor care even to go to the spring-head to gather cress for his meal. So he withered bodily and became afraid lest he might die, for death, that once had no terror for him but was prayed for, had now become a consuming fear in his heart. If he were to die he would not see Crede again. For him to see her years would have to pass away, and she would not return to him as he remembered her: small and dimpled, with blonde hair curling round her pretty ears, and eyes that smiled always. Smiles and blondeness will have gone from her, he said, but she will not be less dear to me. But the waiting is long. The days will seem like weeks, and the weeks will seem like months, and the months will seem like years. Time will flow like the torrent. And listening, it seemed to him that he heard time flowing—slowly, oh, so slowly, and he fell upon his knees and prayed that he might think no more of Crede as he remembered her, but of the Crede that would return to him sinless.

At the word sinless he bethought himself of her welfare, and one day yearning to know what had befallen her he left Glen Bolcane for his monastery, and from the porter he learnt that she was in the south of Ireland, where there were many hermits; and he said to himself as he returned to Glen Bolcane: She will become the spiritual helpmate of some great old man. And some years afterwards he went again to the monastery, and got news of her—that she had acquired great fame for her piety and that the prayers which she composed were murmured in the churches by the people waiting for the priest to celebrate the Mass. On hearing these things Dinoll was glad, and then his gladness turned to jealousy, which he had to bear, reproving himself for his weakness and his unbelief, for had not Crede told him she would return to him sinless? But Crede had promised him once to become a nun, and if she had kept her promise he would be living contented in a monastery among his friars, and she too would be living contented among her nuns, a thing she was not now; for he knew that far from him Crede could know no contentment nor happiness, though indeed by living apart from each other they might be earning high places up in heaven, where they would sit, their hands linked, looking on Christ, his mother beside him in the midst of chaste saints, men and women.

Years passed away, and when jealousy began to gnaw at him again he set forth for his monastery, but before he came to the end of the dell his feet faltered and he said: Twenty years bring grey into the hair, and if I should leave Glen Bolcane and Crede should find me gone, what despair will fall upon me! And on his way back to his wattled hut the thought came to him that if Crede returned she might not know him. So greatly changed am I, he said. But this is not so; my hair may be grey and there are wrinkles, but grey hair and wrinkles will not hide from Crede's eyes the Dinoll she loves.

On coming into his dell the sound of water falling set him thinking that he might scoop a pool out among the rocks which would give him an image of himself, but he had neither pick nor crow. So much the better, he said, for the work will last till time brings Crede back to me. And for years he worked at the pool, and the image it gave back to him of an old man with long grey hair and wrinkled skin overjoyed him and he said: If time has changed me that much, time must have changed Crede. She must be even as I am, yet she does not come. The sun rises without showing her upon the ridge above me, and the evening darkens and I hear not her voice calling. And all manner of wonderings began in his brain lest

Crede had sinned and could not return to him, or that some miracle had kept her hair as blonde as primroses and her flesh white and soft to the touch as wool; and going to his praying stone he prayed that God had not stopped the course of time for Crede, not wishing them to see each other again till they met in heaven. But he was to see her once more before Christ taking pity released them from their bondage and on rising from his knees that day he saw Crede coming down the hill-side, seeking her way along the path that wound among the rocks.

The good Christ has answered my prayer! Thou hast come to me after weary wanderings, grey, with the darkness of age on thy face; and though thou hast lain with four men since we parted, thou returnest sinless to me. Thou art pure, without sin from man, and dear to me as thou ever wast and ever wilt be on this earth and shalt be in heaven. Great is the welcome that I give to thee, and great will be the days that we shall live together, kneeling on the same praying stone, lying side by side in warmth on the winter's night without the dread of sin to keep us apart. Crede, I know all. The great world of Banva is full of thy fame. Far and wide thou hast wandered, leaving an example that earnest prayer to God is no fallacy. Then may God grant us peace and happiness; may the countenance of the King shine brightly upon us when we leave behind us our withered bodies.

CHAP. LIX.

'TIS PROUD of you they must be in London for the great shanachie that you are; the greatest in all the world, I 'm thinking. But maybe, Alec continued, interpreting my silence as a confession that London had not done justice to whatever small talent may be mine, they are passing you over for the bitter jealousy there is in England always of everything that comes out of old Ireland. And didn't they strip us of our lands and our laws, of our own language itself? and aren't all the old houses being emptied now of the fine furniture we made in Dublin? and the pictures, and the silver spoons and dishes, all our handiwork, sold in London, bad cess to them? And aren't they still at the same old scheming, ferreting out our old stories, turning them all into rags and tatters, for not understanding the significance of anything in them. Isn't it the truth I 'm telling your honour?

Before I could answer him, Alec began again: But you 're a Mayo man like myself, and if you should think it worth your while to be writing out any of the stories I 've been telling you, it is meself that will be the proud man, for it won't be taking back a pailful of potato skins you will be doing like the lady in Galway, but fine spuds in which there is a rich diet. Faith and troth, that is why I have opened my mind to you, for I wouldn't have our old stories betrayed and destroyed any longer than I can help it. 'Tis the nature of stories to be travelling; always footing it one way or the other. So 'tis no use trying to keep them to ourselves, I know that, but I would like them to appear in their emigrations clean and tidy, just that, so that they may see over yonder that we have a shanachie as good or better than their own. The stories you have told me, I said, are the gift of the shanachie of Westport to the shanachie of Ballinrobe. If your honour likes to think of it in that way, he answered, 'tis a great honour you 're doing me by comparing me with yourself. Comparing myself with yourself? I rapped out. Why, Alec, we have been telling stories one against the other, and the best of the bunch is 'The Nuns of Crith Gaille'; and by far. We will never be agreed about that, your honour. Well, more is the pity, I replied, and if we aren't agreed among ourselves I don't know how it is to be settled unless we ring the chapel bell and call a meeting with the priest in the chair.

At the word priest Alec's face turned grave, and it came into my mind that I was just about to lose the original Alec which it had taken me a fortnight to evoke. It wouldn't be fair, I said, for me to tell stories against you in your own parish, and the words had no sooner passed my lips than I regretted them. We should do well not to be talking about the priest at all, Alec said, for the clergy do not take kindly to hearing stories told against themselves, even if they be in the years back. And not another word could I get from him. He sat, as it were, frozen in his meditations, and was not roused out of them till at last I said: There have been great shanachies in this world, Alec; greater than we. Now do you think there were any greater than yourself, your honour? I do, indeed, Alec, though I admire 'The Nuns of Crith Gaille' more than any of my own stories. You'll be turning my head if you say any more about that story, he answered, and he asked me who were the world's great shanachies. Had I shaken hands with any of them? With one, I have. An Englishman? Alec interjected. No, Alec. The Englishman, to my thinking, isn't a story-teller at all. He tells of parsons and croquet lawns, and is home-sick when he leaves them. He tells a tea-party well enough, and has a quick eye to spy out the difference between one woman's talk and another; whether she visits the big houses and if she have the talk of the gentry tripping on her tongue. But there is no diet in the Englishman's stories, if I may borrow one of your own expressive phrases. But there was a great shanachie over in France in the years back. Was there now? Alec interjected. There has been one, troth and faith, I answered, one that overtops all the others, wherever you may go looking for them. Now, your honour, Alec cried, you will be delighting me, begob you will, by telling me something about the great shanachie. Balzac, I said. But no sooner was the name out of my mouth than I began to regret having mentioned him, for it is difficult to pick a story out of the great Human Comedy that would appeal to an imaginative, uneducated fellow, and of all something that could be related on a June morning in a sunny wood by an old deserted mill.

At the end of a long silence, Alec said: Was this the great shanachie your honour shook hands with? No, Alec, the shanachie I shook hands with was a Russian—great fellows the Russians for the telling of a story; the best story-tellers are the Russians, and the best amongst them was Turgenev. And I told him how I had seen this great man in the gardens of the Élysée Montmartre. Public gardens, I said, in which a band plays, and the people dance in the open air under the trees, if it be fine, and in a ballroom if the weather be wet. So it must have been wet on the occasion that I saw this great man, for he was walking down the ballroom, a great man and a big one as well—as big as Maliche Daly, standing six feet four at least, and with a head on him as white as Croagh Patrick's peak after a fall of snow, upright as a tree, and a walk on him like a stag: a noble, knowledgeable man, one that had lived a long time in the world, but standing apart like a mountain among hills. Like the peak, your honour, said Alec. Just so, I see you understand him: and his stories, too, are as beautiful in outline as the hills, sometimes a little dimmer, like—— Like the Connemara hills in the gap beyond, Alec interrupted, and I answered: Precisely, I see you understand. Did he speak to your honour? Alec asked. He was kind enough to speak to me, though I was but a boy in those days; and I told Alec that the great shanachie's words had remained with me all my life, so wise did they seem; but as they were spoken in the French language, and about books that Alec had not read, it would be useless for me to try to translate the shanachie's wisdom. Alec accepted my judgment as to what could be told and what should be left out of a narrative, and asked me which was the greater of the two, Turgenev or Dostoieffsky. My vote was given long ago to Turgenev, Alec; I plumped for him. And myself wouldn't be saying that there was anything amiss with that plump, Alec returned. But would it be asking too much if I were to ask you to tell me what t' other was like? I never saw Dostoieffsky in the flesh, but in the portraits that they publish in his books he appears like an unhappy, almost afflicted man from the working classes. There is a good deal of Tartar blood in Russia, and Dostoieffsky's flat, shallow face, with insignificant features and eyes turned up at the corners, recalls the Tartar or Chinese type, and were it not for the agitated eyes no one would suspect he was looking at the portrait of a great man. But the agitated eyes tell that something awful had happened to him, and something very awful did happen to him in the beginning of his life; not many years after writing *Poor Folk,* he was on his way to the scaffold, on the scaffold maybe, when the reprieve came, altering the sentence of death to one of banishment to Siberia. His face in the portrait tells of an unfortunate man, one who was unlucky from the beginning; an epileptic he was, and his life was lived in great poverty; in such poverty, Alec, that there was no time for him to read over his manuscripts before they went to the printer. Turgenev admired his genius, but—— Were they friends? Alec rapped out. They must have known each other, but they couldn't be friends, for they were too different, coming from different classes, and out of a different tradition. Nor were they even of the same race, I muttered. Two great men writing prose narrative in the same language, that was all. There are stories going about, Alec, of a strange visit that Dostoieffsky paid to Turgenev. Dostoieffsky had come to Paris once to arrange for the publication of his works in a French translation, and it is said, mind you, I don't vouch for the truth of the story, but it has got about that one evening, overtaken by his conscience, he rushed off to Turgenev to confess a crime he had committed years ago in Moscow. There being no priest handy, I suppose? Alec interjected. I'm afraid neither of them set much store on priests, I replied; but even those who do not believe in priests like to unburden themselves sometimes; a man who has committed a crime cannot keep his secret always; a secret will out, as you've often heard, Alec. I've heard, Alec said, that murder will out. A much worse crime than many murders was the crime that compelled him to seek out Turgenev in Paris. You must know, Alec, that houses in Paris are very big; and on every storey there are as many rooms as in a whole house here. I suppose that this plan was adopted with a view to fewer servants, for there is no going up and down stairs in a flat; the rooms open one into the other, and Turgenev had come through the folding doors from the dining-room into a white-painted, low-ceilinged saloon, which would have seemed somewhat finicky to Dostoieffsky if he had had eyes to see the grey silk curtains and beautifully bound books. There were comely little book-cases hanging from the walls and standing in corners, filled with choice volumes which could not have failed to attract anybody except a somnambulist, somebody walking in a dream, and that was how Dostoieffsky came into the room: like one in a trance. He knew Turgenev was there, and that's about all—Turgenev only concerning him. He was not aware of the hour, which, as I have said, was an hour after dinner, somewhere about nine o'clock. He was not aware that Turgenev was busy; nor of the embarrassment his name created when the servant announced it: only aware of the torture he experienced in the few minutes he had been kept waiting in the ante-room. For every moment in that room was terrible till the moment came for him to unburden his conscience of the crime committed in Moscow years and years ago. Remorse, he said, has got hold of me now as it never did before, and he stood looking at Turgenev hardly seeing him at all; Vera's face, the girl that had sent him, was much clearer to him. Didn't Turgenev offer him a chair or say something to him? Alec asked. Yes; Turgenev came forward with a chair, but Dostoieffsky waved him aside and walked up and down the room, finding a way through the furniture instinctively without falling over any chair or table, which was wonderful, for he seemed like a man without eyes, and after a while he found his way back to where Turgenev was sitting. It was last night, he said: She was by me, and it was she who sent me hither. The dead have a strange power over us, and she is dead many years: ten years ago at least. It was at Moscow. One night, Ivan Sergeivitch—— Who is that one, Ivan Ser . . . vitch? Alec rapped out. Turgenev, I answered. Russians who are strangers address each other as son of—— Like the Irish Mac, Alec said, and I answered that it was so. And Turgenev would address Dostoieffsky as Theodore Mikhailovitch. 'Tis a terrible way of saying Mac, said Alec, and to escape further questions I repeated Dostoieffsky's last words. It was one night in Moscow, at the hub of the streets, I met her, after a long day's work, and so brain-weary was I that I could hardly see or hear when a girl's voice awoke me. I'm afraid I frightened you, the girl said. You startled me a little, I answered: but my appearance must have frightened you, my mind was far away. You're not even awake yet, she said. Oh, but I am, I answered, and we walked on together, myself listening to her story of herself, glad to listen to it, to anything that took me out of myself. She told me she wanted to learn English, and the only way, she said, is to get a situation in England. I'm after one, but I 'm not certain that I shall be able to get it, for you see, I 've no reference. And how is that? You seem a good little girl. I used to be, but I don't know that I am any longer. How did it come about? I was looking, she said, after some children in a tradesman's family, and one day in the park a dog attacked the children, and all three might have been bitten if a student had not come forward and driven off the dog. We met again the next day and the next and the next, and all might have gone on very well if one of the children hadn't walked into the pond after his boat, and when I was asked to explain how I was not by to prevent him doing such a foolish thing, one of the children answered: Vera was talking with the student who drove the dog off. The student returned again and again, and the upshot of it all was that I lost my situation, being deemed, so it was said, unfit to look after children. As I was in love with Ivan and he with me, I went to live with him, and when he left Moscow I took on with his friend, a Roumanian. And what then? I said. When he left there was another and then another. And then? And then, she said, I found myself obliged to go out into the thoroughfare to find somebody to whom I might take a fancy and who might take a fancy to me. As it happened to-night, if we have taken a fancy to each other. But I 've only been out here once before; my word on it; and I assured her that I believed what she had told me, though it seemed to me to matter very little whether she had given herself to three men or to four, for money or caprice.

She had a pretty face and an engaging manner, and every word she spoke revealed a beautiful mind that circumstances could not defile. Now what have you been doing? she said, to change the subject, which was becoming a bit irksome to both of us, and I told her that I was a man who wrote stories for a living, and had come out to escape from the people of my imagination. But why do you wish to forget them? I would forget them, I said, to-night, so that I may remember them better to-morrow, and I'm grateful to you for speaking to me, for if it hadn't been for this little talk with you, perhaps I shouldn't have closed my eyes to-night. And to-morrow will be a day of twelve or fourteen hours. Must you work as hard as that? I must, indeed, for I have no money except the few roubles that publishers pay me for my stories. And I don't know if life will ever become any easier. You see I've only just returned from Siberia: I worked in chains for five years, because I wished to free the people from the police. So you're a convict, I heard her say, and I expected her to drop behind. I don't mind that, she said, for it was for having a better heart than another the police were down on you. Perhaps you're right, I answered, but I thought it well to tell you who I am, for it may do you harm to be seen walking with an ex-convict. I'm not afraid of that, and I saw that my confession, instead of estranging us, as I had intended, seemed to unite us, which is only natural; the outcast can only speak intimately to the outcast. We walked on, discovering ourselves one to the other, and when I stopped to bid her good-bye it seemed to both of us that for a night at least we were destined for each other.

It was then that I began to look her over, and her clothes, her accent, told me she was a workgirl, the typical workgirl of Moscow, and, I said, she has told me the truth; she has been a nursery-maid and needs money, and I've none to give her. You need money, I said, and in coming with me you are leaving money behind you. Never mind; I would sooner go hungry to-morrow than lose you to-night. But I have some money, very little it is true, so little, that if I were to call that cab I should be ashamed to offer you what remained. We can walk, she answered, and it was not till we were fairly out of the city that her legs began to ache. Let us rest awhile, she said. I shall be able to go on presently. But my lodgings are not very far off, she replied, her eyes fixed on the last cab on the last rank. But I 'm dead-tired, and it wouldn't cost much to ride the rest of the way; it isn't more than half-a-mile. Which is lucky, I answered, for the last cab looks as if it has accomplished its last journey. The horse too, Vera said, is near his end; his head is sunk between his forelegs; and it was with a view to shortening his journey by a few yards that we crossed the road. An absurd thought, I remarked, and Vera agreed that the extra yards could not make much difference, but like me she felt she must save the horse from the labour of dragging the cab across the street. As the cab came towards us the horse fell in the middle of the road. He 'll get up when I 've loosened the traces and drawn away the cab, the driver muttered, as he bent over the harness. He plied his whip, but the horse was dead, and we turned away, frightened, myself wondering if we should accept the horse's death as a warning, as an omen. I think even little Vera was frightened, moved by the untoward occurrence, but at fifteen one isn't given to the reading of omens. You see she was only a child, and I listened to her prattle, my thoughts wandering between the magnitude of the universe and the accident that had forced this long walk upon us, robbing me, perhaps, of the love night that I looked forward to so greedily. She will be too tired, I said, and that was all I thought about: whether she would be too tired for love.

Vera, I 'm trying to confess all. Have patience. Have I not come to him to whom thou didst send me? Am I not telling all? Thou knowest that I am concealing nothing. I had looked forward to seeing thee unpin thy pins, and untie thy bows, revealing each delicate form of thy body to me, and so great was my disappointment that there was no candle that I confided my chagrin to thee, and having thought only for my pleasure, thy hands drew a curtain, letting moonlight into the room.

I can see her still. Certain parts of her are before my eyes; her talk is ringing in my ears, will ring in them for ever, for we may not escape from the dead; the dead never relax their clutch, and it is more often a dead hand than a living that urges a man to his doom. After all, did she not love me? But did I love her? How could one such as I love her? To love one must have leisure, and there was none in my life. For bare life I had to sit at a writing-table for ten, twelve, fourteen hours a day, and the police are always at the heels of an ex-convict, and as she strove to detain me, her hand on the lapel of my coat, I began to regret that we had met each other, for I foresaw the necessity of breaking with her. When shall we meet again? she asked, in her simplicity. When shall we meet again? I repeated, almost ironically. Have I not told you, I said, folding her in my arms, that I am a penniless convict from Siberia? Why should you wish to see me again? For what? That I do not know, she replied, but I promise not to disturb you while you're writing; I'll sit in a corner very quiet, reading the pages as you throw them aside. Tears were on her eyelids, and I looked away. I cannot, I said: I'm a convict; the police are always watching me. You're a child, and—— If you're afraid to let me come to see you, tell me where you walk in the evenings, and, not foreseeing that we should ever run up against each other in the Nikolskaya, I told her that I walked there nearly every evening, and bade her good-bye, going back to my garret, thinking, not of her, but of the work that would have to be accomplished before the sun set again.

My work left me too tired to go out, and the next day was the same, and the day after; but after several days of work there came a swimming in my head, and I went out to get the air, and to try to forget the people my pen had called into life. It is necessary to forget them sometimes so that we may not forget them when the time comes for work again. The very first thing I saw that night was Vera looking into the faces of the passengers, and turning away from them as soon as she had scanned them, seeking somebody whom she could not find, looking into their faces and turning away again. She is seeking me, I said, and passed up a side street, thinking to escape, for the sense that she was a danger to me was stronger than ever. We're a mutual danger, I said to myself, and perhaps it was the sense that she was a danger to me that drew me to her next day, for I walked out into the Nikolskaya, asking myself if she was still looking for me. She was there, and I saw her, as before, looking into the faces of the passengers, turning away from them, refusing many men who came and solicited her. She is refusing them, I said, because I am upon her mind. My misfortunes have attracted her. And then I began to argue with myself, asking myself: What imagined doom can there be for us? A girl like any other girl, and, I repeated, a man like any other man, but when I uttered these words I knew I was speaking a lie. For I'm not like any other; and, my thoughts travelling over my past life, I sought to discover if I were as different as I imagined myself to be, but after scanning the terrible history that every year unfolded, I closed the book, frightened, and fell to thinking of Vera. A thirst was upon me to see her; it was not the thirst for her body, not altogether, but the thirst for companionship: my life was lonely, lonelier than it had ever been in Siberia. I reasoned with myself. I said: I must bear with myself, I am done for, but let me not drag her down with me. And I swear that I kept myself for days and weeks from turning into the Nikolskaya lest we should meet. But at last the day came when I began to feel that my dreams were becoming me, and the hallucinations of my people mine. I began to fear my people as one fears spectres. I must escape from them, I cried, else I shall not be able to recall them again. . . . If I do not drive them away to-night they may refuse to obey me to-morrow. And as I jostled through the crowds, neither hearing nor seeing, a voice awoke me suddenly. It was Vera. So I have found you at last, she said. Why haven't you walked here before? I looked into her eyes without speaking. Aren't you glad to see me? she said. Yes, I 'm glad to see you, I answered, but my mind is away, and I neither see the people about me nor have I any mind left to understand what is being said to me. You 'll be better presently, she answered. Let us walk on together. Your mind will return to you presently. But if you work so hard you will kill yourself, and then what shall I do? The words touched my heart and I awoke from my dreams of a bastard son, an epileptic like myself; one that had committed a murder and had forgotten it—Smerdyakov.

I am myself again, I said, and remembering at the same moment that I had money in my pockets, having sold some manuscript, I said: Let us go into an eating-house and have some supper. I should be very glad, she answered, for I 'm hungry. You haven't eaten to-day? and she answered: I have not. It was unwise for me to take her into an eating-house, for when she had eaten and drunk there was only one thing to do, to take her back into my garret, and after I did that, would I be strong enough to turn her out of it in the morning? I knew that I should not turn her out, for reason is not listened to in such moments. Were it listened to, the world would have ceased long ago; it cannot check even the philosopher; we belong to ourselves, to our instincts and passions, and, forgetful of aught else, I listened to Vera, who said she would be the happiest girl in the world if I would share my garret with her; and we were happy for longer than I thought it possible that I could be happy—for nearly three months. But all the time Vera's golden ringlets and happy smiles were setting the tongues of enviers and rivals wagging, and the police are adepts at indirect means of compulsion. It may have been the police and it may not have been the police, but objections to my work began to arise. I lost some of my customers, and feared that I should lose more. It was not an imaginary persecution, I swear it. Every day it became more intense and determined, till the old fear awoke in me, and my thoughts began to talk to me again, saying that I had dragged this poor child into a whirlpool of misfortune, for you are that and nothing more, my thoughts muttered. And I yielded to the belief that my life in the world would drag on as it had begun, in disaster. Vera, I said, I am as a leper; you would do well to leave me. Do you care for me no longer? she asked. And there was no strength in me to answer her: Vera, we have had our time of life together; be wise and leave me, for I can only bring misfortune to you. Had I spoken these words she would not have understood them. She might have said: You 're talking to me now as the people talk in your books. So I said nothing. She asked me of what I was thinking. Of you, darling, I said, but I was really thinking, though I did not dare to tell her, that it were better that she should return to the streets than remain with me, for on the streets she might meet any evening an honest fellow who would be tempted at first by her child beauty and learn to appreciate her gentle nature and marry her. Many men marry off the streets. Every good girl who goes on the street marries; we must believe that goodness rises above prejudices and conventions. But to remain with me would be certain ruin for her; we had entered the danger zone. We had been together three months, and after three months the flesh wearies a little. It may be that I am wronging myself and that it was the persecution of the police that forced me to persecute Vera. Persecution begets persecution, and every day the desire to get rid of her became more intense. I counted her steps as she descended the stairs, saying: She is farther from me than she was a moment ago, and when she returned I counted her steps as she ascended the stairs, saying: She is nearer to me than she was a moment ago. Something had to happen. Oh, it wasn't murder. I should never have had the strength to murder, I couldn't walk upon a fly on the ground, but it would have been better if I had murdered her, for she would have suffered less at the time, and I should not have had to come here with a tale of cruelty: determined, premeditated cruelty, intended to drive her away. She never got a kind look or word from me, till I told her one day that she must leave me to earn my living; and you would do well, I added, to be about earning yours. She made no answer but left my rooms without a word, and I continued to write; ten thousand words had to be written that day; they had been promised; and when I had written the last page my brain was so unsteady that I seemed unable to write the address, and it was whilst I sat, my fingers tight about my forehead, that I heard her feet on the staircase. She will be here in a moment, I said, and I cannot look her in the face. I'll go out. But when I return I shall find her waiting for me. The rooms in which we lived were divided by a partition, so that I could not move without her hearing me, so I sat very still, saying to myself: She thinks I am out. At last I heard something drop, and what dropped sounded like a coil of rope—a rope drops differently from any other object, and when I heard her pick up the rope, I said: She has bought a rope to hang herself. But, if she means to hang herself, she will open the door to see if I'm out, and at the sight of her face all misunderstandings will be wiped away; we shall fall into each other's arms more truly in love than we have ever been. . . .

But she has drawn a chair forward and is going to step from the chair on to the table, and when on the table she will tie the rope—to what? I asked myself, and tried to remember if there was a pole above the window. My thoughts slipped away as thoughts do in a dream, and just as the dreamer says: I'm dreaming, I too began to think I was dreaming. She is writing a letter, I said, giving the reason for her suicide; and I became strangely curious, asking myself what reasons she would give, and if she would find the right words. I must have lost consciousness, if not for long, for some moments, for I remember a table being kicked aside. She has hanged herself, and if I do not strive to shake off this lethargy, and run to her and cut her down, she will die and I shall be responsible. There are moments in every man's life in which he is not himself, in which he loses possession of his free will, if there be such a thing as free will. I must hasten, I said, lest I be too late; but I could not move, and then the song began to sing in my ears: Her death will loosen her clutch upon my life, and in spite of my efforts to rouse myself the time went by. I do not know how it went, and when I awoke, I said: She is dead; it is all over; and dipping the pen into the ink, I addressed the envelope and walked to the office of the newspaper and handed in my copy.

I said just now there was an interval between the tying of the rope and the moment when she kicked the table aside, and that interval was occupied in writing a letter. That is so. She wrote a letter before hanging herself, explaining her suicide. The porter came upstairs, and the police came, and she was carried away, and buried, and disappeared from every human mind except mine. But in my mind she persists, becoming every day clearer, more distinct, and more authoritative. I feel her behind me in the streets; I wake up in the night and see her in the darkness; and last night she bade me go to you: Thou must go to Ivan Sergeivitch, she said, and tell him all; and I believe she sent me to you that I might get peace from her memory. But it would seem that the dead do not know all, for you have listened, not as she thought you would listen, but as I knew you would listen, without pity, almost with contempt. You are incapable, Ivan Sergeivitch, of a noble action or of a noble thought except when you are interpreting the souls that your imagination reveals to you. You're not a Russian but a Greek—a Greek from the Crimea. All the while I have been telling you my story you have been judging me. . . . True that I came for judgment, but the sympathy of a Russian Mujik would have served me better. Repentance is a word without meaning to the philosopher, and confession disgraceful and unworthy of man. Why did I come here? Did I not foresee you? But Vera sent me, and I did not dare to disobey her. She said that I must unburden my conscience to you else I should have no peace. Why did she send me? She sent me to you, Ivan Sergeivitch, that I might learn from you that there is a worse criminal than I. You, sitting in your palace of art, waiting for me to leave you, saying: How much longer will he keep me from my manuscript, a manuscript in which, no doubt, a nightingale in a wood hard by is singing her honeyed song while a heart yearns in a shadowy saloon, like this one. Rich furniture, vases, pictures. Very sordid and disgraceful my life must seem to you. But I would not exchange mine for yours. Cold-hearted sentimentalist! Dostoieffsky on these words dashed into the ante-room, and Turgenev heard the door close that opened on to the staircase. And what did Turgenev do then? I answered: He dipped his pen in the ink and continued revising his manuscript. Are you sure you've got the story right, your honour? And seeing that Alec was beginning to lean towards Dostoieffsky's view of Turgenev, I said: A man is not necessarily cold-hearted because he knows he cannot allay another's remorse. Remorse, Alec, must burn itself out.

CHAP. LX.

ALEC HAD gone to his tea, and I sat for a long time wondering, so strange did it seem to me that he could have listened to the story without perceiving that Turgenev could not have intervened, violence and passion having no part in his life or in his art. And recalling Alec's outburst: And did Turgenev sit there letting the other fellow barge him for an hour without a word in his chops? The Murrigan should have been at him, leathering him all the way down the staircase to the very bottom and into the street! I was annoyed, and left the high wood considering my country's failure, the ineffectual Celt, till the comic spirit getting the better of the solemn, I laughed outright and walked towards my friend's house, to meet him on the greensward with simple, homely talk. After moments of enthusiasm it is pleasant to hear the plain man say: The weather seems settled at last, and to see his goodwife coming from the garden laden with fruit and flowers, to hear the wheels of the pony-chaise, and to meet the young girls returning from their different adventures, a tennis-party or a picnic on one of the islands in the Bay, to watch the young rooks, not yet fully fledged, flopping among the high branches, waiting to receive food from their parents, and, having received it, to see them return to the nests for the night, in response to the impatient cawing of their parents. It is always, I said, out of meditations of what always was, and is and ever shall be, that the best and most moving stories come, and my thoughts going back to the story that I told Alec, I said to myself: Turgenev was right to withhold words; his silence was better than words, for Dostoieffsky would seek to interpret his silence, and would be led towards peace as day is led towards night. Where have you left your new friend? my host asked, startling me out of my meditation. He is having his tea, I answered, and repeated the phrase, delighted by its homeliness. He is having his tea. Could a man be about any more useful business? He is having his tea, and no doubt devoutly, I said to myself, and my host asked me if I was going to see Alec to-morrow. He has been a delightful adventure, I replied, somewhat sententiously, but the adventure has come to an end, and it doesn't seem to me that anything will be gained by continuing it.

Another story from him or myself I could not bear, and to escape from Alec for the next few days I remained indoors till the news came up from the town that he had left Westport, and was not expected back for a week. He is sometimes away for weeks at a time, my host said. I shall not wait his return, I remarked—a remark that prompted my host to ask me if I were going to Moore Hall. And after putting the question he stood by the fireplace pulling at a cigar, still uncertain that it was fully lighted. At last a huge puff of smoke cleared his doubts away, and he turned out of the billiard-room, thinking, perhaps, that I should be left to my memories of the great square Georgian house, one of those built at the end of the eighteenth century in Ireland, atop of a high flight of stairs, atop of a pleasant green hill with woods stretching right and left down to the shore of a lake flowing round headlands, past islands, and finding a passage between the great oak wood of Derrinrush and the Partry shore, widening out in front of the great feudal fortresses of

Castle Carra and Castle Burke into what is almost another lake, passing round Church Island, and ending in a great snipe marsh under the walls of the old Abbey of Ballintubber, built by Roderick, King of Connaught, shall we say in the thirteenth century; a crescent-shapen lake with Moore Hall at one end of the crescent and Ballintubber at the other—a lake on whose every shore is a ruin, an ancient castle, a burnt or an abandoned house. Even the lake islands were once strongholds, and we dream of these defended fiercely against boat-loads of pursuers till portcullis and drawbridge came to be forbidden in Ireland, and later-day chieftains deserted the strongholds of their ancestors for manor houses, retaining their vassals under the name of tenantry, the village supplying the big house with hewers of wood, drawers of water, ploughmen, reapers, gardeners, gamekeepers, huntsmen, jockeys, maidservants, menservants, even mistresses. As late as the 'sixties the Georgian house killed its own mutton and beef, baked its own bread, brewed its own beer, and the last brewer at Moore Hall was John Malowney; his wife, Mary Macdonald that was, and her sister, Betty Macdonald, were cook and housemaid. These Macdonalds were probably the descendants of former chieftains, and the original owners of some of the lands my great-grandfather purchased when he returned from Spain. Whilom chieftains descended into the service of landlords, and the new landlords fought duels, there being no castles to besiege! The Irish castle flourished if the cattle-raiders returned with numerous beeves, and the Georgian house if the blood stock were speedy; it showed signs of declension as soon as the 'crack' began to lift his leg when the back sinew was pressed after the morning gallop.

My father rose at half-past six to see the horses gallop, though nothing else could persuade him out of his bed before ten. He was a good judge of a horse, given overmuch, it is true, to partial and unsatisfactory trials, but able to bring a horse fit and well to the post. Wolf Dog won a great many Queen's Plates, Coranna the Cesarewitch, just failing to get his head first past the post in the Cambridgeshire. He cantered 'home' in the Chester Cup, and this win kept Moore Hall out of the Encumbered Estates Court. Croagh Patrick won the two cups at Goodwood, and Master George all his races till the suspensory ligaments began to swell. I remember the day my father came up from the stables with the evil news on his face, and his valet, who was fussing about the hall chairs with one of my father's silk hats in his hands (in those days men did not go to the stables except in silk hat and gloves), confided to me in the pantry afterwards that he was afraid Master George's forelegs must have shown some slight puffiness, adding: We shall have the veterinary surgeon down here with his irons. Don't you believe in firing? I asked. Joseph did not answer. Back sinews and suspensory ligaments are treated differently in these days; how, I have no knowledge, but in the 'sixties firing was a great device, and Master George's forelegs were fired; and I believe it was the memory of this brutal remedy that made it so difficult to remain on his back when he was put into training again. Be this as it may, he had me off three times one morning. Slieve Carn was the last of the Moore Hall horses that showed 'form,' but he was too beautiful for a race-horse, 'only a Harab,' as the bookies used to say at Newmarket. His box still is there, and it was a sudden sight of this loose-box that incited me to cry after Tom Ruttledge: No, Tom, I 'm not going to Moore Hall. You 'd better make sure that you don't want to go, he replied. . . . I 'm going down to the office; perhaps you 'll tell me when I return.

It seemed unkind to refuse to spend a few days at

Moore Hall, but it was impossible to commit myself definitely to the visit. If a visit there was to be it should come about naturally, and I told my host that I would try to come to a decision whether I should visit the house of my birth or go straight to Dublin in the train. I shall be able to come to a decision, I said, between Westport and Castlebar; not before. There's an excellent inn at Castlebar, and I can get all the food I shall require for a three days' visit. You will save yourself a great deal of trouble, my host replied, if you decide now what your journey is to be. I'll order a hamper to be packed for you. No, no, I replied; and invented on the spot some specious reasons for wishing to go to Castlebar by train. I should like to see the railway bridge again, I said, and half an hour after the tall arches that spanned the valley called forth my admiration once more, and I fell to thinking that if both ends of the bridge disappeared into the woods the bridge would be the most romantic in the dis-United Kingdom. The eastern side of the valley should be planted, I said, and while considering who should undertake this reafforestation, the pretty shapes of the Westport hills came into view, beguiling my thoughts so completely with their pretty outlines that at Castlebar my mind was not yet made up whether I should proceed on my journey or drive to Moore Hall. The road from Castlebar is not a cheerful one; a certain long stretch of bog rose up in memory, and I began to think that it would suit me better to alight at the next station, at Balla. But the train did not stop at Balla, and at Claremorris the stationmaster told me that I should not be able to get a car on account of the races. How very unfortunate, I answered; I should have liked to have seen Moore Hall. I should have gone over in Mr. Ruttledge's motor. That would have been better than a car, the stationmaster replied and the guard blew his whistle.

CHAP. LXI.

BETWEEN CLAREMORRIS and Ballyhaunis there is nothing to attract the eye, and the people that entered my carriage and left it at Castlerea were of a class unknown in Mayo in its feudal days. It was vain to try to decipher the markings on the shells; the kind was unknown to me, and I returned to my own thoughts, remembering that when my mother lived at Moore Hall (which she did to the day of her death), she used to say, when I jumped off the car that brought me from the station: Why that gloom upon your face, George? It would seem as if the sight of your own house is displeasing to you, and not wishing to distress her, I answered: You are mistaken, mother. I was thinking that more trees should have been planted to shut out the view of the lake. A frivolous answer truly, but the best that I could find in those days for a singular aversion. Why should I feel diffident?—why should I feel shy, almost ashamed, among the old places? I often asked myself. Yet that is what I do feel, and unable to find a reason to account for a feeling that seemed inveterate in me, I fell to criticising the alterations that my father had made in the house, trying to persuade myself that it was these alterations that prevented me from feeling at home at Moore Hall. The one that provoked me most was the raising of the roof some ten or a dozen feet for practical reasons, the beams no doubt having rotted under the low eighteenth-century roof. But I could not forget that the small green-mortared slates, like scales, were much more beautiful than the modern slates; large blue slates give a Georgian house the appearance of a lord mayor's mansion-house, and only look well on a high-pitched French roof. My father substituted plate-glass windows for the small panes with eyes in them like grease spots on soup. . . . How lovely! and it was with such æsthetic reflections that I tried for many years to account for a strange aversion. As late as last year, I said, I walked up and down the platform at Athlone, seeking the reason why I was always diffident, shy, ill at ease at Moore Hall; and feeling myself nearer to apprehending a reason that had till now eluded me, I repeated the words: diffident, shy, ill at ease, ashamed, frightened, overcome by the awe that steals over one in the presence of the dead.

Moore Hall is a relic, a ruin, a corpse. Its life ceased when we left it in 1870, and I am one that has no liking for corpses. The wise man never looks on the face of a corpse, knowing well that if he does it will come between him and the living face. . . . That is why I am unwilling to go to Moore Hall, and why I avoid the Quartier St. Georges, and the two streets leading to the Boulevard Montmartre, the Rue Notre Dame de Lorette and the Rue des Martyrs, for these streets are so intensely my past life that I should feel shy and diffident, just as I feel at Moore Hall, in intruding myself on their presence. It would be painful to me to cross the Place Pigale and to enter the café in which I used to spend my evenings of long ago with Manet, with Degas, with Pissarro, with Renoir, with Cabaner, with Alexis, with Duranty, with Mendès. I have heard that it is now the haunt of ponces and punks, and it is well that the Nouvelle Athènes should descend into animal life, for life is always ascending and descending, and the ponces and punks that assemble there to-day would shock me less if I were to enter the café than a group of modern literators discussing —ah, what do they discuss? is there anything left to discuss?

I turn aside from that café and would not enter the Rue Pigale if I could avoid doing so, for however fair the moon might shine it would not shine as fairly as it did the night when I walked there with Mendès, turning to the right, making for the Rue Mansarde, where he lived with Augusta Holmès. Nor would I enter the Rue Amsterdam again; Manet forbids. Three years ago the mistress of a friend of mine asked me to dine with her, and I did not dare disclose the truth to her that I could not venture into the Rue Amsterdam. A shameful cowardice it was to accept her invitation, and my punishment began almost as soon as I crossed the threshold, and it continued all through dinner, for she lived in 73 Rue Amsterdam. Some sense of premonition propelled me at last to the window, and looking from it down into the deep courtyard I cried out: We are certainly in the house overlooking the courtyard in which Manet painted. She said: You must be mistaken, for I could not have missed hearing that so great a painter lived here once. But if you think that this house is the house, go to the concierge and ask him: which I did at once, you may be sure, and he said he had heard that a great painter once lived in the house. But that wall? I asked. The wall, he answered, was built a few years ago. The courtyard is changed, I said; but is there a studio yonder? and he answered: Yes, and showed me into the studio in which I had seen so many masterpieces painted, now, alas, an art class for young women. Not another instant will I remain here! I cried; and I returned to my friend's mistress with these verses on my lips:

Triste sous le baiser plaintif dont tu m'effleures,
Oh! combien ton baiser de jadis m'est plus cher!
Les choses du passé, ma sœur, sont les meilleures.

CHAP. LXII.

WE MUST love for the sake of our remembrance of the kiss we receive, but not for it, and of all, we must not hesitate to resist whatever piercing longings rise up in us to return to the things that we loved long ago. The woman may be more beautiful and more intelligent than she was when we loved her; and the prospects that we remember are, perchance, more romantic to-day than they were when they stirred our imagination, but we must not try to return to them; we shall lose them if we do; by our fireside we can possess them more intensely than when they were illusive actualities.

I can see my father more clearly to-day than I could when I was a child, shall we say, as he sat at the breakfast-table reading the newspaper, suddenly remembering the horses in the stable, and laying down the paper and going into the hall, picking up his silk hat and gloves, that a valet had carefully brushed and laid on the chair for him. I can hear him call to the red setter that has been waiting for him on the steps. I can see the great hay-ricks over against the stables and the old pine in which the gold-finches built their nests, and brighter than day now is the day when the old servant took me out one morning and showed me the nest up in a high bough. That high bough may not exist to-day; and if it hangs as it did in the 'sixties, it would not be as clear to me at Moore Hall as it is by my fireside in London. By my fireside in Ebury Street I can relive the delightful life of the 'sixties again, seeing everyone in his and her occupation, and every room unchanged, unaltered; my nursery with a print between window and door showing three wild riders leaping a wooden fence in a forest. The school-room overlooking the yard is before my eyes—the yard is in ruins but its homely life lives on—the old mule toiling always, bringing up water from the lake. The mule is dead, and my old governess, too, may be under the ground, but she lives in my memory and will live in it, becoming clearer day by day. It would be a misfortune truly to meet her, for no longer would I be able to go with her for long walks beyond the domain out into the high-road, over Anney's bridge; through the long bog to the next bridge, to discover a crayfish in the brook—it is a wonderful thing to see a crayfish and not to know it is a crayfish—and to remember Primrose and Ivory, two ponies dead fifty years or more, and the day my mother drove me to Ballyglass to see the mail coach swing round the hill-side. The coachman held the reins grandly. The guard blew the horn. Why should I go to Ballyglass or to Lough Carra? The boat with sails made out of sheets stolen out of the linen presses lies rotten, or has utterly passed away.

But if Moore Hall lives in my mind completely and independently of the house that stands on the hill-top, why do I continue to refuse to accept my agent's advice to sell the timber? He says that a thousand pounds worth of trees can be taken out of the woods without injury to them, and if he could see into my mind, he would add: The trees that are growing to-day are not the same trees that were your wont to climb in boyhood. In fifty years a tree changes, even as a man; for better or for worse, all things change. Why, therefore, should you hesitate to fell every tree on the hill-sides, to tear the lead from the roof, to leave Moore Hall a ruin like Castle Carra? Rid yourself of Moore Hall so that you may possess it more completely.

CHAP. LXIII.

THE TRAIN passes on through West Meath, and I am puzzled to find an answer to Tom Ruttledge's subtle reasoning, and am forced to plead an invincible repugnance to the felling of the trees, to the selling of furniture and pictures. No; I cannot, I cry, do what you ask; to me the removal of a chair from one room to another is a pain: any change would hurt me almost as much as the selling of the lead coffins in which my forefathers are enclosed.

But even if you succeed in preserving Moore Hall unchanged for a few years, says my agent, whom I have cast for the part of the tempter, Moore Hall will certainly fall into ruin. As soon as you have gone, the trees will be felled, and the lead taken from the roof; Moore Hall will be a ruin within a very few years; for not a great many years of life lie in front of you. A fact that cannot be gainsaid; yet for some reason hidden in me, and which I may not explore, I dare not order trees to be felled at Moore Hall. You forget, Tom, that everything came out of Moore Hall: if Moore Hall had not existed I should not have existed, not as I know myself to-day, for it was Moore Hall that enabled me to go to Paris, and to sit in the Nouvelle Athènes with Manet and with Degas; to gather a literary atmosphere from Hugo, Zola, Goncourt, Banville, Mendès—and Cabaner.

CHAP. LXIV.

AS THE train drew near to Mullingar, I said to myself: Moore Hall was built with Spanish gold, and it was the peasants around the house, and the peasants of Ballintubber, and several other properties that enabled me to go to Paris. It is therefore to Patsy Murphy that the Carra edition of my writings should be dedicated. A strange dedication it would seem to my readers, but if justice were weighed out evenly the Carra edition should go to Patsy Murphy, but in this world we do not get the things that are due to us; in Ireland things always take a crooked turn, and instead of dedicating the Carra edition to Patsy Murphy I have decided to dedicate it to my agent for his good offices in obtaining from Patsy Murphy, without unduc coercion, the money that I so advantageously laid out in the Nouvelle Athènes. Patsy Murphy has been a patron of literature without knowing it.

CHAP. LXV.

OUTSIDE OF the circle of your own life you are unconcerned with the fate of Moore Hall, my agent's ghost insisted as the train passed by Maynooth, and I answered to the ghost: That is not so, for I would prolong the life of Moore Hall beyond my life if it were possible. What is Moore Hall but one of a thousand other houses built in the eighteenth century? he replied. The Nineveh into which Jonah marched for three days before he began to preach passed away so rapidly that the shepherds who fed their flocks among the ruins could not tell Xenophon the name of the bygone city. Why then, said the ghostly voice, should you trouble about Moore Hall? nobody will live there again. It is true, I answered him; time overtakes the most enduring monuments, but men continue to build, for they are created with that intention, and every day we strive against death. Why then should it be very foolish of me to dream of Moore Hall as a hostel for parsons and curates when I am among the gone? The Irish Protestant Church is very dear to me, and Moore Hall might serve as a token of my admiration of a Protestantism that has given to Ireland all our great men and our Anglo-Irish literature. In conversation with Hugh Lane I once said: I will leave my Impressionist pictures to Moore Hall, if you will include some pictures; together we might found a museum that would attract pilgrims. But Hugh Lane, who was something of a sciolist, answered that a museum was useless unless some hundreds of people visited it daily. Three appreciative visitors, I said, are better than a crowd of holiday starers. At this Lane giggled, but his prejudice in favour of the starer did not relax. Hugh Lane was undoubtedly something of a sciolist. But we are not yet at the end of our imaginations. Another destiny than a clerical hostel might be devised for Moore Hall; a rich American might buy my house. Ireland is nearer America than England, and sooner or later Galway will become a Transatlantic port. A steamer plies from Galway to Cong. Cong is but a few miles away from Moore Hall: why should not some rich American take the place from me? and may this book fall into his hands and inspire him to do so.

CHAP. LXVI.

THE TRAIN passes into Dublin, and I remember that if I hasten I may catch the train to Kingstown, and cross to-night. Why wait a day in Dublin? Let me hurry to my fireside in Ebury Street. An hour later I am leaning over the taffrail watching the wake of the ship as she pierces the waveless Irish Sea. It is the past that explains everything, I say to myself. It is in our sense of the past that we find our humanity, and there are no moments in our life so dear to us as when we lean over the taffrail and watch the waters we have passed through. The past tells us whence we have come and what we are, and it was well that I refused to allow the trees to be felled, for sitting by my fireside in Ebury Street I should hear the strokes of the axe in my imagination as plainly as I should if I were living in Moore Hall, and the ghosts of the felled trees would gather about my arm-chair in Ebury Street.

THE END